THE CUB-H
SEASO

Steve Ferris works as a kitchen porter in a Cambridge college; he is also a prolific painter and has a degree in History of European Art from the Courtauld. Chatto will be publishing his first novel in 1997.

Steve Ferris

THE CUB-HUNTING SEASON

VINTAGE

A VINTAGE BOOK

Published by Vintage 1996

2 4 6 8 10 9 7 5 3 1

First published in Great Britain by
Vintage 1996

Random House, 20 Vauxhall Bridge Road, London SW1V 2SA

Random House Australia (Pty) Limited
20 Alfred Street, Milsons Point, Sydney
New South Wales 2061, Australia

Random House New Zealand Limited
18 Poland Road, Glenfield
Auckland 10, New Zealand

Random House South Africa (Pty) Limited
P O Box 337, Bergvlei, South Africa

Random House UK Limited Reg. No. 954009

A CIP catalogue record for this book
is available from the British Library

ISBN 0 09 958071 3

Papers used by Random House UK Limited are natural, recyclable
products made from wood grown in sustainable forests. The
manufacturing processes conform to the environmental
regulations of the country of origin.

Printed and bound in the Channel Islands
by The Guernsey Press Co. Ltd., Vale, Guernsey

Ils ne servent de la pensée que pour autoriser leurs injustices, et n'emploient les paroles que pour déguiser leurs pensées.

Voltaire

For
Bjorn Meier
(because of the above)

Contents

Flight

THIS CONCERNS SOMEONE called Beaver Toadstone.

Many people just don't consider their children when they have them christened. It's bad enough to be born with a surname as clumsy as Toadstone, but to be doubly afflicted by the addition of such a bizarre forename is to start life already disadvantaged. It borders on the criminal, on the insane. Luckily, the boy had an extraordinary gift to go with his extraordinary name. He could transform himself at will into the shape of any animal you cared to mention, from streptococcus to stegosaurus. Not that this incredible ability ever lent him much fame, fortune or happiness, because intermittent ineptitude came with the package in the form of wrappings and string that caused a constant tangle. He did make a short career as a circus performer, but the audiences weren't that easily convinced, because in order to demonstrate his skill he had to go behind a screen to take off his clothes. Hence everyone suspected some trick, some trapdoor. It wouldn't have done to have a naked man in the middle of the ring, now would it, a top hat proffered by the ringmaster to hide his dignity, as Beaver announced, 'Now, ladies and gentlemen, I propose to transubstantiate myself into the form of a living, breathing tiger, king of the jungles of Bengal, renowned man-eater and destroyer of herds.' What a frightful spectacle that would create, and did create. Indeed, being a bungler of the highest quality, one night he forgot to go back into his star-spangled cage and turned himself into a faultless copy of the Man before the Fall and – my word – before *his* fall too, which was mighty when it came, crashing amid screams of surprise masking

1

delight from the women, and from the men shouts of consternation along with demands to have the lunatic locked up.

The master of ceremonies rushed to mask the horror with his cape, dragged him out and told him, 'Thank you *so* much, Mr Toadstone. The company shall no longer be requiring your dubious services. Collect your wages and make yourself scarce!' The ferocious captain had poured all the venom he could muster into the nominative disyllabic, but Beaver wasn't good at making himself scarce. The problem had been that as an elephant he couldn't possibly have squeezed himself into the tiny changing cubicle, the size of which usually limited his shows, except, that is, at the stage when the audience were invited to shout out the names of animals and he'd go through a prodigious sequence of mammals and reptiles, usually weird, to test his ability: from aardvark to pangolin, from okapi to Komodo dragon.

To avoid being menaced by angry fathers, soon after his rude and ruddy downfall, he changed himself into a monkey-eating eagle and flew off home, dropping the bundle of fivers somewhere over Scunthorpe. (Whoever found the windfall didn't report it to anyone. Well, it'd sound pretty silly saying, 'Yes, sergeant, it just dropped out of the sky in the middle of the street!' They'd probably have been arrested for drunk and disorderly behaviour along with theft.)

There were other times when Beaver created problems making himself into a pachyderm. Once he did it in the bedroom while secretly rehearsing a set before the wardrobe mirror and a lapse in concentration or a sudden whim (to which he was rather prone) made him turn into the massive bulk of an African bull, weighing over a ton and swishing its trunk like a hurricane-tossed palm. He broke the lightbulb and crushed the paper lampshade against the ceiling. He pushed the bed against the bedside table, knocking over the Dresden figurine that belonged to his wife's great-grandmother and, executing a tiptoe manoeuvre, smashed a bottle of Gee's linctus which left an ugly brown blotch on the carpet. It can still be seen today if you are accorded the privilege of being invited into the bedroom of the infamous Mr B. Toadstone. Though his circus days were over by then, his wife allowed the occasional lapse. During the impromptu performance, the floor began to give under the strain and, before he managed to flip quickly from impersonating an endangered leviathan to being a moon moth, he had split two of the floorboards and made half the ceiling fall into the teacups of Mrs T. and her cronies who were having their regular Sunday tea-leaf reading. Miraculously, he brought about little other destruction besides. Edith, by then more used to mishaps, was unmoved but Mrs Syringe, her neighbour, an old maid always sheathed in black crêpe, wearing jet beads and lorgnette, was so surprised she spat her mouthful of Madeira cake and Darjeeling clear into the fireplace. Poor dear! If she'd swallowed instead, who knows, she would likely have choked to death. Heaven forbid!

When Beaver first discovered his mysterious talent he caused his mother great distress without ever letting her in on the actual secret, which was good enough reason to be distressed in itself. Secretive children are always a worry. It was not the wealthiest of families, his father being a schoolmaster in a tiny colliery village in the north. Mrs Toadstone senior hadn't an idea why her little Beaver, her one and only, repeatedly turned up on her doorstep with his shirts split at the seams and all the buttons on his flies hanging by frayed threads, clutching his waistband and swearing he'd not had a fight. He'd remembered to take off his shoes before the transition; a good job, because they were much too expensive to mend every other week. He hated shoes anyway and usually walked up to the copse on the hill behind their house with them tied together hanging round his neck. Once he changed himself into a ring oozle and was chased out of their kingdoms by a succession of feudal blackbirds, and by the time he had caught his breath and swapped shapes again, he had forgotten where he had hidden his clothes. By then he was twelve and generally a bit more careful – who wouldn't be after being told so many times not to get into fights, and not to lie about it afterwards, when all the while he knew he was innocent, but dared not try to explain the truth? On that particular occasion he turned himself into a timber wolf and went howling and prowling about the woods trying to discover the whereabouts of his missing trousers and T-shirt. He could always say they'd been nicked while he was swimming, but then he'd been warned not to play up by the pond since Johnny Braker had been found drowned last March. But dare he go home in the disguise of an extinct Britannic lupine and then sneak into the house as a woodlouse, to report the disappearance of more garments? No, he thought.

He was normally very careful. And what if he was seen while still covered in fur, padding on all fours, dripping saliva from lolling tongue and staring sheepishly with glaring, golden eyes? In fact he *was* seen, by Miriam Moorgate, the 'Gypsy' who had come down to wash her shawl in the stream. But when she reported the incident later, everyone said she was either a simpleton or a witch haunted by unfamiliar familiars. He eventually recovered his things by sheer chance, when he darted into the undergrowth at the sound of Miriam's approach. He feared the gamekeeper with a gun, and wasn't sure what to turn into to avoid being shot . . . a natural ditherer, our Beaver. He got home very late and had to say he got lost coming back from the next village. Toadstone senior wasn't convinced, verging on angry. But he wormed his way past his father's objections and slunk off to bed, where his mother brought him a snack and a glass of hot milk.

Beaver was never what you'd call a popular specimen, partly because he was always reading books about exotic animals instead of ones about football and war, and especially because he was the teacher's son, so you couldn't tell him who'd broken the toilet window in case he then told his old man, and you couldn't joke with him and talk about playing doctors and nurses because he was too bookish. Little did his classmates know that during the ages of thirteen and fourteen he spent a lot of his spare time as a fly on the wall in Jayne Graye's bedroom. She was a vain child who often sat in front of her mother's dressing-table mirror, in all sorts of novel positions, to inspect her newly acquired characteristics, or simply lay on her patchwork quilt in the attic, catching the May sunshine as it fell through the open skylight, letting it caress her bare flank for a near-eternity of

4

dusty tenderness, not thinking about boys, but sniffing the vagrant scent of blossom, listening to the birds, just letting the hand of whichever god it was tickle her sides. On one occasion she noticed the motionless bluebottle on the windowsill and hurled a comic at it in mock disgust. Beaver barely had time to wake himself out of his reverie and slip out of the dormer casement. He collided with the net curtain and then with the windowpane and then with the frame and then with the curlicue latch before tumbling out into the dizzy sunshine and the buzz of second cousins. He missed the spider's web by a fraction of an inch. Now he knew what it was like to make the jerking journey of an insect and find himself bottled in by corners and glass. How horrible!

Then the time came when he needed the group, when he'd grown up into the big boys' school and had to travel by bus every day to the neighbouring town. No longer were his contemporaries worried about 'Hoppety', his father. (The little monsters called him that because of the way he pranced around in front of the class and because of his name, of course.) The new tribe began to tell him their adventures and misadventures. Acne swarmed across his face and perniciously spread to his shoulders and chest, and the bum-fluff began to grow, but he was scared to shave in case he knocked the heads off all his spots. He looked like a walking disaster, so he was no longer out of the ordinary. They were locked into the fraternity of virgin males, talking about all the things they would do as though they had already done them. Beaver tried to entertain with his knowledge of the sexual habits of various creatures, such as snails, worms and protozoa, and the story that the first explorers to see elephants suspected that the male's genitals were put on back to front so he could reverse up to the female for coitus since he would be bound to crush his partner with his passion. When this failed to impress, Beaver took the decision to exhibit his wonderful gift.

Like all those his age, he wasn't sure if what he had was precious metal or simply dross; if it was worth sharing, if people wanted to share it, or if he cared to reveal himself fully. But one day, in the tumbledown building by the pond during the August holiday, he declared to Thomas Jonas and Meredith Baxter (another ridiculous name), 'I can be any animal I want!'

Meredith, by then an expert in schoolboy sarcasm, remarked, 'By waving your arms about in front of your face, making a farting noise with your mouth and trying to flap your ears and twitch your tail . . .'

Goaded thus, Beaver transformed, remembering it had to be something that could wriggle out of his clothes and yet be impressive enough to make the other two utterly convinced. He chose a giant horned toad. Silly, really, considering, but there you are.

His jacket fell in a heap on top of him and he had a bit of a struggle to pop out through the dirty collar of his regulation greying shirt. The onlookers were petrified. Then Tommy, who'd been squatting, fell over backwards into the dust and guffawed, rocking to and fro, releasing the nervous tension. And it wasn't such a bad trick after all, though where Beaver had gone he couldn't imagine (not the brightest of boys, that Jonas!).

Meredith also broke from his trance, leapt forward, seized Toadstone and held him up to his face. 'Well, bugger me, that was pretty goddamn impressive! Say, how d'y' do it?' As though to extract the information, he dug his thumb into the belly of the unfortunate Beaver, I mean Toad. As you might expect, the animal's natural defences, the boy's automatic systems, came into play and he squirted a jet of pungent, warm pee down the captor's sleeve. The latter dropped the fat amphibian and was about to kick it when it changed into a bright-red boy, one paw hiding his privates, the other rubbing his hip where he'd fallen to the ground.

'What d'y' do that for, eh? It hurt.'

'What d'y' do this for?' Meredith held up his arm and added, 'Piss all over me, you slug?'

'Toad!' squealed TJ, resuming his rolling in the dirt.

'I'm really sorry, really I am, but it's like that sometimes. I was a fly once on somebody's wall when they threw a book at me and I had to bump my way out of the window.'

'And what exactly were you doing?'

6

'None of your bloody business!' Beaver had turned away and was trying to extricate his underpants from the pile on the grass. He succeeded in getting them on back to front, and turned round, holding his jacket like a screen in front of him. 'Jayne Graye was ... you know!' he muttered half blushing, half triumphant, disconnectedly.

'Oh, yeah? And how was it for you?' This from Baxter, who was clutching his ribs which were aching from so much laughing.

'She looked like a *Speyeria idalia*.'

'Like a what?'

'A regal fritillary. It's a kind of butterfly. She was lying with her arms and legs open on one of those old-fashioned quilt things made out of hexagons of scrap material, like lepidopteran scales under the microscope. And the sun was dappling her skin.' The smithereen effect of compound eyes had added to the sequining.

'Is that how you see everything, in terms of microscopes and telescopes?' asked Baxter with a smirk.

'And what do you arseholes think I was doing in her room half the afternoon? Measuring sunbeam intensity?'

'OK, Superman, what's it like to be a fly?'

'Sort of jerky.' He couldn't think of any better way to describe the sensation, and even as he spoke he knew he'd get nothing but abuse for his hopelessness of expression.

But, remarkably, more questions followed, in earnest but necessarily cloaked in sham inattentiveness. Bax was in control of the situation now, and Jonas only contributed the odd clever interjection or bar-room snigger when he thought it merited it, when he pictured Miss Graye looking as erotic as an insect pinned on a microscope table. He wasn't capable of imagining butterflies with breasts and things, and said so with a lewd grin.

The following Saturday afternoon the three were back at the mill, stretched out on sacking under shafts of sulphurous sun, near to what had once been the state of the art in flour machinery. Tom had brought his cousin, who was staying with them at the time. He was a very thin, very tall, very serious chemistry student from Aberystwyth University.

Jonas minor was all concerned with giving the impression of being a mature sophisticate rather than a pimply sixteen-year-old obsessed with hairy-palm syndrome and potential virginity-losing proposals, if such things existed. He was more subdued than before, but nonetheless allowed several inanities to escape, almost despite himself. This time they really put Beaver through his paces: boa followed white mouse (lab variety), agouti followed hyrax, mandrill turned into segmented annelid (at which point Meredith, in a sudden rush of puerile vengefulness or sheer stupidity, tried to stamp on him). Worms may be blind, but some unnamed sense detected the descending foot of apocalypse and he changed into a flea, leapt aside and became a snarling dingo, then a grizzly, then a mountain lion. He scooped his clothes up into his massive mouth and disappeared behind a rotting partition to change.

The student was all agog but kept his seriousness to ask how Beaver did it.

He hadn't the faintest idea. 'I don't say abracadabra, if that's what you mean. I just concentrate very hard on all the details, a sort of 3-D picture of the animal, and there you are! If I don't know what the animal's like, I can't do it, or rather I can but I go all blurred at the edges and often feel sick.'

'How do you know you go all blurred?'

'I do it in front of the mirror.'

Don't we all? thought TJ, but only smiled to himself.

'What's it like to be a kangaroo, for instance?'

'I've never been one.'

'Oh, all right, an Alsatian?'

'If I stay inside it's OK. No problem. But if I do it outside I'm more animal. I cock my leg all over the place, sniff dog turds, dig up things and want to growl at people and bite old ladies.' This wasn't strictly true, but he thought he'd give them a good run for their money. He'd only transformed himself in the wood, but it was true about peeing on everything and smelling indiscriminately. The scents in the bracken were so strong it was like experiencing smell in Technicolor, and when a seed went up his nose everything went green and purple, blue and orange.

As the interrogation continued, he began to wish he hadn't shown off in the first place. They obviously were fascinated but horrified in equal measure, envious but not wanting to be in his shoes – as the uninitiated would stand naked before a woman for the first time, desperate to consummate the affair but anxious about the irreversibility of the step. They enjoyed being this ordinary when the other was so incredibly alien. He knew they wouldn't tell (no one would believe them), but felt he'd separated himself from the group rather than integrated himself into it.

Luckily, the family moved shortly after that, when Mr Toadstone got a tiny headship down south. Beaver vowed he'd not exhibit himself again. But while he was at college, reading, of all things, the ancient world at UCL, he couldn't resist the odd spell as a pigeon flying off to Trafalgar Square, feeling suddenly part of a vast community. Shame they couldn't talk, one to another, these birds of paradise. Often, he found himself strutting after some hen or other, doing that ridiculous head-bobbing, tail-fanning dance. The quick shudder of fluttering orgasm was different but hardly satisfying, and he returned to Cartwright Gardens utterly exhausted. The morning light woke him with no desire whatever to go to lectures on Ur or Persopolis.

As the three years passed, he, like other students, grew to accept the perversities of intercourse as all part of the act and took to slipping into the cages in Regent's Park to copulate with alligators or gazelles and once even with a hippo in a muddy, lukewarm pond. It was ecstatic, the dropping of barriers more complete than with girls on the floor below in the hall of residence, but he always worried that he was on the verge of becoming a degenerate. He gained a reputation for being extraordinarily athletic in bed, and was in demand as such among the experimental females of his own species.

He only managed a third and wasn't sufficiently qualified, therefore, to pursue a career as an archaeologist or museum curator or even poly lecturer. He wasn't that interested anyway. Now the dilemma again. Should he use his talent and make himself famous or should he find some nice sinecure in the country, like his father before him, a teacher of juniors? But that would be unthinkable.

He spent several years working, on and off, in factories or picking fruit during the season, seeing Europe and even rekindling some real interest in the past. The reliefs at the palace of Ashurnasipal held him in thrall. The Lamassu, the winged, human-headed, tutelary genie that guarded the gates of Sargon's palace, tempted him to try new compound transformations. But he held back. Until one day he went to a circus in Barcelona. There was a contortionist who was able to wrap herself into the tiniest ball of flesh. The ringmaster invited the audience, in several languages, to try their hand at copying the young lady's antics. After the show, Beaver went backstage to offer his services. Needless to say, the manager was amazed and saw dollar bills go swarming round his head, swarming round his head.

They spent three months playing to packed houses (or rather tents) all over the peninsula and on into the south of France. The special skills of Castor, *el hombre-animal*, gained a certain notoriety, but because of the obligatory screening Joe Public suspected trickery and contrivance. That was why the finale of quick changes was incorporated into the show. But this innovation had to wait for their arrival in England in the spring of the following year. Beaver's learning Spanish, French and Flemish animal vocabulary was despairingly slow for both him and the boss. He had the idea of hiding one of the boys in the magic box to relay what he was supposed to conjure next, but there was room for confusion if the interpreter got the wrong idea or translated badly, or if Castor misheard the heavily accented voice, and furthermore, getting out of his clothes and making the change in the cramped confinement, with someone looking on as well as filling up a large portion of that space, was too, too much and the trial run was discontinued after a couple of nights. The ringmaster used to announce, 'And now, ladies and gentlemen, Castor *el magnífico* proposes to confound your reason with the shape and semblance of such-and-such an animal,' doing it according to a prearranged sequence, but this had to be extended once it became apparent that many were coming back for the late show expecting something different: a dolphin or a condor, perhaps. The fruit-bat routine failed to surprise after you'd seen it the once. He stuck to medium-sized mammals and birds with the occasional reptilian thrown in. It wasn't possible, for example, to turn into a horse in the claustrophobic cabinet. There simply wasn't the room. So it was decided to use one of the wagons. This had a double advantage. It could be wheeled out uncovered, the spectators seeing an empty cage beyond the bars, draped with an improvised curtain, bespangled and beribboned, that had previously been a saddle blanket for Bertha the Bachtrian before she died of heart failure, combined with a piece of speedily painted tarpaulin normally used for patching the big top. It had large doors at each end so Beaver could enter one end, do his stuff and emerge by the ramp at the other. It wasn't very tall so he frequently banged his head or gave himself a crick in the neck when he made himself into a baby giraffe or a dromedary. But then everything in this universe has a habit of being good one minute and bad the next. Heigh-ho!

So it wasn't until they arrived in Newcastle, by ferry from Esbjerg, that true fame and fortune would be theirs, or so they imagined. It was decided that a tank of water should be hauled into the ring as well, so that shark and squid could feature in the drama. Indeed in Middlesbrough the magic of the sea lion, hammerhead, barracuda and osprey went down a treat. People had always been more startled by the transition than by the end product, but with the water slopping about, the evolution from piscine to avian was sufficiently veiled. His dorsal fin disappeared, his air bladder became a lung and each scale lengthened and spread to form a feather. He felt his bones grow hollow and brittle, his face round out and his jaw project into a shiny, hooked beak. His vertical tail tilted through 90 degrees and his lateral fins sprouted claws or stretched to become wings. He flew up to perch on the trapeze to thunderous applause. He was overcome with giddiness, which may well be the reason he finished with an elephant and a man, a man with no clothes, down below the fig leaf even. He might have wriggled into the wagon as a camel, but as an elephant! The axles would have snapped.

He was given £135 of back pay, all rolled up together. If he'd stopped to consider, he would have realised he'd been cheated out of hundreds more, but in his plight he omitted to count, then in his flight he forgot to hold on tight and so some native of Yorkshire received more than just pennies from heaven. All his father could say when he turned up on the doorstep, penniless and without any luggage, was, 'The youth of today!' He'd taken the precaution of slipping into his old room to put on a tattered pair of jeans, sandals and a sweater. His mother was too overjoyed to notice that the things he had on had been left behind in his chest of drawers. She thought she'd had a premonition of her son's return earlier, as she pottered about upstairs, when in fact she'd heard him creep downstairs and then loudly knock on the front door as if he'd arrived that very minute: 11.26 p.m. British Standard.

Soon he was off on his travels again. Not to have a second bite at the cherry, but to find himself, sort himself out and to work out just what to do with the rest of his life. What exactly should he do with this gift which seemed to bring nothing but trouble? He ended up in Bulgaria, in a freak show, trying his hand at mythical mixtures: hippocamp and hippogryph, hydra and manticore. With certain combinations he felt perfectly at ease – man and horse, for instance. His spine experienced a surging forwards and upwards, but with the front half fastidious about the smell of the rear. As a two-headed dog it was a different matter: he saw himself as cloven in twain, fragmented, divided against himself. As a salamander, bathing in fire, he learned a new pleasure, but as a basilisk he was horror-struck when his deliberately averted gaze glimpsed a passing terrier and turned it to stone on the instant. Thank goodness it was the dog and not the master! A unicorn was no use as a part of the display. The villagers refused to believe it was not the old deception of a stallion with a narwhal horn attached to its brow. This was

12

also the case with an imitation of Quetzalcoatl. His audience weren't ready for audacious foreign imports and preferred personifications of the Bannik or some field sprite or other.

He kept it up for a whole season before deciding once and for all to quit the glitzy profession.

He arrived back in the home country a more sagacious individual. He got a job as a trainee accountant for a breakfast-cereal manufacturer, rented a flat above the news-agent's on the corner and joined the Liberal Party. (He had considered the Labour Party, following in his father's foot-steps, but rejected it on the grounds that he wasn't ordinary enough, though he began to try to turn himself into another Mr Average just as soon as he got back.) It was at one of their fund-raising bazaars that he met the comely but intense Edith Lavender, daughter of the Lavender part of Lavender and Cosgrove, the local estate agents. After a whirlwind courtship they were engaged to be married.

Beaver had a sinking feeling that sooner or later, and better sooner, he must tell her about his little problem. Would she believe him? 'Dearest, I can make myself into any animal you might care to mention.' Thinking it was just one of his little games, she'd say, 'I bet you can, Bufo, my darling.' He wished she wouldn't call him that, but never mind. Expecting a multiplicity of facial gestures, noises or shadowplay, she would demand he show her. He'd stare at his hands, not daring to go on until she had goaded him for many minutes. Finally he handed over a clipping from the *Gateshead Gazette* with a write-up of the extraordinary abilities of Castor the Magnificents (a great piece of proofreading, that!). It praised his miraculous tricks, but was concerned not to make it sound too credible, too incredible: go and see if you can fathom out how they do the thing. Better than an advert. Shame it hadn't made the front page.

Edith read it and asked if he'd been to see the marvel when he lived up north. He said he'd done more than that, he'd been the amazing Mr Castor and done all that the rag said and more. 'How did you do it?' she asked. By way of answer he turned into a sparrow and flew up into a tree. They were out for a walk down by the river, mauve twilight was closing in, the grey-green water reflected an amber sun. Beaver felt oppressed by the growing gloom. He transmogrified in desperation.

She stared at the pile of clothes on the olive grass, unable to take her eyes off them, as though he had vanished into the earth for ever. He fluttered to the ground and looked up at her, putting his head on one side, imploringly. 'Oh, Beaver!' she managed and sat down heavily on the bank. He changed into a badger and muzzled her hand.

A passing youth asked her, 'Is that a pet? If it's not, they carry rabies, y' know. You ought to be careful.' Involuntarily, she withdrew her hand.

All this had taken many more minutes than would appear from the telling of it, but as one day you'll find out, or conceivably know already, the spell love weaves is time-bending, lengthening moments into ages. With the withdrawal of the fair maiden's hand from the trembling nose of Badger-Beaver, the poor bungler became terrified that she was about to refuse to marry him. She stood and whispered, 'Oh, I must go home and think about all this,' or some such thing, as though entirely to herself, only recollecting the animal at her feet when a last ray of the dying sun caught his beady eye. 'Come round tomorrow while Mum and Dad are out and I'll give you an answer.' Her voice trailed and she trailed off home. Beaver, who found thinking in badger thoughts a most tiresome process, turned back to a man and sat huddled and shivering a good fifteen minutes more. When he told me all this, he remarked that, though badgers are great sages, they only arrive at a conclusion after painstaking consideration of every side of the question, and for that reason he returned to the more hectic brain-jumble of human love.

Next day, with heavy heart and patches of bristle on his chin where his automatically performed shave had failed in its objective, our hero, head down, scuffled his way round to Cambourne Cottage, so named because the previous owner had pretensions to being Cornish, though actually a native of Macclesfield. His beloved let him in, vainly attempting to disguise her anxiety with a tight-lipped smile which looked more like a rictus and with chatter about the weather and how it'd favour her father's marrows and tomato plants. In the middle of all this nonsense Beaver asked, 'Well . . .?' in such a way as to make answering unavoidable.

'Look,' she said, 'I had an awful dream last night.' She looked for encouragement but found none and so launched into her attack haphazardly. 'You were changing into every kind of beast you could imagine, all creepy-crawly or dangerous, and finally you slid under the covers as a black and green snake with golden eyes and ruby tongue. I'd jumped into bed to get away from you and then I couldn't move even as I felt you slither between my legs. I opened them wide because if I'd closed them you'd have bitten me. But still you kept coming, so I threw off the blankets and saw the tip of your tail vanish. I pulled my knees up ready to spring out of bed but I could see you through my skirt and you were just about to sink your teeth into my tenderest spot, and maybe you did, 'cause I woke up at that moment, all of a quiver . . .'

She might have begun a course in sociology and psychology at North Cheshire Poly, though not actually completed it, but Beaver would have never thought her capable of telling such a lurid tale in such graphic detail. He was burning red with shame and she with embarrassment, and they both stared at their hands, unwilling to acknowledge the other's predicament or maybe even presence. She wanted reassuring that it would be safe to marry a man at least half animal, and he wanted her to rid herself of such foolish fancy, though he recalled for a moment some of the grosser exploits of his college debauchery and shuddered to think he could have ever done such things, and enjoyed them into the bargain.

How would you allay fears like that? I guess that in this case, as in many others, they bumbled through it, he telling her things that she never heard and he unable to listen to the things she told him, and neither answering one another's questions, as they each kept up a staccato soliloquy, pausing to allow the drone of his or her voice to fill the gaps she or he left, much like the speaker's hiss between consecutive tracks on a record. The outcome was that she demanded he

15

stop and he decreed that he wouldn't do it again. They went on repeating these perfectly congruent decisions, as though they were both diametrically opposed to the other's standpoint, until they finally realised they were saying the same thing, he saying yes, she saying no, then the other way round.

And then, if it were a video instead of a real-life idyll, there'd come piped music out of the sofa and dusk would fall prematurely outside the glassless window frames at the flick of a button or the slide of a dimmer switch, and they'd hold hands (camera close-up) and kiss, eyes closed (second close-up), and the whole would fade out, to be replaced by a view of a church (long shot) filled with expectant relatives looking over their shoulders and waiting for the organist (angled zoom-in from organ loft) to spy the bride, to strike up the none-too-joyous wedding march from 'Saul'. Followed briefly by the 'I do' scene and roll the final titles, devoid of that other pompous-pious gobbledegook that comes with the retailed-to-your-spiritual-needs marriage-ceremony package.

Anyway, as this isn't a video, but nonetheless a thing sewn together with many a well-worn cliché, let us just say that the inevitable happened and they tied the as-long-as-you-both-shall-live knot and Beaver agreed to do a PGCE and settle for the life of teaching squealing brats that he had sworn he would never be forced into after seeing the trouble and strife it had brought his parents. Since he had not been the most brilliant of schoolboy academics, it is strange to report that he found himself a very comfortable little slot in a minor public school in Hertfordshire and Edith came with him to be a junior house-mother and in due course just the common-or-garden variety of mother, when she gave birth to a series of babies, none of whom appeared to inherit their father's propensity for aping the antics of any number of endangered primates or nocturnal poikilotherms. This fact gave Mrs Toadstone utterly sublime relief. She had spent the morning-sickness period of her pregnancy extending bouts of antiperistaltic activity well on into the afternoon under the influence of oppressive worry and the strange urge to cultivate her own string of psychosomatic ailments. The

16

rubber-band-devouring and coal-gnawing was accompanied by an aversion for all things furry and she had to plan her constitutionals so as to avoid all masters and wives who had bulldogs or fox terriers as pets and mascots.

She saw that Beaver missed the conjuring and relented slightly, allowing him to practise in private. He would disobey her precise prohibitions just once, when their youngest child woke from a nightmare about things invading the house from sidereal skies. Beaver took him for a trip around the fields, getting him to promise never to tell his mother. The child got out of bed the next morning convinced that it had been a dream, the first of the happy oneiric wanderings that came thereafter. If he had broken his promise, would anyone have believed that his father had become a grey horse just to calm him?

There was once a minor crisis when Jonathan T. made his father certain he was about to divest himself of a normal little boy's shape in favour of that of a conger eel or something equally unsavoury in order to wash himself more playfully. It was in the grand cast-iron tub that the incipient transubstantiation was about to be worked when Beaver, a devoted if inevitably bumbling and inconsistent father, was bathing the dreamer one spring Saturday just after taking the Third and Fourth for cricket and marginally before rushing over to Netherhurst for dinner with the Goslings. Edith was fully occupied with reconstructing and rearranging a heaped-up hairdo, when she heard the grunts and monosyllables of her husband's consternation.

In the pale turquoise twilight of the north-facing Victorian extravaganza, Beaver had been splashing around with the plastic ducks, the tugboat and the hippo soap dish, as much as if not more than his tiny son, when the latter had said, 'I feel funny!' He stood up to see his son's sun-tanned shoulders turn silvery-grey and become crisscrossed with a net of incised lines, glisten with the oily sheen of fish scales, and begin to sport the jut of a sprouting sail-fin, and he thought the youngster's head tilted backwards, narrowed and lost its mop of dark hair. But it was just a trick of the light, Beaver told himself.

17

Trip

Territory:

THE WORM WENDS its way to the Wash. It wanders disconsolately about for want of a more determined course, for lack of gouge or gorge. It wriggles around in a valley as slight as the meniscus on a rather flat pint of beer, or as deflated as the contours of the coagulating batter in a Shrove Tuesday tosser's pan. Within the pancake's rim the chef has created an amalgamated geography made up of the ingredients of his odd recipe: a crêpe suzette sprinkled with motorway escarpments, rift-valley underpasses, and roofs substituted for mountain ranges against the broad, broad expanse of steely sky. Road and rail add their coloured lines to the OS map, but any journey undertaken within its confines contravenes the regimentation of grid-line rectitude. There are dotted sites where recent developments become transformed into archaeological ruins waiting to be more fully excavated and charted: playgrounds like ancient observatories, with complicated architectonic sundials; industrial buildings becoming Roman bath complexes; slag embankments doubling as earthwork defences, remnants of an Iron Age. On the edge of town there are water meadows, a scrubby common and a series of paths and bridges seemingly arranged at random, beside and across the river and the railway. The area has seen many successive occupations.

Time:

The not-so-naughty nineties. Summer. Sun up early, the night air not given long enough to chill. River-borne mist. The pubs close and spill their dregs into the university-city streets, all sleep and boredom. The students ignore the citizens; the citizens try to ignore the interlopers. If our three fellahin leave the public bar at 11.30 and get to the post office at midnight, the amble over the grassy plain will last till 5.30 a.m., though the boys themselves will feel they have filled five times those four hours with their ritual voyage. Saturday night. Recovery by Monday, storming through an elongated Lord's Day hyperactive and without rest.

Taking part:

They are all male. They look young, though one of them is exactly the sum of the ages of the other two. They combine almost like an oxygen ion with the two hydrogens. One of the paired atoms is smaller than the single round O, the other much bigger. They have white, white skin and dark, dark hair. Their names do not matter. Let them be chemically replaced with a P, an S and an N. Elementally. They are connected not because they come from the same estate, not because they are related, not even by sex. S is homosexual, a youth-club leader. P and N left the club a long time before. They know. They couldn't give a fuck. S is safe, inert.

Trade:

Obtaining three tabs, Lysergic acid diethylamide. The list of 'brands' is huge. The compound differs little. Purple Oms engender psychedelia, supposedly; Jokers, like Jupiter, bring jollity; Red Dragons rearrange the cosmos by biting their own tails, turning the psyche into a practically closed circle. The size of the piece of cardboard varies, and the number of times they are dipped. Some that drop into the trough of ambrosia are fished out afterwards and carry sufficient potency to bring flight, shift shapes, move mountains. Then the unwary animal can convert from man to sea cucumber, his inner facts can become externals, extend from him like spines, can search and destroy. In his rush from imagined harpies the poor, sad sap, the pointless, hopeless soul, can fall under buses believing himself invincible; drown assuming amphibious adaptability; dropping a few feet to become impaled upon palisade poles, when the perceived multiplication of distance causes a quantum increase in shock.

Tickets:

S and F both work in a large supermarket. S goes to F and asks him to score him three Black A's. F is very sexy, but no deal there. He scooters into the labyrinth of identical houses grouped round strange keyhole-shaped culs-de-sac, barricaded by garage doors, interlocking with other clusters of inward-looking homes, gathered round patches of gardened landscape: a lone shrub, barbed-wired saplings, dogpiss-irrigated flowerbeds, concrete benches, concrete playthings. He gets the last three of a batch, stashes them in a leaf of clingfilm, stuffs them in his wallet and rides off on his extended phallic symbol. He gets them for the knock-down price of £3.50 apiece.

Taxiing:

They meet in the Frog and Parrot. It is renowned as a hard place. People sport denims and tattoos. Fights are frequent. The public bar is very public. It has a monarchic pool table, a brace of dartboards, a triumvirate of fruit machines, a CD jukebox and a TV suspended from the ceiling for the Cup. Ancient and modern. It boasts a football team, two darts teams, a crib team, two quiz teams. The walls hold commendations for fund-raising activities. Many bars have their quirky collections: banknotes tacked to the chimney breast, stuffed fish, postcards from peregrinating customers missing a wifeless haven. This one has a massacre of masks. Some come from a colonial past; some are Halloween souvenirs; some are cheap imitations from Third World countries suffering from the blight of being 'opened up to tourism'. There are some valuable Noh-drama props and a couple of grotesqueries from Venice. The effect on passing trade is startling, but always a good conversation starter. Loquacity leads to a parched throat. The pub is popular and sales are strong.

The landlord and lady have recently taken over from a couple noted for their chalk and cheese ménage: he a sot, she a puritan with a mouth like a mouse's arsehole. The large number of regulars are very regular, many trying blindly to escape one fate or another. Itinerant shades mass outside, under the lilacs, and whisper the imminent bad ends of each of their haunting partners. A sound of shifting leaves. Broken-marriage wayward sons. Prohibitive progenitors.

S arrives first, to hear the litanies of the gang of boys and girls whose adolescence is marred not so much by zits and exam trauma as by the collective feeling of being unloved, unwanted, bound to end on the scrapheap like their mums and dads, the ones that have used them as punch bags, paramours or levers against one another. S stands for sympathy but, for all his brimming over with an urge to help, is impotent to communicate the desire. It passes for the usual type of imitation. A bleeding-hearted faggot more likely to be the butt of jokes than relied upon for aid. His money counts and his ineptitude proves that the disease is not confined to the young, the poor, the dispossessed, the disenfranchised. A freak within the circus of aberrations whose quiet acceptance of unacceptance endears him to them even though peer pressure disposes of all visible signs of communion. He has seen their scars, drawn breath and sighed. He has heard the torrid catalogue of depravity and neglect, and despaired. He shares their drugs. They share his.

P and N arrive and immediately want to see the merchandise. In a plastic film container for greater safety the triumph of alchemy: three blue-grey squares of cardboard less than

21

half a centimetre along each side still in their wrap. Coarse perforations and a printed capital 'A' off-centre in each. There is some threat that the drug squad will raid the pub some time soon, but no one believes it will happen when they are there.

Takeoff:

S has never done it before. P claims he has but S is in doubt. N has, definitely. In the event his takes the longest to have any effect, or so he says. After a couple of pints each, the three put the imitation sugar cubes in their mouths, chew them, swallow them and smile. People say, 'Have you dropped them yet? Are you buzzing?'

Last orders come and go and still they hold back from leaving. Then the landlord decides to thin out the crowd and bolt his doors. Most topers troop out, reunited on the threshold with their personal ghosts. They slip out from under the bushes and march off with the skein of revellers, headed to one of the nearby houses to smoke while the neglectful parents are away in Tenerife.

The trio heads for town. N keeps asking if they are getting afterimages, multiple freeze-frames in the shapes of their hands as they flip them before their eyes. No. Perhaps. They pretend. Perhaps. That depends. Yes. Yes, they are, aren't they? Aren't they? They sit under a tree and have a forced fit of giggles, maybe heralding the arrival of the mage, secretly praying for the imminence of the light-bearer. Odd motes of colour flash across their retinas as though the entoptic debris of dead cells has been resurrected, each fragment momentarily phosphorescing. They take this as an indication of failure, the slight tremors indicating that they *have* come from some factory or other but that the processes have not worked. Their fingers begin to tingle. This may be the only buzz they'll get. Indeed, N pronounces the nonviability of the pieces of card and disclaims any magical sensation.

They walk on, past the cop shop where there is an increase in paranoia, but N still says that nothing is happening even as P and S feel the tingling spread into their legs. They make the post-office playground and sit on the swings to protest. Then the hurricane hits, the breaker rushes up over the shingle. S is swamped first. He feels the ground turn to sponge. He feels a creeping, crawling web of spidery gossamer wrap the whole of his body, moving to the blowing of a nonexistent breeze. Every tiny tilt translates into soaring and plunging. He gets down on all fours to observe the ebb and flow of the rippling concrete. He touches the rough surface and the granules and grit cling and dig into the cocoon of threads. The field of vision widens and the detail multiplies. On close inspection the iron supports of the swings look like sequoia trunks, the chains leave marks in the air and the ground swell continues. He appears to grapple with the onset alone. But soon P is catching up and the neap tide of sensual information takes the pair of them and they are unable to stand still. S feels the precipitous slide of time, past him in the wrong direction, condensing being and doing into nanoseconds of awareness, scintillating battalions of chronophotographic outlines speeding by, radiated from the most mundane objects, encrusting grey bollards in diamond dust, expanding the road to a Champs-Elysées studded with emerald and ruby chippings, all catching, refracting and redoubling the orange glow from sodium sunflowers circled with concentric layers of isoclinal light-crystals. They shimmer and dance and dazzle like diadems of tourmaline, beryl and chrysoprase. Crossing the boulevard is difficult. S still hasn't become used to the warp that wraps him and that certain unwillingness to respond in his limbs. Too much else going on.

The road is now the size of the Field of Mars. They aim for the large roundabout with its underpasses. N recommends it while still maintaining he is not buzzing, speeding or tripping. He shows the signs in his babel of words and his fidgeting. The minute, transparent spinners have got him.

The trouble:

Those of us who know and know too much see the problem
and feel impotent before it. Our words are like the words of
a politician, pie-crust promises, the rhetoric of failure. The
rage bottles up inside us and finds few outlets. These beautiful and not so beautiful young men bound for the knacker's
yard may have their share of looks, their silky penises, their
sea-smooth flesh may entice, entrance, but shortly they will
be manacled to pathetic jobs and termagant spouses, mew-
ling kids and mortgage repayments. And in the meantime
they take the gilded pills and smile inanely at the time-lapse
camera. They see as much as we, but their clear understanding, uncluttered, views their futures as all they can expect,
all that is on offer. The glamour of the advertising hoardings
is the only glimmer of better prospects.

The three of them arrive at the football-stadium circus.
They enter the caldera via a downward-sloping ramp and a
six-foot-wide tunnel lined with rectangular tiles arranged in
exemplary histograms. Around the rim of the circle the
coping stones spin at meteoric velocity as they swing their
heads in chase. The truncated tops of vans and lorries race
ahead of their gaze, dashes of blazing colour encoding some
indecipherable message. The Andean peaks of gabled offices
serrate the brown-purple-black-orange of the sky. It is all
these colours, not a mix, all these colours at once. By spin-
ning S multiples these mountains into a vast cordillera
encompassing the arena they stand inside. The four exits,
with their violent hidden neon, also grow in number. Three
can be seen at once, then four, and he guesses that there are
as many again grouped behind his panoramic perception.
The quincunx of hardy shrubs and stretching trees sinks into
impenetrable blackness. Crown-of-thorns edges slash the air
with malevolent intent, waiting for the capsize of any passing
ship and the depositing of any wrecked sailor on isolated
shores. N disappears into a clump of bushes and his voice
gets bounced from places where he can't possibly be. All the
while the number of coliseum entrances grows, the threat of
gladiatorial conflict growing with it. Soon, snarling dogs or

24

even lions. Soon, men with helmets and burnished short swords. Soon, the anxious desperation will pass out of his control and the monsters of his own private abyss will come bounding out to terrorise him, shred him, flay him. N jumps out at him and drags him down into the tangle of briars, the jungle of thistles, nettles, sundews, liverworts, pitcher plants, earthstars, cacti and obvious nightshade. Poison, poison, poison. He gives a strangled squeal, mind in bits, trying to tie it all back together. Clawing, he falls, tensing, struggling, gulping down breaths full of venomous pollen, spiked vanes, veined scimitars, sickle-shaped barbs assaulting his fragility.

P intervenes and helps him up. N is unrepentant and the three momentarily become three again, disparate, no longer three-in-one. 'I've got to get out.' S succeeds in getting out.

'Which one of them, oh God, which one?' The five plots of darkness hold an army of mad warriors, soul-strippers.

'The river.'

'Which side?'

'Near the school. Quick.'

They get out just in time. Moments later a crew of brutes leap from the cover, naked except for bronze penis guards, an ornamentation of prongs and copper arabesques, bearing tridents and star-shaped bucklers, wearing harnesses of black leather and iron rings, studs, genital-shaped masks with perforations unrelated to the eyes, nostrils and mouth beneath. The three escape the clutches of their enemies by clambering up a heaven-high flight of steps, the walls tipping inwards, the railings at the top about to enmesh and close the Venus flytrap. A regrouping and an attempt to re-establish the triune wholeness.

A very gentle incline leads past the abutment of the bridge to the road beside the Worm. It, too, is lined with foliage, but this *forêt sauvage* holds no horde of barbarians. However, they are not out of the wood yet. At one point N drops his jacket. They all look. It is crawling with miniature pea-green dragons, carapaced and polypodal, war-gaming over grey. They definitely move, charge, withdraw, alter formation, horse and rider in one. No clear division between opposite sides. N brushes them off, but doesn't put his coat back on, for fear this new-model army might interfere with the fields of turbo-electricity fluctuating round his body. Still he refuses to admit he is on the same planet as P and S, but then S has been temporarily transported to another and has only just landed back on the right cloudbank moments ago.

At the bottom of the slope the concrete bastion supporting the flyover emerges from the frets of branches. Concrete ashlars decorate the false fascia in a granitic charade. Flint or chert chipping in first pinky fawn, then milky white, are embedded in alternating slabs. The vertical rhythm ripples down to the road by the river. As the boys look, this curtain wall snakes like a drape disturbed by an on-and-off breeze. The parapet above cuts into the sealing sky like a gigantic cornice or pelmet. A wrongly proportioned door keeps padlocked shut a man-made cave. N pounds on the wood, demanding admittance. The echo dies and the secretive chatter of the leaves or the susurrus of waving walls sounds from deep inside. A score of tramps or a nocturnal secret society are pretending not to be within, but are unable to refrain from plotting their next move even as they are being found out.

Leaving the strange creatures to debate their position and their strategy, they go to the bottom of the path and turn right under the bridge. The road carries on to the common. It is quite wide, but to them it stands open like an American twelve-lane highway, its gentle curve as expansive as the largest ocean bay in the world. The gasworks, half way along, appear like a mosque or a cathedral.

When they reach it, N spews out a description whose intricacy borders on the baroque, though his lack of vocabulary is replaced with incredible syntax whose repetition and tiny variation at each turn seems better able to encompass the composite of Perpendicular crocketing and metallic filigree. Its vastness rivals Hagia Sophia. The splay and interconnection of girders and cast-iron beams mimics flying buttresses in Chartres. The tetrahedrally arranged rods within each of the supporting pillars combines Neoplasticism with Jugendstil design. The main arches of the ambulatory,

26

baptistery or chapterhouse are surmounted by a clerestory and a triforium. A tracery of mullions and transoms pierces the openings like stained-glass windows. The capitals at each level spread like acanthus. The vault holding up the sky is ribbed with pale echoes of the soaring columns. The malachite dome of the sanctuary within does not reach to the full height of the lantern, but in their mind's eye the three see themselves climbing up the stair turrets and looking down on the marble-smooth cupola. They walk past, watching the dance of the colonnade and the pinnacles against a sky of violet-green-black-blue.

The trail:

To the cattle grid, through the wicket gate, on to the common. Just beyond the second playground a tarmac strip connects the cluster of tacky starter homes with the pub on the opposite bank of the river, its metalled surface like a starting grid for a Grand Prix or a cross-country rally. Beyond this ribbon of bitumen and granite, tonight, a choppy sea of frosty tussocks extends, the merest hints of mist rising along the line of the railway embankment. The domain occupies the combined areas of Hyde Park, Green Park and Kensington Gardens. The olive blades catch the light of the moon, the light of the stars, the lights of unseen scintilla and arrange the tiny particles in a crystalline lattice over their cellulose surfaces even though it is not cold enough for actual frost: chameleon nature has taken on a disguise to merge into an acid-bleached background. The becalmed Sargasso of grass has a rubble causeway stretching across it towards the obsidian shrapnel of combined trees and steel, a tiny underlining of the white-yellow-mauve, where the vanishing points of three sets of eyes rove left and right along the ocean's horizon. The stones of the path are of two contrasting types. There are a myriad limestone fractions and a scatter of industrially wasted grey nuggets thrown up by blast furnaces or some other form of man-made vulcanism, all too small for a stoning, too large to be classed as gravel;

27

a false beach, a Red Sea part, a beckoning necessity of a track whose distant line has reduced itself to a hairlike structure, a silver strand from the cloud-god above. The speckled skin of the attenuated sea monster looks deceptively secure, yet the incursion of clumps of lizard green suggest that the track will only last till morning, when the snake-thing will submerge once more, like Zaratan, into the greasy deep verdure.

There is a havoc of miracle horses able to tread on the skin of the weedy water without sinking into its blanched depths. S has always had a rapport with animals and as he clicks his tongue they come to gather round him, their breath visible, their smell palpable, their eyes fathomless. He strokes their noses in turn as in some valedictory blessing, some clear announcement of departure, a reassurance, a promise of return. P and N don't like the ponderous bulk of these sentinels of the shore and demand that they set out on their quest immediately. S acquiesces and bids the herd leave him. They lope away, to walk on the white waves and nibble foam on the crests.

Now, without the need of thought, the tripling of his individuality, the concordance of himself and his surrogate sons, makes the glow outside glow within. He becomes ecstatic. The drug has reached the height of its growth. The blossoming of luminosity inside him takes over the whole of him. The lanterns in the distance beyond the spalls of volcanic glass seem to move, to go out and come back on again.

They set out at a brisk pace. They stay on the path as if the meadows really were a swamp or a lake. The brightness of the sky and the surroundings are of dream clarity. It is definitely night, this is a night journey, but the separate sources shine like multiple suns.

Next they distinguish a set of lights which seem to move, going gradually towards the north, along the line of the tracks, among the scrubby trees, under the electricity gantries. Acetylene sparks puncture the dark. As they manage to disentangle the shadows from the glare, they realise that there is some kind of train trundling in the direction of the footbridge. The tingling in their hands, then in their calves, has spread and a sensation like that of going fast over a humpback bridge in a car has made the awareness of their testicles increase. They seem in imminent danger of disappearing. A sickly warm emptiness engulfs that part of their bodies, a numbness resulting, a prepubescent lack: no balls, no balls at all. By the time they get to the bottom of the steps they are accustomed to the chemical castration, they even welcome the unsexing, the regression to a purer state.

Another Hammerite-clothed pile of girders, bolts, rivets and the flight of wooden steps climbs heavenwards, a Jacob's ladder. Were angels to have stood with lyres, shaums and serpents, bedecked with the precious trappings of the antiquated denizens of the empyrean, the three would not have been surprised. Their boyishness is at maximum. Only three steps above the other two, S sees them as diminutive figures, wide-eyed innocents. They swap places. He is back at school, out hiding after a day's truancy. He used to be a model pupil. Now he is playing Peter Pan. Successfully until they come down from on high.

They clamber up the Brobdingnagian staircase and across the boards which, though only spanning forty feet, look like a Blackpool promenade. They promenade to the centre and look out over the studded balustrade, above the steel crisscross, along the line, south towards the minuscule station in the far distance. The bolt-heads and rivets of the balustrade map the places of the stars from the bridge on to the arcing sky, or vice versa. The rails have been hand-polished with Silver Dip and they gleam like splinters of light, light broken off the glassy globes at the tops of the flowery lamps.

Midway along the lines the maintenance vehicle idles, surrounded by lights, some blazing from brackets on the low wooden platform that supports the crane, some on the guard's van, some on the dumpy shunter, a dragon from an unknown cavern attended by acolytes: feeding it, caressing it, taking its energy to weld rails together. The jib or neck of the leviathan ends in a prognathic pulley-skull. Rays like flame shoot from its mouth. The cervical bones reach up at a steep angle and the lattice shows the cables of its oesophagus and trachea. It cooperates with its attendants, moving

29

loads of metal and sleepers for them, lifting them from its back on to the clinker bed of the tracks, where the sapphire sparkles spread their molten fire on the ground beneath its paws, fire for it to walk upon. It advances towards the bridge, its brontosaur head towering high above the level of the transfixed threesome, inexorably descending upon them, nonchalant but undeterred. It looms out of the solid black-navy pitch, nodding, staring, fixating on the figurines ahead. As it nears them it bows to them and slides beneath their feet, yards in front of their paralysed faces, the orb of its light illuminating the cloud of dust or breath that hangs about it, ringed by burning moths and insects. They turn as one to see it raise its head again on the other side. It smiles. It has winked.

They watch the monster for a little while longer before continuing across and down. It is amazing how the flame-jacketed marshals don't seem to notice three space cadets on the bridge. They enter the trees at the bottom of the flight. A gravel path runs through the arcade to a shallow stream, the stones underwater the same as those above, reflective skin drawn up over them like a lid. The overhanding twigs try to reach their doubles sweeping up from below. The group walks the plank above the mirror-smooth brook and into the field beyond, which is under a blanket of lunar-toned mist. Looking straight down they can see the earth beneath; looking forwards no margin between the land and the water can be seen.

The dragon up on the embankment scrapes forwards, nod-ding, flashing. The boys, or rather the man and the boys, the priest and his offspring, scamper away. They pause to check if the wetness on their jeans is wet, or just another manifestation of the brigades of microscopic forces acting out their Agincourts and Waterloos on the fog-traced cloth. Then the rocks they hadn't noticed when fishing or playing round the riverbank move and arise and turn into cow-shaped things which plod off, moons between their horns. Laughter and mooing.

The dragon is about to cross the drawbridge and return to its invisible lair. It slips its head under the girders and noses its way past triangular superstructures. The swirls of vapour evaporating from the river are cut into wedges by the metal shadows. The blades tumble from the bridge to the banks and bang into the three watchers before folding up into nothing, as each segment catching the preceding one concertinas the white into the black.

When all the triangular beams of solid glow have vanished, the group returns to the bridge. As they walk they see the big sky change from ink-ebony-crude-oil to ultramarine-gold-opal. The transitions and gradations of colour are clearly discernible. The dragon has dragged the night from the canopy above them as if it were an umbrella or a fold-away wing, batlike, enormous, antediluvian, eternal. The unwrapping of the Christmas present of heaven exposes layer after layer of water-thin transparency, air-brushed with a hundred thousand hues, each successive one a degree lighter, more luminous. The light does not come from the sun, from a single centre. It comes from the whole dome, from without, diffuse, all-embracing, a protective goldfish bowl with every-thing inside it. Unquestionable, unquestioned perfection. N mentions that this was the place he first fucked a girl, spoiling the show of the *deus ex machina*, for this theatrical paradise is most certainly *not* the place. P looks up at onion-skin observatory coffer. He has a telescope in his eye. So does S. Does N? Are the lines separating, are they edging apart?

Tail-lights:

The red, green and blue zigzags on the wall chart reconverge and the single unity, entity, entirety, continues. The rest of the night need not be meticulously described. The dawn comes to dispel most of the paranoia, with a paradoxical descant of vague depression as the chemical comes undone in their blood. But a few notes need to reproduce the final movement of the symphony: rallentando, minor key, cello, no pizzicato, largo, piano, pianissimo.

They decide against the bridge, exit from the grassland over a fence on to a railway track which looks unused. Lost, disoriented. Set of points merge their path with the main line. Orange-yellow-rose-madder over platinum skate scratches, dots of red and green of irrelevant signals. Infinity both directions. Over barbed wire on to a mound of grey stones, dull metamorphics; scramble to the top and then the vision of the sea turned back to drought-parched soil, desert cracked. Boulders, ochre grasses.

They go back to the bridge by the pub and cross after S says hello to the horses once more. Over the water, right past two pubs and on to the towpath. On the way down. All the way along the river they see bats flapping above the shreds of mist. Swans and ducks reflecting elephants and aardvarks. Back towards home.

At the level crossing they look for signs of the dragon. Nothing. Silence. Absence. Nonsense. At the third playground a pause, flopping on the ground, to decide how to end. S feels that the other two are closer to each other than to him. And so it shall be for ever. He doesn't want the pair of them to come home with him, so lets them go towards N's house. They are arms round each other's shoulders, singing, when he looks back, as he completes the circle. Almost finishes it.

Prolegomenon

THE ROCK AT the bottom of the mineshaft was soft and dark and hard and bright.

The pithead lay only half a mile or so from the cliff edge, but once upon a time the ramparts of the railway embankment, the complex of buildings and the ever-growing slag heap had obscured that fact completely.

Today there is no trace of the colliery. It has been swept aside. The slopes leading to the tracks are now shielded with gorse bushes which blaze into a sheet of yellow fire in perfect time for Easter, and the gigantic scab of clinkers, stones and poorest-quality coal that once hid the sea is now covered in topsoil brought from miles away, and carpeted in emerald grass, false and fragile, picnic chairs and tables set into little tarmac islands scattered over the remade landscape, promising only plastic pleasure.

The seam spreads out under the sea, stretching further out than at any other workings in the country. Old black-and-white photos show the little squat trains of wagons that carried men and rock to and from the face. The flashes for the cameras made a synthetic sun, melting the shadows, paling the contrasts. In the good old days, when the industry still fed the village, the grime from the pit and the sea fret combined to render the whole sleepy place a misty painting, *en grisaille*. The darkness below was always the same for the miners, regardless of when the shift started and finished, regardless of whether it was night or day up top, regardless of whether weak summer sun shone on rows of flapping washing in the back streets, or whether lowering snow clouds canopied the sludge-filled gutters and pavements. Forever night down the pit. And whenever the old man got home from work covered in dirt and dark and sat in the galvanised tub, set up in front of the range ready for his arrival, fire banked up and roaring because of the bleazer, the soap rid his albino body of only some of the night. It remained ingrained in his pores, under his nails and clinging to the tangles of hair around his groin and under his arms. It stained the white towel he wrapped himself in and his underclothes always stayed grey, however long they were bleached and boiled in the pot they called a copper. The night stayed with him even on Sundays and holidays, reminding everyone in the terraced house of his livelihood and its dangers, its threat, its continual presence. Yet where it lay, in its lair, for all its brooding strength and power, it spoke of safety and security eternal.

Although cold, salty water seeped into the tunnels and settled into pools like trails of miners' sweat, the mine was warm to work in. They laboured in singlets or bare-chested. Draughts whistled whale song through the gates and junctions and the rumble of truck wheels on metal echoed around the passages in ways that made it sound like the conversation of gnomes, both lugubrious and full of levity.

War artists went down to record how the night was hewn from the friable layers and carted the four and a half miles to the cage and up to the surface to be washed and sorted by women mostly, then sent off to depots or put on larger trains to trundle along the coastal line to destinations all over the north. They failed to capture the look of the stuff. Too much light passed from the paper through the pastel, the ink, and even through the graphite whose molecules are so similar to the coal's, but whose substance is so unlike it in its lack of palpable density. The silver of lead made them shine too bright. The images of men on their knees in cramped galleries, the beams of the lamps on their helmets like needles, captured the claustrophobia, but the fear was the artists' fear, not that of the miners. They respected the mountain of pressing rock around them, feared it when it cracked and fell, when it tumbled down on top of them if the shoring failed, but somehow they felt at ease, felt the

34

energy coursing through their pick-wielding arms to be the same as that trapped in the bone-brittle, bituminous blocks. Dendritic fissures played over the black slabs and the crystals that filled the spaces glittered like pouring water. An intrusion of iron pyrites sparkled with the same vigour as the lights in a lover's eyes. Canaries sang before instruments superseded them and pit ponies traipsed between the shafts all their lives.

My grandfather was pensioned off by the Coal Board when pneumoconiosis was diagnosed. He became ill. The night had lodged itself in his lungs, but maybe it was the daily diet of Woodbine smoke painting the tunnels and passageways with nicotine and carbon monoxide fumes which promoted the disease. He did not die of it, but the surgeons mining his body discovered the boulder of a carcinoma in his caecum which they duly dug out with their pickaxes and needle beams of light. The fortune-teller he visited in Morecambe, or wherever it was, told him he'd live till he was ninety. He did not. My grandmother was plunged into dark despair. They burnt his body and scattered the ashes. There was no return to the earth, but nonetheless unending night closed about him and the depth of its colour holds his spirit still.

Now he is dead I cannot talk to him about the dark. I have been down a cave in Avon, but the rock is different. The guide told us it gets ten times as pitch as it ever does above ground, and we all turned off our torches and the blackness swallowed us entirely. There was only the sound of the boys' breathing and the rustle of clothes, and then the murmurs of growing fright before we banished it with a switch and crawled on over mud-coated rocks and up slippery slopes of water-gouged sluices. We ducked under an overhang with a pool underneath to see the underground river that had whimsically chosen a different course. We tasted the water. Such icy purity. We got to the surface soaked and exhausted. I could say I have been into that dark my grandfather felt so comfortable within, but it is not precisely the same for coal as it is for lime.

He told us a story about how the coal had almost cost

him his life. Most of the time the solid roof pretended to offer its protecting shelter, but occasionally it threatened the miners, as it remembered an organic past and limbered its muscular walls. Perhaps it was simply the goings-on of the greensand or the shale, struggling to assert their dull blandness, their grey weight, their majority. The coal was born from fantastic forests, the other rocks from silts in shallow, tepid oceans.

He told us the story as we stood at the end of the garden outside a group of Aged Miners' Houses in a town further from the fret and the grime, but with its own set of wheels to drag the darkness out of the belly of the earth. It was his sister's house. She ended her days in a home in Durham City imagining my father her brother and me my father. I remember a pair of huge glazed urns the colour of lapis lazuli on her sideboard. They were stolen by confidence tricksters, the same age as me in all probability. My grandfather wanted to castrate them if they were caught, but they weren't.

On the garden steps, then, Joe met one of his old workmates. Mags and I played along the railings, using them as a climbing frame, and the man said it was the manner of children and we should be allowed to wreak havoc and plague the old ladies and the old gentlemen. That was the order of things. Joe replied that the order of things wasn't always right. If it were, the man he was talking to would have been given a medal the size of a frying pan. I must have been nine or ten or less, but I knew that the bond between these two was intimate in a fashion that I could not aspire to, a tie stronger than ordinary friendship. I have not seen the like since then.

My grandfather was a deputy and a shot-firer. I still have the keys he used to blow the charges lodged in the coalface. They are T-shaped, going green with verdigris. They engaged with a circular slot in a box, igniting the dynamite when they were turned. This was not the push-plunger shown in the movies. That could be sparked too easily, accidentally, by a trip, a fall. The top of the T hides a spike like the thing for extracting stones from horses' hooves, the same as the extra attachment on Swiss Army knives. I never found out

36

what they were really designed to do. Now, I cannot ask him.

On that day, he remembered, something went wrong with the firing and he ordered his men out at the double. The chain reaction went through its paces. He followed the others as the shot ignited and as cracks sliced across the ceiling, chasing the scurrying men, trying to dislodge a cascade of boulders to entrap, to crush and to maim them. My grandfather was the only one caught by the shouting, screaming rock. A piece the size of a house crashed from the roof, pinning him to the floor. He exaggerated, but I can imagine him there in the dark with a column of carboniferous stone resting on his spine, waiting for it to snap, a pyre of petrified wood balanced on his shoulders. The man who was standing on the steps outside the Durham garden came back and was instructed to leave with the rest. My grandfather could feel the imminent collapse, could probably bring it about by flexing his breaking back. The man disobeyed and, either by propping the boulder up or manhandling it, dislodged my grandfather, dragged him out for the crew to carry to a safer zone, before the crumbling sky brought down a night colder and denser than night itself.

I can imagine the weeks of recovery and the necessary reports, but know that the red-tape industry and efficiency of bureaucratic measures were in their infancy then. My grandfather would have blamed himself. I wonder if the man who didn't get a medal is still alive today? Probably not. I wonder if the accident happened before my father was born? If so, the man's disobedience ensured my grandfather's survival and the engendering of my father and the engendering of me. Otherwise I mightn't be here. That is possibly what I felt in their company. The two men were not only reminded of the past, their past, but the futures that hung from that moment. Part of that future stood fidgeting at their feet wanting to go back to their improvised playground. 'Boys as young as you used to have to work down the mines,' the hero said as I went to hang upside down above the marigolds.

Now my grandfather has gone. The winding gear has

37

gone, too, and some of the grey debris has gone, probably tipped into the hole left by the pit itself. There has been talk on the parish council about getting the wheels back to stand as a monument to those killed or hurt beneath the rolling hill. The underground network of roads and chambers has filled with salt water as if the light that penetrates the North Sea were attempting to filter through the tons of rock. On the surface the sea-coal, and the waste that was once dropped from an aerial runway directly into the water, has gathered on the shore. The acid green and rusty brown have built up false beaches, and the stack that once stood sentinel at the foot of Dead Man's Bank has all but disappeared, that massive geological remnant which had resisted so long, pounded to pebbles, wiped out in the space of half my lifetime.

Memories often come randomly. They lie in a pile of waste, mostly unsalvageable, not ready for reuse. Before it was redesigned as a thing of beauty, I used to scurry over the slag heap hunting for fossils. The industrial midden yielded figured stones with textures like Art Nouveau designs, petrified wallpaper with scientific tongue-twister names like *Lepidodendron, Stigmaria* and *Sigillaria*, barks of diamonds, dots and stripes. I regret the fact that I gave them away years ago. I imagine the new strata of compacting grey and black rubble under the blanket of earth and green. I wonder if it will form a new rock in a million years' time. I wonder if the palaeontologists will dig plastic traces out of the crust and puzzle at the mesh's resemblance to fossil plants, ponder over the possibility of its being a sport of Nature, rather than a sport of Man. My grandfather milled similar patterns on the handles and levers he turned on his lathe in the lean-to shed at the bottom of the yard.

One of the things I most remember about the hazy days in the north is that cavelike den, down the big steps, past the makeshift bathroom resting on brick pillars, next to the pantry where the old steps had come down from the door to get to the privy and the coal shed up against the wall. In retrospect it seems to have been an exclusively male domain, the forge of Vulcan. There were lumps of metal all around and the smell of lubricant. There were shreds of silver that had been cut by the tools from the revolving pieces of soft steel. There was clutter everywhere. The mechanisms were cannibalised from others and patched up with patterned globes and acorns attached to their once plain features. Wooden laths, steel oddments and tools hung from the sharply sloping roof, like weird stalactites. Rows of chisels, bits for the brace, files, rasps, surforms, planes, hacksaws, spare blades, spanners and ratchets, all lined the windowsill, fitting into semicircular bulges made from a thick leather strip stapled into the rough wood. The windows were covered with sticky-backed plastic up past my eye level, frosting the glass with ripples, lozenges and lines. There was very little space even for a tiny tot like me. It seemed I never would grow much bigger. I am sure my sister never went there, or perhaps she never went there with me. My grandfather was always making things, doodling home improvements on scraps of paper, then turning them into reality, using whatever he could salvage from the racking above his head, or improvising them from some discarded thing or other, inventing new things, most of which I didn't understand, but whose ingenuity I could feel. The little ornamental crisscrossings around the crown or base displayed the pride lavished upon their construction, his hard-won skill and his spontaneity.

Now the shed must be gone, and the stalactites. Now the imitation frosting must have been removed, the house modernised and made fit for people without a pit to work in. My grandparents moved into an old-people's flat further down the coast, impeccably planned by town planners to stand at the bottom of a hill that for rheumatics might as well have been a mountain. The policy of making the rough places plane evidently only extended to some old slag, not to some old codger, struggling up the face of K2 to the newsagent's at the top and back down again, all in a single day. After the flat they transferred to a bungalow in the same complex and there the night closed in on old Joe. He had given up smoking and his bulk had swollen, as though he had taken to consuming vast quantities of Cameron's or

Castle Eden. The dust in his lungs settled and the explosion in his digestive tract finally took him away.

He and my grandmother had begun using a knitting machine to augment their pension and pass the time. Joe had to tinker with the beds of needles and rig various improvements and innovations. He was reminded of the hours he had spent in his private cavern, designing a rug-making machine. It would have been named after him and his immortality would have been guaranteed. Now he has gone and his name too. He probably wouldn't approve of the way I run my life, make my living, and other things besides, and I am left the legacy of a black shape as big as a house resting on my back and the feeling that I am banging my head against the same walls that surrounded him.

His son, my father, went through many jobs but the idea of his working in the mining industry appalled my grandfather, even if it was as an accounts clerk in an office on the surface. He studied to become a teacher. He taught metal-work and woodwork and I think the lathe from the dark at the bottom of the steps now languishes unused, unuseful, in the garage. The first subject I gave up when I was sent to the *proper* school was woodwork, ostensibly because the teacher was a sadistic bastard, but really because the magic of my grandfather's skill showed as nought in the hands of my father, or so my jaundiced view declared. Sons reject the achievements of their fathers as a matter of course. They want to leave their own mark, to wipe out the previous ones in the process. Recently I started to take scraps of wood and metal and assemble them into sculpture whose archaic lines look totemic, primeval, permanent. One of the first things I ever made was a sort of model of the pithead using bits of driftwood from the false beach below the K2 foothills.

My grandfather did many jobs during his life, as did my father. He kept pigs and killed them. He was in the Home Guard. He won medals he never received. He kept a shop. He ran a delivery service. He fought his own court cases. I went to a good school, they tell me, and now unload lorries and work in a shop, shelf-filling. My grandfather loved my grandmother and their family stability seemed archetypical, or maybe it was merely what we little-legs saw or wanted to see. My grandfather was too young to fight in the Great War, though one of his brothers was one of the fallen.

Their father, my great-grandfather, was a wealthy man. The inheritance, to be divided at his death, included eight houses. He committed suicide. The power he abandoned kept it out of the papers. He couldn't go on living when his wife died. There were two other sons in the family, besides Joe and the glorious martyr killed for king, country and sweet fuck all. At the time my great-grandfather hanged himself from the back of the pantry door, Joe was too young to inherit. His two houses, and the dead son's two, passed to the eldest surviving child to be kept in trust until my grandfather reached the right age. By the time he did, the property was gone. It had been drunk. My grandfather was, not surprisingly, a teetotaller. I was an alcoholic. When I made a frenzied attempt at killing myself, Joe said I should be thrown out of the house. At the time we were already in the mineshaft of the distant south. I did not know then what I know now. I did not know what happened in 1921. The pressures to recoup the family prestige are vested in me. I will disappoint all those ghosts, for the surname will die, with me and my incompleteness. The night will get me. I shall have no children.

I still have my grandfather's books. The rules of safety in the coal seam. Ways to detect killing gases, exploding gases (firedamp, in the air, in the ground, the four elements combining), first-aid manuals, copies of relevant legislation, geological timetables. In all the papers my father and I cleaned out of his desk there were no plans for his amazing invention, but my grandmother gave me the one remaining letter she'd saved from a shoebox-ful. It had one of those mysterious addresses the Post Office miraculously manages to locate, as if there were a bank of bizarrely labelled pigeon-holes in each sorting room with tags waiting to be matched with improbable directions. *To the man who recently appeared in the press because he invented a rug-making machine for the home market. I think he lives somewhere near Hartlepool. Please try to find him.* He did live near

Hartlepool, and the workers at the PO did do their job. I think George VI was on the stamp. I cannot find the memento mori in my inadequately systematised lot of pigeonhole shoeboxes in the loft, but I will.

The next village along the coast, a ribbon of houses up a hillside, stood within walking distance of where they lived, but my grandparents decided to buy a six-berth caravan as a holiday home and install it on the site across the main line from the cluster of building-block homes. My parents also bought one and that served us in a similar fashion. We had already moved south, to a little town on the banks of the river Sept. There was a wonderful curving beach backed by dunes which overlooked the boxes on wheels. My grandparents named theirs after me, my sister and my cousins, taking the first letters from each of our names and conjuring up an acronym. My initial came first: I was the first-born.

There were some carefree breaks before the strain of a family disintegration and the mounting mass of homework and pressure from school rendered them less cheerful. We kids went off one day with a much older boy from the next caravan and we scrapped and played among the pillboxes and the mountains of sand. Complaining that the grains were chafing at the top of his legs, he went into one of the concrete war memorials to brush them away. I casually followed him in and watched, transfixed, as he dropped his jeans and white Y-fronts and lifted up his T-shirt to remove the offending silicon chips. He had a crop of pubic hair and I was fascinated. Neither I nor any of the boys I knew had reached that stage yet. I remember the odd low light bouncing off salt-whitened concrete as it fell from tiny windows that once held gun emplacements and allowed soldiers not much older than this youth to scan the horizon for invading ships, subs or landing craft. I remember the pointed gather of his foreskin and the way he jostled his balls around to get at the irritating particles. I remember thinking his penis seemed enormous even flaccid and I felt sure my smaller erection must have been obvious. When he told me to take a closer look for him I must have reddened, but the dim glow would have covered that. 'I think you've got it all out,'

I said. I really wanted to ask if he wanted me to brush the rest of the sand from between his buttocks where he had even greater difficulty seeing and reaching. I didn't. That was that.

On the tramp back to the zigzag of steps up the hill to the site he told us a joke that we laughed at but didn't get: 'There was this sadist and this masochist and the sadist made the masochist take all his clothes off then tied him up. He got out a bullwhip and said to the masochist, "You'd really enjoy it if I used this, wouldn't you?" – "Oh, yes," said the masochist. – "OK," said the sadist, and walked away.'

The grey sea pounded the rocks and the oil slick of black shingle and the leopard-mottled sand as I went beachcombing at the age of seventeen, with the darkness laughing at my shoulder. The shoreline was deserted. I had explored the caves and wondered what number of sexual scrapes must have taken place inside their womblike vaults. I collected a handful of penny-flat stones and skipped them three, four, five times over the opaque breakers. Then I selected a handful of the white ones and, on the wet sand in front of the encroaching tide, spelled out J-o-h-n-n-y before the waves took the plaintive concrete poem out to sea. I grabbed the first and last dot before that happened. Those two points of reference must lie in the piles of junk upstairs, somewhere.

The beach had been condemned by the European Commissioners because of the refuse from the belly of the earth and the effluvia from the belly of the people, which turn the sea a viscous grey. There is, or was, a sewage outflow just north and one just south of it. I saw three dead things delivered by the water to that beach: a porpoise, a dog and a boy. The first was well decayed and stank and hummed with flies in the cracks of its skin. The second was strangely without hair. It was thin, like a whippet, but might not have been. The lips curled back from the teeth. The whole carcass was parchment yellow, skin, eyes, canines. It was twisted up like a dog poisoned in a volcanic eruption. I buried it under sand and chunks of Carboniferous limestone. The boy's corpse was recovered by a pair of frogmen. He was younger than me and had got his foot caught in between rocks as the tide flooded in. He was carried up to the waiting ambulance in the diver's arms, a bizarre pietà, the place of the Virgin taken by a black-rubber-clad male and the Christ by a child with bright red trunks, his arms stretched straight and his head hung back, his body the colour of paper. We watched the scene, as if in slow motion, from the top of the bank, the ashen sky like a tarnished cleaver slammed down on the chopping-board slab of a marble sea. I didn't go down to gawp like some, but went back into the caravan to read Rupert Brooke or something similar.

My grandfather spent thousands of hours on the drawings for his invention and thousands more building working mock-ups, but I cannot imagine or describe the manifold complexities of the mechanism. I can work out the basic premise because they taught me to think that way in my *proper* school in the flatlands of East Anglia. My grandmother still makes rugs, though the arthritis makes it a labour of pain, rather than a labour of love. I was told she used to stretch the coarse webbing between two chairs in front of the blazing hearth while my grandfather was in the depths of his night-in-daytime, and that she was thus able to thread from above, pass the wool or rag back through with the other hand, then knot it and cut it, while sitting at a third chair in between the others. So basically a needle had to thread the stuff from a bobbin through one hole and out of the next, secure a loop to something, like a sewing machine would, then either tie off the doubled cord in turn or fix it using a second reel, and finally cut the tuft at the same height as the preceding one, in rows, backwards and forwards across the diamond weave. Simple! The device must have been something similar to a piano hammer (or a clavichord's, which plucks rather than hits). I can see Joe planing, filing, sawing, calm, then cursing, in the inner sanctum of his temple of industriousness, unheard by his wife, or, if she happened to cross the yard, allowing herself not to hear, or choosing to interpret the imprecations as propitiatory spells to the fairies and goblins that hid away in the pitchy hidey-hole. How many failures of carefully constructed prototypes were there before the final one? How did he feel when all

44

that hard graft finally paid off and he finished the scheme? I wonder.

Lyell, Cuvier and Buckland were pioneers of the idea that the fossil record can be read from the pages of the rocks once the language is properly understood. I was a little less sentimental, more acquisitive. One day while down on the beach near the caravan park with my geological hammer, I was surrounded by a group of jeering older boys. They threw sand in my eyes and taunted me. They challenged me to climb the cliff. The particular bit they had in mind stood an eroded promontory with the yellow limestone exposed and rainwashed into a petrified waterfall, with clumps of tussocky grass interrupting the cascade's flow. It was about forty degrees from vertical but the islets of greenery seemed to plot an easy ascent. The muddy river was actually quite slippy even in the dry weather as the tiny humps of fossilised water tumbled one over the other in a fine rain. You had to dig your trainers in before they held, and a handful of vegetation was just as likely to come away in your hand as hold fast. I clambered up the first part of the slope after the other boys without difficulty, but as they reached the top I came to a lumpy knoll projecting from the face like a nose and couldn't manoeuvre my legs over the bridge and hold on to the eyebrows at the same time. I was stuck.

Everything went slowing down to a stillness. I couldn't call out or wouldn't because of stubbornness and yet my fear must have vibrated through the air or the smell of me carried over to the youngish man on the steps. He came down over the beach and bounded up the cliff with consummate ease. When he reached me I'm sure he must have asked something pointless like 'Are you stuck?' but I can't remember. He put his hand on my backside and pushed me up on the forehead of the monster and then got to the top before me to haul me up after him. 'Thank you, sir!' I said and he must have been surprised by my accent and by being addressed like that so young, by one so young. I was effusive, but he said it was nothing and strode off.

Only later did I recall that his helping hand was shoved unnecessarily far forward between my legs to give me the boost to get to the top. I must have been wearing short trousers and, thinking visually about the positions involved, imagine he had ample opportunity to press his chest against my T-shirted back. But perhaps I am inventing all that? At the time I was deliriously grateful for his timely intervention – my guardian angel, if I have one, interfering with me again.

My grandfather, when he completed his work, must have felt the same. He was almost at the top of the ladder, needing that little intervention to turn invention into viable proposition. When the company he applied to agreed to help, he must have thought he was safe, standing looking down from on high.

He went to a carpet manufacturer and I can imagine his harsh bluntness actually helping his endeavour rather than upsetting people, as was so often the case with his relatives. The board of directors would have argued that it would diminish sales, but he would have pointed out that they would be tapping a section of the population which didn't have the wherewithal to cushion their floors with square feet of portable fields of orange and brown; that if they controlled the sale of backing cloth and thread, replacement needles and the back-up service engineers, they would expand rather than reduce their share of customers; that the inroad into Commonwealth countries would be greater with machinery, especially that designed for small-scale use, than with luxury items like carpets to replace their matting or bare boards; markets always operated on swings-and-roundabouts principles and the company could win only if it had exclusive access to the patents. They listened patiently and were persuaded . . . provided that the rights were signed over to them.

In the heat of success, my grandfather made a move that was uncharacteristically foolish. He allowed the contract to be drawn up and ratified. Maybe he was simply relieved, like me at the top of the cliff? Only when the manufacture and promised marketing campaign didn't materialise did he realise that the helping hand had been placed aggressively on his balls, not as a pat on the back at all. He must have been discouraged and demoralised, especially as the patents pending, numbers so-and-so and so-and-so-on, lay in the self-same hands that had touched up his commercial acumen. He must have felt bitter, must have seen the boulder come crashing down to crush him.

On the day we stood in the chapel in front of his pale, shiny coffin, pretending to be a happy family, united in our feelings of mortality and desperately hoping for better days, I could stand in my one scruffy suit and be glad that my father had only asked the question about drug-taking as we drove from the station to the mining village and that because we were both staring ahead and had no eye-to-eye contact, I was able to lie, almost convincingly. The divorce and my own sins still lay in the future, the book had not yet been written. The predominant feeling was that the stuff of life is both soft and dark and hard and bright.

Butterfly

MARTIN WOKE UP with an erection. He always did nowadays. He never used to, but now he did. And he'd deal with it in the usual way. In just a minute. But he liked to savour the moment first.

He woke up on his back with his right hand curled up on his left shoulder, his left arm by his side and his right leg bent so that the ball of his fist rested near the other ankle. He flattened out his hand, allowed it to linger on his collar-bone before sliding the palm down his chest and across his stomach to touch the waistband of his boxers. This particular pair were relegated almost exclusively to use as truncated pyjamas, though he would occasionally wear them to school if he wasn't doing PE that day and his mother hadn't washed the others. They were covered with alligators, jaws gaping wide; pink and orange alligators. His aunt had assured him they were expensive and had insisted that he model them for her last Christmas. He had done so, a little embarrassed but without protest, certain that she was a little 'funny' because she was forever touching his hair and putting her finger in his ear. He was also sure the designer of the fabric must have done his foundation course at somewhere like Bradford Poly and then his degree at Chelsea, sitting all day dreaming up psychedelic animals he could never quite get right. These particular beasties crawled at all sorts of angles over the white background, and when he looked down at the snapping mouths that were the wrong way up, the curving bulges of the eye sockets, the straight lines of the jaws and the vaguely bulbous tips of the snouts with their flaring nostrils looked just like brightly coloured pricks, only the incisors became serrations on the upper side, and he sometimes imagined that one day he'd slip his hand down to find teeth among his hair, rather than the other way around. A crude joke. 'Cor, that'd do some damage!' he thought, but like most thirteen-year-old boys, his calculations in that area far outstripped his practical knowledge.

Sometimes when he woke up, his erection would poke out the fly of his shorts or, less often, out the cuff, uncomfortably pinned to his left leg; more frequently it lay along his hip or nearly perpendicular to his body, pushing for all its worth to get out. He always stroked all round his waist, feeling the elasticated wrinkles of his underpants, as far as he could without changing position. It tickled a little and made his dick tingle with anticipation. Right side to left side, then back to the middle, just below his bellybutton to finger the button at the top of the fly, then to undo it, holding his stomach in, so that, as he let himself relax, the flaps opened to let his exploring hand brush ever so lightly past the head of his penis and down the shaft, under the cotton, to cup his scrotum with his four fingers and to hook his thumb over his phallus – a word he loved – to nest in his pubic hair like a tiny tusk. He didn't have that much growth yet, but it was jet black so looked quite impressive, whereas some in his class were practically bald, naked. He was a clever boy, brilliant at English, the teacher said. He used long words such as 'expostulate', 'archaeopteryx', 'amanuensis', and 'horripilate'. He didn't always know what they meant, however, and assumed the last one had something to do with sex. His favourite combination at the moment was 'psittaceous paraclete', which his older brother had told him came from Beckett. 'The one who got murdered in the cathedral?' he queried. But early in the morning his mind was not occupied with entomology.

Under the hot duvet he was always surprised to find how cool and clammy his testicles were, but his brother had enlightened him on that score too: that bit of him was the coolest part of the body and had to be in order to produce healthy spermatozoa. He added that he actually enjoyed

49

going into the walk-in freezer at work on Saturdays. It was part of his productivity deal, he said.

The duvet was printed with lots of cars being raced by Mickey and Minnie Mouse. He'd got it when he was eleven, but was a bit fed up with it now, especially when his mates came round and they sat on the bed while they played games on the telly. It was partly for this reason – to avoid looking at signs of a childhood that he wished to get rid of – that he kept his eyes shut, but also because the sun, blazing through the curtains, made the insides of his eyelids enfold him in the great red light that somehow went with the sexual arousal. Martin had the second biggest prick in the class. How the other boys knew was a mystery, but everyone always knew who had the biggest and who the smallest. Strange, since at that age boys are very coy and cover themselves with towels to change for swimming, or put their shirts on so that the tails hide their tails as they whip their shorts off after football. It was as if some crowd of birds watched each individual separately through their bedroom windows and, in council later, discussed their findings and then crowed their news to all who'd listen. Everyone knew. Somehow.

He squeezed his hand and adjusted it so thumb and fore-finger met, squeezed some more, and slowly pulled down-wards. He felt his foreskin retract, smoothly like the shutter on his brother's loading bay, but without the clank of metal and whirr of motor, though the humming of the blood in his ears was similar to the noise of a distant engine room. The cargo in the hold needed unloading fast because his mother was calling him to breakfast. 'I'm coming,' he shouted, as he let the rhythmical piston action accelerate. Firing on both cylinders, he simultaneously shot his left arm under the bed to pick up a Kleenex and mop up most of the oil slick before it polluted the beaches, and flung the cover off with his right. He'd noticed that a little went a long way and that it showed up even worse on dark sheets than on light ones; very scientific. When his mum came to change them, she must notice. He felt guilty and resolved not to do

50

it in bed any more. His resolve usually failed. One more stroke and he was spent, target practising with the tissue.

Sometimes he did it when he got home from school as well as before getting up, but the morning was peak time, rush hour. In the evening it was just a matter of a quick shake, between getting out of uniform and into jeans, frequently still on his feet, staring into the garden, thinking about nothing, waiting for relief. Mornings he coherently thought about Simon. Martin might have had the second biggest prick in the class, but Simon had the most experienced. He'd been caught behind the bike racks with Melanie Travis, banging away against the corrugated iron. A prefect heard the racket and went to investigate, only to see trousers round ankles and skirt almost to shoulders. The discoverer had laughed at the explorers and told them to do it more discreetly, and privately he had asked Simon if he had taken precautions. Simon said, 'No, 'cos she said she was on the pill.' (At fourteen!) He was advised to be more careful. The older boy said he wouldn't report him, though the story still got around, as did the one about his exploits with the woman down the street. But that was less likely to be true.

Martin didn't feel any guilt about thinking about Simon, but somewhere in his thinking he half calculated that it was just a phase he was going through. The thing was, Simon was so athletic, brilliant at football, always suntanned (even in winter), well-muscled and looked-up to; by many for his worldly wisdom, and by most because he could beat almost anybody in a fight. When he thought about him it was with what a jargon generator might label a pan-visual psycho-physical comprehension, seeing all of him at once, that is, and absorbing the image. It was as though concentrating sexual attention on certain parts of the body was actually a learned way of seeing, or at least one reinforced by taboo and pornography. Martin had not really learned that lesson yet. A baby feels itself to be continuous with its environment, a child is happy having its integrity broached by attacks of tickling, but the late adolescent guards bits of himself as though they were secret missile bases.

Martin had seen *all* of Simon in the changing room, but

51

all glances had to be furtive. In Simon's case it proved quite easy, since he didn't have the excess self-consciousness of the others. He had done earlier on in his career. He had reached puberty in the first year and had been at pains to hide this fact, until most of the rest caught up to some extent. Luckily, the early onset of hairiness had not led to his becoming baboon-like. Now, he'd quite happily walk round completely naked and talk to people who would quickly get embarrassed and turn away. If you were caught looking, you'd get jeered at as 'bumboy' or 'bender' and, in their particular school, as 'ballboy' or 'bagboy'. Firstly, because it was cripplingly humiliating to be considered worthy only to be a linesman: so bad at games you were left on the side to pick up other people's balls. Secondly, because a previous PE teacher, one Willy Williams (as warped a Welshman as you could ever hope to find), had once picked on the prettiest boy in the school to run an errand, and shouted at the unfortunate, 'Go grab my bag, boy. In the showers!' Often the terms were reduced to just B.B. and this appeared as a graffito on boys' lockers, such as, 'P.P. is a B.B.' There was a boy in the fifth form called Brian Butcher who had been made miserable for four years because of his blasted initials, but ended up nicknamed 'King' because by the time he was fifteen he could play the guitar like a genius; evasion by compensation, compensated by excelling.

Martin got up and dressed, dumping the blotter in the wastebin, the one with the picture of the Altamira cave paintings that they'd got free with washing powder three years ago. There was additional dry debris in the bin and he crumpled up a sheet of rough-book paper covered in algebra to partially disguise its contents. He picked the alligators up off the floor and inspected them, and also the backside of Minnie and Mickey, before straightening them out. By then his hard-on had completely disappeared and he slipped into white M&S briefs and his shirt and trousers and ran downstairs to scrambled egg on toast and 'I wish you'd put your socks 'n' shoes on before you come down,' from his mother.

'Yes, Mum!'

'Did you have a wash?'

Did she know? 'No.'

'Well, make sure you do before you go. Now, hurry up. Scramble!'

Upstairs again. On with blazer, with its anchor on the pocket, tie, top button left undone, socks, shoes. Kit into duffel bag, books into briefcase. Thunder downstairs. Into the street to see his bus stopped at the lamppost at the end of the garden. The others had got on and for some reason there were more members of the public than usual, so there were no seats downstairs. Top deck as crowded. He made his way to the back. Simon motioned him to sit next to him and asked him if he'd done the maths homework. Simon hadn't done his and so copied Martin's jolting along the country lanes towards Elderton, the village where their school dominated everything. They didn't talk as the task in hand was pressing.

In maths, first thing, Simon sat as far away as possible, so that any of his wrong answers wouldn't tally with his neighbour's wrong answers, but in English they sat together again. This wasn't a common occurrence and Martin felt a little apprehensive. Untidy youth, he felt himself stiffening, while Eddison was droning on about the witches' recipe book, or so it seemed. Blokes sit with their legs apart, whereas birds keep theirs together. Martin felt Simon's leg budge his and then not retreat, stay put. The muscles must have been tensed to keep that position. Simon whispered, 'I've got a stork-on.'

'So have I,' replied Martin, not a little shocked.

The pressure relaxed and their attention was captured by the teacher's raised voice demanding of Jean Fitzpatrick who exactly she thought Hecate was. He guffawed derisively when she confidently replied, 'Macbeth's wife, sir.' (Not such a bad answer after all, it might be reflected.)

PE could have easily been a total disaster third lesson as Martin discerned that his shorts had mysteriously vanished, or been pinched as a joke, or simply been left behind in the rush. (A boy will usually attribute any explanation, be it theft or magical intervention, rather than admit his own culpability.) Simon was changing next to him. He lent him

53

his and wore tennis shorts instead. He would be staying behind for a club match against a school from the next nearest town.

At lunch the two boys managed to arrive together and so sat together, eating burgers and chips and raspberry trifle. Simon said, 'You should pop round and see me some time, you know. I only live at the other end of the estate . . . oh, you *know*? Well, come on Saturday afternoon.'

Martin was amazed because they'd never actually been that close, though the one copied the other's homework from time to time. Simon had lived in town before and only within the last three months gone to the outlying village where his father bought a better house after a major promotion, though only major enough to move halfway from town, halfway to the ludicrously expensive village where the school was.

'And bring your swimming things. We'll go down to the millpond.'

This was a large inlet on the river, above the lock, long without a mill, and consequently quite secluded even though it lay just behind the village. Impossible, Martin thought.

The next day was a bore and most of the time the two were in different sets, and Simon got a detention at lunchtime for not doing his French homework. Martin was in the top group so didn't do the same exercises.

Then, Saturday.

Martin woke up with an erection and a very giddy feeling. He sometimes got butterflies in his stomach, but this time it seemed to be all over. He slid his hand down in the usual gesture and felt as if his skin was hardening as well. The now infrequent wet dreams left a crusty deposit by way of evidence of their having happened. But this was a different crustiness. He also felt as though there were suddenly hard, hairy bristles or something prickling his palm as he neared his goal.

He unglued his eyes. The room was somehow fragmented. Little prismatic rainbows slithered off all shiny objects, in all directions, like a swarm of disturbed bees. He tried to fling the mice off his chest but found that the duvet felt

54

horribly heavy. He felt he should be sweating but his skin was awfully dry, even crisp. He wriggled up towards the pillow and thought he must be going mad as he appeared to have turned black. And, my God! The hair! Even on the wrong side of his hands. So it was true what they said? The room seemed to be getting bigger, becoming immense. He felt his shoulders seemingly split, the shoulder blades burgeoning forth. He tried to call out to his mother, but no voice came, only a dry, metallic rasping.

Managing to pull himself further out from under the duvet, he saw that there was a multiplicity of variegated chitinous setae armour-plating his thorax. It must be a trick of the light, he thought. It's so bright this morning, and everything seems to be vibrating, as though they were demolishing the street, or the next street, or Simon's street. Now his waist should be surfacing and his knob, but, oh no – it wasn't there! His arms, he noticed, were all jointed wrongly like . . . like a flaming bloody insect from one of his brother's weird books. His legs came clear of the eiderdown, the mountains of crumbled autos, and they were too short, foetally contracted, followed by a second pair and still his body kept on going down into the heaps of linen and duck feather.

Pushing with all six arthropodal limbs and feeling very, very sick, he got the rest of his tail out as if he were emerging from a chrysalis. He rolled over and pushed himself up into a squatting position. 'This fucking nightmare metamorphosis better stop! I've got to see Simon this afternoon. And I can't swim like this, now, can I!' he clicked inside his head, which, he realised, didn't want to go up and down, only from side to side, almost full circle, too. Over his shoulder he could see his wings. They were stupendously beautiful, covered with glistening scales and showing two huge peacock eye-patches, half hidden by a pair of more autumnal fans. He couldn't believe it. He also found it hard to relate to the room. It had grown incredibly large. He was now about the size of his pillow which was growing larger too. No, it was he who was doing the altering, the shrinking. The sun went in for a moment and left him devastatingly cold.

He jumped up and seemed to float and then sink softly

on to the back of a blue racer. The weave of the cover was like a *Kon-Tiki* raft or, at least, bundles of papyrus. 'I'm so sorry,' he wailed inside his helmeted head. 'What have I done? Touched Simon's leg? I must go and tell him. Get him to help.'

He flew, fluttered to the window and got through the gap that flapped open between the curtains. He landed on the sill. He realised that he had got from a to b without using the $x \times 2y^2$, where the 2 were his legs, y the distance and x the amount of energy required to do so. 'What am I thinking about? Maths and Simon. M & S.' Crazy.

He walked along the girder bridge of the latch and saw a mass of buddleia below, like a burning bush. He leapt and drifted, wafted, sank, coasted against the warm, turbulent, sticky-scented air on to the ice plant. He stuck his proboscis into a tiny cup of nectar and was electrified by the all-pervading sweetness. 'Oh, to linger here, on and on and never swim, I mean fly, again. I must get as far as number 17 by some means or other. This brazen pink will await my return.' He set off.

His flight was, he felt, more like jumps from one clump of air to another. It seemed uneven in density. The temperature seemed to be responsible. Aerodynamically, his kind are supposed to be impossible, their flight unmathematical, but then the coelacanth was supposed to be extinct, and here he was proving that real or imaginary numbers were the same, provided that you had adjusted your field of vision correctly to accommodate them, to fit them into an insect mentality.

It must have been earlier than he thought as there was very little activity in the village. His mum and dad would be off to Marks' and/or Sainsbury's in town soon, in order to miss the traffic and find a space to put the Astra, assuming it was around eight thirty, as he had thought before the incipience of lepidopteran exoskeletal rigidity had impinged upon his consciousness. He still liked words even while he was mulling over the disappearance and replacement of certain bits of his body. They had done insect anatomy two terms ago, but he hadn't revised the topic since. It was an age to the end-of-term exams, if he ever resumed his normal shape.

More flowers, pansies, peonies or some such, not so sweet, more like whisky or beer compared to the syrupy liqueur he had sipped earlier. Simon's house. Which room? Or should he try the kitchen? He knew it was at the back because Simon had said that he could see the earth-mover laying the pipeline along the beechwood's boundary. Round he floated in a dream. The sun went in again and he felt the freeze.

There were three windows. One was obviously the main bedroom. It was a bay and had velvet *and* net curtains. Then came frosted glass and a large area of brickwork, with some creeper crawling up it. He landed for a moment, but the tiny flowers smelled utterly disgusting, excremental, not sacramental.

He could hear heavy metal, not very loud, coming from the wide-open casement beyond the mass of foliage. In he went. This was obviously what he wanted. Football stuff and American football stuff and certificates and medals and a trophy or two and a lot of mess on the floor including some antique lead soldiers and a space-age, sci-fi-film metal monster, half horse, half tank, standing proud in the middle of the rout. The duvet had a naked woman on it, her head was all wrinkled as the thing had been pushed back and a pair of boxers lay on the pillow. They had 'kiss this' and red lip prints scattered on a mottled pink-and-blue background. A porn mag lay dropped on the floor beside the future dinosaur and a box of Scotties. On the bedside table a student edition of *The Tempest*. Funny, we aren't doing that at school, thought the butterfly. A door cut into the far wall led into the bathroom. It stood ajar and The Destroyers could be heard through the crack, accompanied by a rather gruff, flat voice that went a bit squeaky on the screamed notes. It was a song about 'go get me a woman and make her my slave'.

In through the open door following the flex to the portable. A room big enough for a shower, a washbasin, a toilet, a mat, a boy and a butterfly. Lit by a window set into the end wall of the house, high up, shallow and broad unlike the one Martin had passed outside, the tiled sill cluttered with bottles and sprays and an apparently brand-new safety razor and a pack of blades, unopened.

The shower was on and steam billowed around the ground-glass panel. The boy, with his back to the rest of the room, was rinsing shampoo from his golden-brown hair with almost caressing motions of both hands. Martin had alighted on the cassette player. The music died at the end of the track. 'Bugger it,' said the voice through the torrent. The boy turned and opened the door. Steam. Simon stepping out, drenching everything, throwing a white towel in front of the machine and crouching before it to press 'Eject' and turn the tape. He noticed the flash of some moth he'd scared with the blizzard of his towel, pressed 'Play' and hopped into the shower again.

The vapour in the room was making his wings damp and slow, so the boy who became a butterfly crawled up the wall and over the edge to the Blue Stratos and Kouros, a vantage point from which more of the soaking footballer could be observed through the cloud and crashing downpour. He must have turned the pressure up. Martin had seen everything by the time the Destroyers had been changed to Battleship Potemkin, but in his new guise a reflex action had taken over and he had leapt, he had launched himself heavenwards to avoid the avalanche. Settling next on the basin rim, he had needed a minute or two to stop the lacquered armour segments of his abdomen clattering together, fit to burst, a knight recovering in the lists between jousting bouts. Some of his finery had come unstuck as he scaled the cliff to the light, a smear of moments-ago splendid paint from dusty wings. He felt elated but a little lopsided, as if a breeze were blowing through a hole in a shirt he didn't have, on a roller coaster he wasn't riding. He hoped no permanent damage had been done, and for an instant or two pondered the possibility of his never becoming a proper boy again. Off he flew and settled on the edge of the shower door. Evidently the wing hadn't suffered unduly.

He hadn't realised before, but compound eyes somehow shattered Simon's image without destroying any of its coherence. In a kaleidoscope you see the pattern knowing that it is made of slivers of see-through plastic in a tube held to the eye, and only when the far end is rotated so that the compounds jiggle between the two mirrors do you see the parts rather than the whole device, and only once they have come to a stop once more does the symmetry of the complete design become more apparent than the overlapping of the pink triangle and the green ellipse, multiplying in the centre, as if by magic, to make the bright shape of the glowing carnation. Thus it was that the young boy became a myriad of interlocking sections, each with its own distinct outline, fitting together to make a jigsaw which, when finished, mysteriously showed no lines between the pieces, the chocolate-boxy mosaic being substantially clearer than the flecked and streaked tesseræ composing its complete, unified form, the form of a boy, stood stock still. The machine had stopped turning. Martin was amazed.

'Bugger it!' again as Simon finished, thrust the glass against the wall, switched off the jet and stooped, one foot forward, to pick up the snowfield and wrap it round him as he stepped back into the cubicle to let the excess water trickle down his legs and down the plughole. Martin had been jolted off his perch and on to the lino, recovering enough to feebly flap after a thousand feet of free fall, or so it seemed. He looked up, by tilting his whole body, to see Simon dry his hair, fast and furiously. He saw him envelop his entire head in a halo of cotton fluff and agitate it as if it was a snake in a sack. He could see the darker hair under his arms and, lowering himself as if he were doing a press-up, the network of golden down stuck on his shins, like a mass of flow markers in a mock-up of the Mississippi Delta; and, allowing his bulging eyes to move up again, or rather by pressing his back end down and raising his head, straightening his fore-legs till the joints locked, he could see between his legs from a most unusual angle. He breathed out, which left his whole thorax throbbing with effort.

Simon, like some inappropriately Oedipal figure, unwrapped his head, unbandaged his eyes, the hair springing up like the massed pikes and stakes in a romanticised medieval battle. He began to rub his body, which was already partly dry, the moisture having continued to descend under the pull of gravity while he was worrying his hair. His trunk didn't take long and he went down to clear the droplets from the rest of himself, taking care not to trail the towel in the pool left at his feet. He put it down outside the cubicle and stepped on it to dry his soles, then on the mat to check the places he might have overlooked. He held the towel to his neck with both hands a moment before allowing it to drape his back like a small cape, sliding it laterally to blot each shoulder in turn, then pulling one end round to his stomach and releasing it with the right hand which he then brought up to his neck again, in the same fashion as Martin had his that morning. The white wet cloth hung in front of him like a long loincloth.

After a pause Simon tilted back his head and closed his eyes, his lips slightly parted. Martin flew with difficulty to settle on his shoulder but the boy instinctively brushed the tickling feet away, missing the insect by half an inch or so. The butterfly-boy tried to bellow as he hovered by his ear, 'Simon, it's me. It's Martin.' A butterfly's roar would not scare a flea. Its voice matches its delicate frame and even the dragon-eyed variety has a pale, thin echo, not a hurricane to compliment its blazon.

Simon's eyes had opened a slit and saw the flashes of colour. He closed them again and moaned, 'Ohhh, Mart!'

The standing boy stood steaming. He lowered his left hand the short distance to his midpoint, the towelling foaming down his length and below, in a cascade to the floor. Martin had gone back to the floor, as staying aloft without another sip of nectar was proving too great an effort, even if the breeze from outside was finding its way across the bedroom and past the bathroom door. Simon bent his legs and flicked from tape to radio before continuing. He remained on his knees once down.

The rubbing had dried him and increased his stiffness. He let the weight of the towel go and continued his rhythm, out of time with the music, but gradually synchronising. 'Build

prisons for these madmen, madmen . . .' the rock channel
wailed. 'Martin, Martin,' he whispered.

The scale-wing had walked on to the mat, its shaggy fibres
a mangrove forest, creepers and air roots clogged with humid
air. The damp trunks moving nonetheless, swept by the
draught from the door. Martin was losing more granular
patches from his battered wings and tiredness made him
want to close his eyes, even though he wished to see the
climax. Luckily his eyes had had their lids removed during
the metamorphosis, so he had no choice.

Simon's breathing came faster, through his mouth. He
opened his eyes and looked down and saw the butterfly
beneath him. 'Come and land on my flower, little peacock,'
he hissed. He saw the creature climb on to the fallen mound
of ice and take off in slow motion. He took his hand from
his erection and pushed it between his legs, as though grasping the butt of a revolver instead of its barrel. His cock was
trembling, his finger on the trigger. He held his breath and
the pulsation spread till it reached the base of his skull. The
cream and purple and brown fragment let its six clawed feet
and spiralling proboscis trespass upon the waxy petals of the
glistening orchid which instantaneously began to explode. A
convulsion. A geyser erupting. A huge sigh and an evacuation
of boiling snow from the depths of the volcanic flower's
corolla.

Simon collapsed backwards, his buttocks on his heels,
spine curved over instead of arched in tension as it had been
a moment ago. Eyes shut, hands both closed over collapsing
tower. As his panting slowed, he dared to survey the damage.
Most of his emission was on the now grubby towel, but
some was on the mat and some was on the butterfly, glued
upside down in among the trees on the fringe of the forest.

Martin had been blasted in midair and the extra weight
had somersaulted him to earth. It had hit his body and his
legs were coated. His new senses felt the gumming-up of the
works and the pungency tasted of urgency and emergency.
His eyes were clouded and his tongue coiled and uncoiled
as the salty-sweet mixture, both honey and Dead Sea, made
his whole head feel swamped in one all-embracing sensation.

It was as if his brain were made of it. It burned and put out the fire. It quenched his thirst, but fuelled his need to get out of a desert of howling wind and glacial shadow. He was more exhausted than ever he was after his morning ritual and infinitely more refreshed, though the realisation that he was losing strength and in a terribly vulnerable position began to assert itself on top of the kaleidoscope of interlocking sensual stimulation.

Simon reached down his hand, feeling pity for the drowning, broken-backed butterfly. The combination of sawlike footpads that can grip glass and the glassy liquid glaze allowed the thing to be easily picked up on his finger. He got up and walked into the bedroom, took a tissue and wiped his prick with the other hand and crumpled it into the corner. Then he took another, put it on the woman's breast and persuaded the butterfly to crawl on to it, dragging itself across the fibrous wastes. He watched it recover somewhat, and though its wings were a little gelatinous when they were brought together, he thought the thing would survive. He transferred it to the windowsill in the sun, lifting the hanky carefully. He went back into the bathroom to clear up, taking a pair of briefs from the drawer and the jeans and T-shirt laid over the back of the desk chair by his mother the night before. When he returned, the butterfly had gone.

The rays of the sun had rapidly put the life back into Martin and dried his besmirched skin. Though he could tell his wings were ragged, he knew he had enough strength to get home. On the way he stopped off at various plants, but their delights were not as rich. How would he be able tell anyone what he had experienced? He had not for one moment considered how he had been changed, but the notion that he'd never get back was pressing him as he made his way home. There was more activity about the streets, but he didn't really notice it. He wondered why he had been catapulted from one way of living into another, and was in one respect overjoyed at what had happened, but now there was a nagging concern somewhere in his reduced psyche. In most reported instances of metamorphosis, the subject normally finds his brain patterns more or less intact, but in this case the diminution, and the torpidity that accompanies ectothermy, had altered the speed at which he could deduce things. But then, how often is a butterfly called upon to unravel the processes involved that take it from egg to adult? And for that matter, could any lepidopteran ever conceive what it would be like to be magically made a little boy? If that happened, it would probably wish to be reconverted, to be in the air another while.

He got home and into his bedroom. He sank on to the pillow and found he could close off the torrent of light from his eyes, turn the pressure almost off and 'think' about what to do. Adolescents will often pray to be given things they know, or have been told, they ought not to have. Equally frantically they will beseech the wiping-away of guilt. Why should they deserve to pass an exam they haven't revised for, and why beg the Almighty to make their crib sheets turn to dust in the hands of the sharp-eyed avenging invigilator? He did not know why he had become a butterfly, he only knew he wanted to become a boy again, but the rearranged internal organs churned at the possibility that he had failed the test and that the thing that had happened in the bathroom at the other end of the village would damn him to this disjointed existence for ever: a short-lived for ever. He didn't mean to look at Simon like that, but couldn't resist. He shouldn't have been challenged like that in the first place. He was tossing and turning with anxiety when he realised that he had become detached from his wings.

He only saw and felt greyness surround him as if, having switched it back on, the seeing activity refused to work properly. He was able to roll right over and could feel the hard, brittle wings under him, and at the same time their softness and delicacy. He experienced them as fur against the skin, as if he had his own shape and size back. But not quite. He decided that another transmogrification was taking place. The hard plates of his suit of armour dissolved and sank through the warming muscles and sinews, snaking about to realign themselves. The parts that had been outside were reforming inside, converting into bone and cartilage, joints, discs, tendons, ligaments, hardening and lengthening, connecting and articulating. The tin-can tubing that had bent and joined around him formed an armature deep within. He felt organs shift and disintegrate, coalesce and resume their former places and functions. The breath that had come from below was replaced by that which came from above. Eyes shrank, became lidded and shuttered; their multiplicity had become binocular, finely focussed and movable. The proboscis slid back between his jaws, and teeth protruded anew from itching gums. The bulbous bag of flesh dragging out behind deflated and translocated to the front, the bristles replaced by silky softness as the burdensome thoracic carapace lightened and became less intractable, raw flesh becoming cloaked in downy skin. The warmth in the room was a warmth he shared, contiguous and much less dense, less saturated than when he had flown, a warmth so much more human. He opened his eyes as the last mottles of brown left him white and all curled up. His hair smelled of flowers, his hands of another boy, but the complex of data an insect can unravel began to become a jumble and then a nonsense. The singing of the air became the sound of a car engine. He got up, his limbs like lead and like light, and stumbled to the window to see his mother getting out of the Vauxhall, carrying the shopping. She waved and he waved back.

A dream. He must get dressed and then bike over past the buddleia bushes and up the hill to the old estate, with the millpond beyond. White Y-fronts, patched jeans with Bros-type splits and frayings. His brother's old sweatshirt with the Destroyers' tour dates printed on the back and an imploding skull on the front, white; white socks and scuffed Nike trainers.

He was about to flip the mouse Grand Prix back into place when he noticed something on the pillow. He put them in a matchbox taken from the shelf. It had *El pub inglés, Barbate* written on the lid. He stowed it in his pocket and went down.

'Nice to see you're up in time for lunch, dear,' said his mum. 'What do you want? Burgers and chips or Chinese chicken and salad?'

'Whatever you lot have, I guess. Where's Mark?' That was his big brother. He wanted to ask him about the dream because he was doing psychology, sociology and politics A levels at the tech.

'He would normally be at work, dear, but he took the day off. He's gone with Catherine to Alton Towers for the day. He went up to ask if you wanted to go, but you were out for the count.'

'When?'

'When what dear?'

'When was I out for the count?'

'I don't know. We've only been gone since nine and it's eleven now. Well, I suppose around eight.'

'Oh.'

They had the chicken. Then it was toffee pecan crunch ice cream. 'Don't gobble like a turkey, son!' said his father.

'OK," he clucked between swallows.

'And don't talk with your mouth full, you won't taste your food and it sounds disgusting.'

'I'm going swimming with Simon,' he announced as he splashed and nearly smashed his way through the washing-up.'

'All right, Martin. How long are you going to be?'

'I don't know. It depends on how long it takes.'

'All right, I won't do you any tea and you can microwave something when you get back, but phone if you're going to be very late and take your key in case. Your dad and I are playing bridge in Chelsea tonight. Don't forget. And who's this Simon, anyway? You haven't mentioned him before.'

'Just a mate.'

His mother looked exasperated.

'He lives in the big house near the millpond, on the edge of the estate.'

'I hope you aren't swimming there. You know what I told you about that!'

She had told him that a month or two ago a boy had been attacked by a man who liked little boys, which seemed a bit of a contradiction, so he smirked, and she got angry, saying it was disgusting and he should be sad for the poor child and just as sad for the old man as he'd obviously had something awful happen to him to do such a thing. That time he said, 'Yes, Mum.' This time he said, 'No, Mum.'

His bright-red mountain bike got him there faster than butterfly power. He saw Simon looking out of a downstairs window. The door opened before he was able to knock on it. 'Is that Martin, love?' from the kitchen.

'Oh fuck, that means we've got to say hello!'

Martin was surprised at that word out in the open, but followed quietly.

'This is my mate Martin. This is my mum, in case you hadn't guessed!'

'Pleased to make your acquaintance, Mrs – '

'Oh, my God, that was a funny thing to say. "Hi, Mrs M" would be better, or even, "What's up, Hilda?" But it's such an awful name, don't you think?'

'Yes, I mean no, Mrs . . . M.'

Simon was laughing, but not nastily, and Martin was the colour of a red admiral.

'Oh, I'm sorry, sweetie. You just ignore me. And I think it was actually very polite of you to say hello like that. You must be much better brought up than this little sod!' she expostulated, ruffling his hair. 'All he does is drink and swear and play with himself.'

This time Simon coloured and said defiantly, 'Not as often as I used to!'

'I don't believe you. Now take two cans out of the fridge and get out of the way. Your aunt and uncle will be here soon.' Turning to Martin, she added, 'You will stay as well, won't you? He's told me ever such a lot about you and says you're a real brainbox.'

'Yes, I'd love to. Thank you very much, Mrs M.' (No hesitation this time.)

He had expected Coke but got Red Stripe instead. He didn't really like the taste, but the ice-cold lager was very refreshing, and probably way too strong. The room was tidy, the monster under the Anglepoise and the soldiers put away. The magazine was gone, and the handkerchiefs. *The Tempest* was open face down.

'She made me clear up. I had a bit of a battle this morning.'

'I see.'

'Sorry she talked like that. She was actually quite subdued. I'm amazed she didn't ask you how often you play with yourself. And before you say, "She wouldn't," believe me, she would. She once asked another one of my friends in town before we moved. God, I was embarrassed!'

'My mother once said "masturbate" but not to me, and it was about one of the neighbour's sons who'd got caught doing it with a girl, or something!'

'God, how tedious – with a girl I mean, there's far better things to do.' This was mock serious, but with a hint of double bluff about it.

Out of nervousness the conversation rambled on as they downed the beer. Simon showed him his collection of autographs of famous footballers. Then came a new revelation: he admitted the Shakespeare was because he was probably going to act in it, he was auditioning for the part of Ariel. Changing subject casually he asked, 'Do you still want to swim?'

'Yes, why not?'

'Shall we get changed before we go?'

'I don't mind. I left my stuff in the hall. Shall I go and get it?'

'Yes, but be quiet or else Hilda will collar you and start talking about lesbians, or something!'

Martin smiled, hugely.

He came back into the bedroom to find Simon sockless, shoeless, and removing his shirt, casually looking out of the window.

'Did you do what my mother asked you, this morning?' he asked and turned.

Should he feign incomprehension? He nodded slowly. 'Do you do it more than once a day?'

'Sometimes,' hushed.

'Do you want to do it now?' Martin had got an almost instant hard-on seeing Simon sliding out of his clothes. He remained silent, staring.

'I've got the horn.'

'So have I,' he managed.

'Shut the door and come here.' Seconds later on the bed beside Simon he was told to take his socks and shoes and shirt off. As he did so he heard, 'I had an amazing one this morning. This butterfly landed on my dick just as I was coming and I shot all over it. I thought I'd killed it but I dried it out on a tissue and it flew away. I was thinking about you coming round and it just happened.'

Martin stood up and put his hand in his pocket and brought out the box. Simon reached over and unclipped and unzipped him and slipped his hand into the gap and felt his balls. Martin held the box out to him and said, 'Look.' He took his hand away and took the box as Martin knelt on the floor beside his legs, resting his hand on his knee.

He opened the box.

Tower

BARBATE LIES IN the sun, on Spain's southern Atlantic edge, northwest of Cádiz. Without a detailed map I cannot say exactly where, for I arrived from the north and left for the north, after a week's break from a tour of historical sites and art galleries.

It felt as if the motorway had been built exclusively to allow our carload to get from Seville to Barbate and then from Barbate to Seville. We stopped twice on the way down, once for petrol and once to pick wayside flowers to freshen the apartment. They were short, hardy things with very odd leaves, narrow across, deep from top to bottom and practically triangular in section. They seemed somehow related to the thistle because of their radiant purple blooms and the feathery bracts beneath. It is a very hot part of the peninsula and so their succulent hardiness would be excellent protection against the environment. We picked some and drove on.

I asked Cecilia what they were called and she told me lion's claws. I envisaged a very decadent lion, maybe called Sally, sitting with green enamelled paws and a carmine blaze across lips and whiskers. We had seen such a creature stalking through a craft market in a square in an old, but not ancient, quarter of Seville. His cigarette, short hair and slight five-o'clock shadow declaring one thing, his nail varnish and paint another. He asked for the hour, as they do in Spain. I almost told him I couldn't spare it, but would if he'd wait a while.

The country was in turmoil at the time. The moves towards democratisation had allowed some boys to don the robes of queerdom and expose their homosexuality brazenly;

women had at last been given the legal right to divorce their husbands; drug-taking was spreading as the police relaxed and the Moroccans came over from their fields to sell. So it was that Cecilia had begun to cast off her husband. The driver was another man, heavily bearded, very dark, by the name of Alonso.

Cecilia had three sons, one called Pablo with whom I was obsessed but didn't say, didn't dare. One called Felipe who was rebelling like a battalion of nineteenth-century Russian revolutionaries and, although finding his father's militaristic discipline in the new flat too much, hating his mother's liberal regime almost as much and, being a typical little *machista*, blaming her for the break-up of the marriage. The other son's name I cannot remember. We never met.

One night while the lovebirds were sharing Alonso's bed I was left with the youngster at home. He let the ghetto blaster blare into the early hours and when I finally got up to ask for a bit of peace, I found him in the middle of the tiled living room, with his prick in his hand, clothes scattered all around, hissing, 'Ceci, Ceci.'

Almost every day I stayed in Seville, he had called his mother 'bitch' to her face in front of me. When he was caught playing truant, he was told he couldn't come to the seaside. In the event he rode his moped all the way and arrived very late, covered in sweat and dust, stinking like a locker-room. No ghetto blaster, thank God, but I did hear him intoning his litany at four in the morning.

Earlier that week we had been to the Feria, but were fed up with seeing cavorting horses and dancing groups, with drinking chocolate and eating doughnuts at every meal, and with seeing crowds everywhere, always going the opposite way to us. My Spanish at that time was a little faltering, unless well oiled with sherry, and people often remarked on my talking to the boys in English while they replied in their own language, passive understanding coming before the ability to construct freely in another tongue. With Cecilia, however, I had to gear myself up and discuss her liaison with Alonso in great philosophical detail along with the what-to-do-about Felipe. The most demanding exercise of all was talking to one of Cecilia's friends in the coastal town about the finer points of tuna fishing. With his un-Castilian, Andalucian accent and his tendency to clip the end off every other word, it was very awkward. I managed somehow.

In Barbate I was an exotic and people were amazed to see an Englishman where one ought not to be. The Atlantic is not as clear or as warm as the Mediterranean and storms lash the town from time to time. It is devoid of the tourist facilities normally known as 'traps'. Some attempt has been made to give the kids and the up-and-coming somewhere to go to be seen and there are one or two discos and an English pub. We drank there one night, Cecilia and I, and had to shout above the video-jukebox.

We saw an American when Cecilia and I went along the coast to the next village. Alonso had driven back to Seville for business reasons (whatever they were), Felipe had gone round to see his cousins and we had borrowed the fisherman's Seat. The Yank was in the bar we happened into. He was stoned and pissed out of his arsehole as they say (or some of them might, anyway). We were talking rapidly when he tottered over to demand we buy him a drink. His pidgin Spanish made Cecilia only slowly aware of what he wanted and she issued a torrent of words which made the barlady crack up and walk into the back out of the way. I just turned and told him, 'Look! The answer's no, so just go boil your head, and if you need the recipe and a cooking pot big enough, I'll be happy to oblige.'

The grass and the alcohol weren't sufficient to render him totally incapable of grasping the situation. He called my parentage into question and said, 'Just you wait, sweetheart!'

I did, but he staggered backwards and beautifully vaulted over one of the white cast-iron chairs with an applauding clatter. 'Your landing was a bit off, but I'd have to award you nine point eight for that performance.' He got up and promptly sat down sulkily. I asked the returning barmaid to charge me for the drinks, saying she should add a double vodka for the incapacitated, and left.

On the road back we turned off on a track to the right and wound our way higher between some kind of stunted trees. I don't know what they were, so I can't tell you. They were a dark grey-green with very gnarled trunks, which displayed even more pronounced twists the nearer the clifftop they stood. Cecilia told me she collected *setas* here, but it was too late in the season. I had no idea what she was talking about till she showed me an old withered specimen after we got out of the car. It was a kind of mushroom. Not very magical and by the looks of it not very edible.

We came round the last bend and parked the car next to what I had thought was a castle keep as we approached, but it turned out to be smaller than I had expected. It had no castellations and quite large windows, but only near the top. As we walked around it I realised there was no door. There had once been one but it was way above my head, on the side away from the sea. I could tell because the masonry was a different colour and much coarser. I asked whether it was a fort of some kind, but was told no, although it had been used for various things from a watchtower to a smuggler's hideout. I couldn't imagine a more stupid setting for the latter, perched on the cliff like a lighthouse, perfectly visible from the sea below. 'Yes,' she agreed with me, 'but not from the road and you couldn't get up the cliff. Look!' We went over to the edge and I saw a sheer drop. Gulls were screaming about and the limestone was brilliantly lit by the descending sun.

I took out the camera and did some scrambling about and some click-clicking. Meanwhile Cecilia had gone to sit further up the coast on a promontory where the cliffs halted and changed to steep slopes, mellowing into slight hills which went inland to form the basin for the village we'd just been to. The bay was quite considerable, but you could see the resumption of precipices beyond, very small and in dark shadow. I photographed her with the calm ocean behind her. It was not the clichéd ultramarine of most stories, but a leaden grey over which had been washed glazes of cerulean cobalt, viridian, turquoise and deep purple. The sun was not golden but vivid yellow and only when it finally touched the sea did it rapidly shift to vermillion, as if the heat had been drained from it and the water about it boiled. The reflected

72

light made the sea first a pool of quicksilver, then a bowl of blood, then a slab of black marble as the last part of the arc dropped below the horizon. After that the light came more from the sky and the sea resumed some of its blueness. This pale light quickly went. The trees were blue-black and menacingly contorted, whispering their secrets, and the tower was sombre and the white car looked brown.

We drove back and found Pablito had come back early from Cádiz. He was doing his military service there and had the weekend off. We went out and got drunk and when we got in had to share a bedroom because Felipe was still there, unfortunately. I had the bottom bunk and couldn't help stare as the bronze beauty shed his shirt and trousers and pants before he leapt into the top bunk. He stood and talked to me first, so close I could have touched him. He was more beautiful than rain in the desert. Even his cock was beautiful. Some aren't, you know? Some may be big, but they can be heavily veined or odd in the relative proportions of bollocks to dick. Some have bizarre shapes, not straight but curved, or twirled like the porcine. The shaft may be too thick for the glans, the balls may hang too far or be tucked under so tightly as to be invisible. A late circumcision can leave unsightly scar tissue, moles or birthmarks can suggest unwholesomeness. Too much pubic hair and the thing looks totally animal, too little and it looks grotesque, a positive Punch's nose of a prick. There is not the vocabulary there is for describing faces, probably because the features change to express moods, and phrases like 'a bitter mouth' or 'smiling, happy eyes' produce certain standard envisagings. But I sometimes wonder if some of the epithets for expression or character could not be applied to those bits just as easily as otherwise: fierce, steadfast, unshakeable (in resolve, that is), timid, willing or unwilling, feeble? But I am getting away from the point. I am in danger of losing the thread.

As we slept I dreamed. I did not dream about the beautiful boy above me but about his mother, about the moments spent sitting behind her, photographing her and going over the mystery of the tower. I dreamed of times long gone. I saw the tale unfold around me.

*

73

Long ago, an Arab merchant journeyed from the city of Seville to Barbate on his black stallion, in search of the boy his spies had reported seeing there. He had been told to seek him at the school run by the local priest. One of his servants had gone on ahead and, seeing his master in the square, led his mount into a cobbled side street. He asked his master if he would not prefer to wait till tomorrow, after refreshing himself and the horse. No, he would not.

At eleven the clock in the bell tower sounded and the boys came out from behind the church. 'Where is my little urchin?' asked the man.

'He always tarries, my good lord,' replied the servant. 'Here he comes now.'

The wealthy owner clapped his hand to his mouth. The boy was blond and blond and blond, impossibly blond for this bleached place; of heavenly beauty, unbelievable, the stuff of fable, a sport of the devil maybe.

The boy, whose name was Esteban, had lingered with the priest over some Latin text or other, something he often did to the light-hearted ridicule of his schoolmates and the amazement of Father Pedro Diego. The boy's insight was keen for one so young.

He walked towards the side street only to see the black charger barring his way. The rider had white trousers on, gathered at the ankle, and a voluminous white shirt gathered at the waist, but his shoes and his waistcoat spoke of immense wealth and refinement. The footwear was black and the pointed tips curled back, but still they were of the supplest leather and the stitching was all undetectable. They had a silver buckle each with two amoretti firing arrows at a dragon-beast in the centre of the clasp. The waistcoat was sea-grey and over it a filigree of gold and silver embroidered swirls twined and untwined like a map of all the galaxies of an exploding universe.

The man's skin was dark and he had a thick beard like Alonso's, but far finer features. His eyes glittered, but the expression was hard to tell. He had a dark turban with a silver crescent clipped to the front. He carried a scimitar and a kris. His cloak was carmine and so light that it fluttered even though the air was motionless, ready to stagnate around twelve o'clock so people would slow to lunch and siesta, as always.

The horse was groomed to look like obsidian, but it had been travelling hard. Foam flecked its muzzle and there was dust on its fetlocks. Its ears stood alert. The harnessing was of white leather. White! Imagine! Bronze ornaments dotted it and the bit had the same beast on it as the merchant's shoes, tail out of one side of the mouth, head out of the other.

The boy bowed slightly and said, 'Noble sir, I would trouble you to let me pass. I have been hard at work at school, but now must to my mother's house to help her, for my two brothers are out in the field and my father has gone to buy seeds in the city.' He said this in Arabic and when there was no response repeated it in Latin and then in Spanish. Still no response. He turned as if to set off in the opposite direction – a longer route home, but he had to get there rather than squander more time on talking and getting nowhere.

'I see, little master, that your famed learning is indeed true. I compliment you on your speech and your politeness. Let me offer you a small prize for your courteous manner.' He prodded the servant, who produced the salver he had been instructed to have ready. On it a glass dish held an array of Turkish delights. It smelled sublime. Esteban was tempted.

'Thank you, your excellency, but I cannot accept something from which you yourself may gain greater profit.' This exchange was in the oriental language and when the man got off his horse and held the dish in front of the boy and insisted, he took the smallest piece and ate it.

'Amazing!' in Spanish, then in Arabic, 'You are most kind, my lord, but now I must get to my mother's house. It does me little profit to stand and talk when she needs my help in her work. Our conversation is very pleasant but my duty, as you can see, lies elsewhere and I am becoming late.'

The man said in the boy's own tongue, 'Come then, let me ride you home on my poor nag Aristotle. He may be weak but can manage your tiny frame.'

'I have been told to take nothing from strangers, if it so please you not to misunderstand my meaning. I must obey my parents in all things, so it is written, is it not?'

'Then why, Esteban, did you take the sweet and eat it?'

He was momentarily shocked that his name was known, though his fame as a scholar was certainly village-wide, so he had not really been surprised at the earlier compliment. 'I honoured you as you honoured me, and I could not refuse your reward without offence . . . and if you must know, I was hungry!'

'Ah-ha, so you're not quite so formal. Get up and I'll take you back and we needn't mention the bribe, eh?' And do take another bit, you're dying to.' He did. 'Now put your foot in between my hands and swing your other over the saddle.'

Once up, the man got up behind him and pressed him against the pommel, handed him the reins and told him to steer. He put his hands round his waist and the horse reeled round even though the boy had done very little.

Along narrow streets to the edge of the town, along the quay past the fish market on to the road out of town. Esteban held the reins, but a lot of the time he pointed out a direction to the man, who prodded the black animal with his toe or his heel. The servant stayed behind with the tray and the delight.

Esteban's mother stood in the doorway watching for him. The man hoisted him over the saddle and lowered him to the ground. 'My good woman, before you tell off your off-spring, let me say that it is my fault he is late and so I offered to carry him home. I do hope you haven't been put to any great trouble. You must let me pay you if I have. Your son is a marvel to talk to.'

'Your highness, I am too pleased that he entertained you to be cross with either of you, and thank you for your kindness. Now, you go and get on with the chores,' she said to the boy. He skipped away and turned to half wave, half salute from the door. 'Go on!'

'He would make a great asset to serve at table for some lord, my lady, and his intelligence would make him a most

76

diplomatic page. Have you never thought your son could get on better away from the sleepy little town?'

'He is not my son, your worship, but rather my stepson. There is a great deal of age difference between him and his elder brothers and so he is important to me in the house. Having no daughter to do these things, he must be the one to help. It is a pity he is so clever. My husband wants to send him to university in Salamanca, wherever that is, in accordance with the wishes of the boy's mother, God rest her! I love him even if at times I do not show it for he is so naturally affectionate, but I fear his looks will break many hearts soon enough . . . and probably ours.'

'Your concerns do you justice, madam, but if I, or another, were to pay you to take him into our care and to send him to Salamanca ourselves, your problems would be solved for you. You could afford to pay for help around the place. He deserves the opportunity, don't you think?'

'I cannot say, most worthy gentleman, but the price would have to be high to satisfy my husband that your intentions were the best for all concerned.'

'I will pay his weight in silver. He is golden and thus may be worth more, but my offer will stand only until his thirteenth birthday, not a day longer.' Without waiting for a response, he turned and cantered off towards the town.

The following day Esteban's father came home very downcast. He had bought the seed, but the horse and what cash remained from the sale of the bull had been stolen on the return road. It was dark and his assailant was dark. He sprang from behind a rock. He had leapt on to the dappled mare and put a curved blade to his neck. In the moonlight a jewel on the hilt glinted and a tattoo on the knuckles showed a monster with the god of love on its back, wrestling with it or merely tickling its ears. He recalled these tiny details even though the robbery had taken place in the blinking of an eye.

Esteban heard the story from the loft. His brothers were in the tavern getting pissed as normal and so there was little enough noise, enabling him to hear more than usual. He didn't want to listen, though he couldn't help it. He knew his father had been acting when he greeted them both, only declaring his tiredness and saying that nothing else was wrong. It had been late so after a hug and the present of a new belt the boy was sent up the ladder.

He slept in the same bed as the other two and hated their coming in and their waking him up, reeking of ale and often telling him things he'd have preferred not to hear. Nonetheless the warmth of their quickly stilled bodies was a comfort. Usually he was between them but sometimes pushed to one side or the other. They had taught him the things Pedro Diego kept silent about. His father and step-mother had a separate room at the back of the house, the other side of the storeroom, and so realised none of this, perhaps.

He listened on as the two argued about what to do. It seemed the mortgage repayment was due in about a fortnight's time. The Jew would not wait. A nobleman was mentioned by the woman and the price for taking away their troubles and the boy. 'I know you want rid of Esteban but he stays whatever happens. We agreed. I know he is not your kin, but neither are the other boys.'

'The other "boys", as you call them, are men and work well for their living. You could not sell them because you could not afford to do without them and anyway they will soon be off seeking wives and we can sell up and find somewhere smaller, but the child is a rope around your neck. You know the priesthood will take him off your hands soon enough, but this way you can solve all the problems at once. You'd be bound to see him again and you'd keep your promise to your fair lady.'

'You know I love you as much as I loved her before. But I must keep a promise made on her deathbed to see no harm comes to him.'

'Do you think this Arab is a liar and a cheat? I should think even his servant has jewels of his own.'

At this point Esteban remembered something. The tray of sweets had been held by a hand with a tattoo. He wanted to shout this out, but that would give away his being awake and a spy.

When his brothers clambered up he was still awake. They had left their boots by the door, but he could hear them a mile off, bloody drunkards! As they took off their breeches they were chuckling about the two whores they'd just had. Féderico saw Esteban's eyes open in the moonlight. 'Ah, you should have seen mine, baby brother. She had tits like pumpkins and a twat as juicy as an apricot.'

'Both the colour of sour milk, in other words,' put in Andrés.

Esteban could see both were aroused by their talk and was surprised their carousing had not deadened their urges. He knew what would happen next and bit his lip and lay rigid staring at the rafters as they got in on either side of him.

Miraculously, the Jew agreed an extension. Times were good and the family had always paid back in the past and there were only seven more payments to be made.

The merchant came to visit Esteban's father while the child was at school and spoke to him as to his wife, emphasising that the offer would not be repeated.

'I do not need your money,' said Esteban's father.

'We will see,' he said as he rode away. This time he was on a fine palomino with an undressed mane.

Esteban saw him in the marketplace and went to talk to him. He said he'd be prepared to go to a big house away from home if it helped his father, who he thought was in trouble with a moneylender. They spoke in Arabic. The boy worried that someone might eavesdrop on business that didn't even really concern him. 'And I'd like to be out of the way from my brothers. They aren't bad, but sometimes when they're under the influence of whatever it is, they say and do disgusting things.' The tone was becoming confidential and he willingly accepted a ride up to the cliffs.

They went at a gallop and veered off the road and through dense brush, away from the beaten path. 'Here would be a good place,' the Moor said in Spanish.

'For what?'

'I want to build a tower, a place to hide from the world. To live a simple life.'

79

'That'd be nice, but wouldn't you miss anything?'

'Only my talks with you, little one, and my stable of horses. But never mind that. I must get you back home.'

He put him down behind the house and he walked the rest of the way down the hill.

Two days later was his birthday. On the eve his father had a blazing row with the rest of the family. He had to find the money after all and could see no alternative but to let the property go.

'And how shall we live?'

He shrugged. 'We'll survive.'

Esteban sat outside and wandered off to feed the chickens. He knew they'd start talking about the price of little boys (the adults, not the poultry, that is).

His father went off on the mare and Esteban badgered him into promising he'd be back in twenty-four hours. But birthday dawned and no father. He went to school and they all had cakes and orange juice at a quarter to eleven. He was given a book by the priest. He was amazed to see it was love poetry. But he put it away in his bag and raced home. No father.

At six o'clock they had dinner and as they were cleaning away his father came in, all smiles, and immediately dispelled the gloom that had spread from Esteban to the rest of the group. Féderico and Andrés had been ready to go off to drink and get out of misery's way. However, the levity felt false, as if it was a farewell, not a homecoming.

A knock at the door made everyone jump. It opened and in walked the merchant's servant carrying a sack which was obviously very heavy. It clinked as he put it on the table. They all knew what it was. The father looked ill, the stepmother's eyes bulged, the older youths beamed and smirked. Esteban tried to smile. Failed. Tried to speak. Failed.

'Must he go tonight?' asked his father.

'Immediately,' said the merchant entering the room, a look of calm triumph on his face. His eyes glittered like the jewels on a dagger.

*

The dream breaks, shifts, reshapes and time has passed. I do not see the brave faces father and son show each other at the boy's going and the man's staying. I do not see the ride during which, after much coaxing, the Arab lord gives up trying to get a word from the child. I do not feel the burning cold of the wind or the blade-like press of the white-clad limbs scraping against the coarser stuff. I do not sense the tense contraction of those muscles and the hiding of all his past happinesses and his warmth deep inside. I could have conjured the untouched spread of food on the morning after, in the palace in the hills, but kept it from my coastal imaginings. I could have reconstructed terse agreement to speak and the bearded one's hopes that eventually the little statue would come to realise it was for the best. I could.

There would have been disdain in the boy's eyes as he was waited on, knowing that even if he'd been replaced by a servant at home, his stepmother would still wish she were being helped by him. His father's callousness would grow in time as her apparent hardness diminished. He would reap a harvest of remorse and silence, she the scorn of her neighbours at her wishing to undo the bargain. These things in retrospect I can fabricate, but I am still thinking about the boy's time passing and the transfer from the palace back down to the tower above the village. It took only weeks to build. The merchant had decreed it set up as soon as he realised that Turkish delight or more lavish gifts would not conquer the boy's heart.

The time dragged. Masons had left a small gap in their work, and, once the boy had climbed the ladder, they sealed him inside. A pulley allowed him to haul up food every morning, brought by his stepmother. He sat reading the books sent by the priest and studied according to the instructions left him.

'I desire you as you now desire your freedom. You see your family but cannot be with them. I could force you to obey, but I want and will have your willingness. It will come as a sacrifice to unburden your father's guilt and allow you to see the dark pain leave the eyes of the woman who comes to you every day. Your friends have been forbidden to come and I hold the leases of most of their fathers' properties, so they will not, and each one will be made miserable by your torment and their parents will feel as alienated from them as you do from yours. You cannot do this to the people you grew up with.' That is what the dark knight called up to Esteban when he came to view his work.

In my own time, a couple of years ago, in a state of reverie, on the bottom bunk in the bedroom in a flat in a block of apartments built away from the medieval centre, I dreamed up the conspiracy that would liberate the boy. He was given three years to go willingly to the warlord's bed, three years the then people of the then Barbate dreaded they would suffer through in vain, pointlessly. I hear the sounds of clipped syllables in a broad accent, guarded words; fishing for ideas that would free the boy and break the shackles of the invader's power. Plans, plans, plans and most full of a revenge they knew impossible, full of campaigns against the usurper which would be beyond their reach; no weapons no army, no help. But then the tunnellings of the mind of the blond boy's adoptive mother discovered the beginnings of a secret and a solution, out of the depths of her concern and her craving for justice. The meeting I see flash by and the murmur of consent comes to me across the gap of centuries.

Prisoners either try to escape their prison or resign themselves to being already dead. Esteban's heart was heavy and the flights of fantasy brought on by the things in his borrowed books only made him more depressed. He returned to earth with a bump every time. The windows had been made to measure and even if he could slip through, the drop was awkward, the bringing of a ladder bound to be seen by informers, and once he had got away the Arab stallion would carry his master after him and trample him down or take him back to a worse fate.

One morning his mother brought a special cake as if it were his fourteenth birthday already. It was earlier than usual and the gulls made a dawn din beyond the tower and its rocky mount. Other women were busy under the trees, gathering mushrooms, and the gabbled news was that he would find his way from the tower in time to avoid his fate. She did not say how or precisely when.

A long way away the first blow with the pick was struck. They were coming from the town the other side of the hills. In a little hollow they had come to start to move the earth, to dig the child out and foil the schemes of the villain.

It took a long time, but not so long. The limestone yielded and the Atlantic acquiesced in the conspiracy and hid the rubble and the noise. The gnarled trees shaded the site and seemed to cluster around the excavation to hide it completely. The sound of rock giving up its hold echoed through the bedroom as I half slept underneath Pablito that night.

Esteban was freed, of course, but, in an attempt to avert the tragedy of the whole village's extinction because of their trickery, he refused to leave. 'I will come out, but I will return each afternoon as the air slowly stagnates to make us sleepy. For it is then that he comes to ask how I feel and what I have decided. He doesn't come every day, not even every week now, for after these months of waiting for my acceptance of his demands, he has grown weary. I see no despair in his dark eyes, but know well that if he finds me gone, the sword and the flame shall scour this village off the map and only the white tower will stand memorial to my escaping, your courage and the stupidity of all of us. My love is not worth all this.' He stretched out his hand to indicate his world, the town. 'None of us deserves this terrible thing. I wish I had been born ugly, that my hair had been black like yours, or that maybe it could change now and the merchant would realise the worthlessness of his bargain, the emptiness of his contract. If I deceive him into thinking I am thinking about it, thinking about his words, thinking about his hold on all of us and his need for a hold on me, then it will give us all more time, more space to see what we can do with the future, our future, his future.'

'And your future,' his stepmother added.

So it was that, wrapped in a cloak to look like a girl, Esteban stooped along the corridor out to see the sun over a grey slab sea and then walked through the sentinel trees down to his father's house. Always alone and always returning alone to climb up the makeshift stairs in the well of the tower up to the floor of his room in time to see the horse and his rider arrive and to converse more lightly with the man, knowing he was his prisoner now, that the gaoler's keys belonged to himself, not to the one who had put him there. He could get a reprieve for the village, but in the meantime the lord was sentenced to wait and implore, and the glimmerings of hope made the expectation greater and the walls of the prison tower more impenetrable, as if there were a door he could not find, like a dreamer lost in a dark and threatening place.

Esteban had grown more radiant because of his ability to come and go and to convince the man that he was beginning to appreciate his visits more. The merchant had grown tired of his catamites and his sycophantic retinue and the long rides to and from the palace actually afforded him more time to think of the boy and essay verses about him in his complicated language.

They had begun to talk about transformation and the theme had become so important that the merchant was using his money to procure the knowledge of alchemists, charlatans and soothsayers, to foretell the outcome of his yearning, his ruling passion; to foresee whether or not the beautiful creature could be tamed. And he'd smile at what he took to be hints and implications of the boy's unbending where nothing had been meant, simply because those paid in silver to say he'd find fortune had said exactly that, that the richest prize of all would be ultimately his. The seed had been falsely sown, but the crop would prove unexpected.

One old hag saw through the veil and described the boy and his living, without any clues provided, no supposed foreknowledge at her disposal. Not a case of platitudes and things easily interpreted as one wished. She said she saw the crumbling of a tower and the boy replaced by a girl and the village rejoicing on the day of someone's birthday. Thereafter, she never told any more lies for she was made unable.

So it was that Esteban came disguised to talk again with his friend the priest. The priest told him that at he end of the allotted time a solution would appear. 'But consider carefully what you must do, my son,' he warned. 'You must beware of committing some evil, some seemingly lesser evil to prevent a more awful ending taking place, however good and pure your intentions, whatever the motivation. Neither must you consider the brutality of the bargain your father struck out of necessity to be the same as the one the imprisoning khalif wishes to strike with you. He may be driven by a perverse passion, but as yet it remains a crime of thought, not of deed. We know him to be a heathen, but that is not of itself a crime and furthermore the ways of divine intervention in the world are often desperately difficult to discern. You and I know – I have taught you as much – that a good thing may be tainted by the intent of it, and that an act of charity is sullied by hints of self-interest or self-satisfaction. The devil may creep into our hearts and bid us do things we know to be good, but the reasons for doing them may be suspect, and the fruit will become polluted and poisonous. The Saracen consults with dabblers in the occult and wishes to see the workings of the Almighty before they come to pass. We know these wizards to be heretics and deceivers, and he will doubtless find himself deceived. He may want this. He has the prize but holds it not. He thinks you can be bought, but the price is far too high. He has been told of the coming destruction, but will not be undeceived.'

Further questioning about what the priest meant gave the boy no clarification. 'Dream yourself free of him and you will be. We dreamed up your temporary escape and here we sit. You have forgiven your father to the degree you have grown to understand his difficulties. I hope he will forgive himself and that the remorse, which weighs on him so heavily, can be lightened by your ultimate release. We are all happy that you have been reprieved from incarceration, the first part of the trial, but realise that the greatest problems are still unresolved.'

To make the disguise impenetrable, Esteban returned dressed as a girl, down the chalky tunnel by candlelight, up ramshackle scaffolding, into the centre of the tower. He looked out to sea and yearned to be permanently away from the clifftop fortress. Now that he could come and go, his existence was somehow more chained and manacled than before.

I see the boy reading the love poetry the priest had given him. I see him forming images against the stonework, of chivalrous quests, of transformations and strange pictures to illustrate the author's convoluted metaphors: roses instead of lips; coals for eyes; strands sliced from the night sky falling from her brow to her shoulder. Stranger still: girls as Amazonic warriors attacking the heart of the pining lover, firing arrows from heart-shaped bows, string drawn tight to a point; dropping a phial of maddening potion into his goblet that transmutes the shadows into panthers and wild horses which pursue him snarling; girls curled up as moons, stretched out as quiet lakes, roaring and battering like the sea, growing as trees to shade the loved one or as briary thornbushes to ensnare. For a moment he wished he had been a girl, as he glimpsed the water's stillness from his window. Just for a moment, he felt its calm and the legitimate wash of wave on sand, the long-attested lying-down of male and female, the relentless stroke on the hard-edged rocks and the slow but sure eroding and rounding and reconciling of elements. I wonder what Pablito saw reflected on the virgin plaster beside his bed, or on the back of his dreaming eyes?

In the morning, in the half-light, in the half-dream, I saw how it would have ended. I saw the return of the boy with the blond, blond, blond hair to the tower on the eve of his sixteenth birthday, his heart sick with the knowledge that the collective will of the village had come up with nothing and that only he could resolve the contending demands of his feelings and his thoughts, his revulsions and his desires, satisfy himself that the people down there would be set free with his giving in, or else be shackled for ever because of his scruples, and that either way out presented him personally with no hope.

He lay in bed wishing himself ugly, visited by an overnight plague; wishing himself dead, overtaken by angels as he slept; wishing himself old, the years taken miraculously from him; beyond the time of the verdict, whatever its outcome;

wishing himself the owner of a quiet life; wishing himself never born; wishing himself a member of the other sex; praying for divine intervention or retribution, or the less divine intercession of some champion, or magicking of some charm or spell; wanting the dark-skinned oppressor to relinquish his hold, abandon the demand for so vile a fulfilment, but nonetheless still incapable of wanting his death, his removal.

Sleep would have come with lame slowness and meanly. He could have rehearsed a hundred variants of refusal or acceptance, knowing full well that it would not come out as planned. The image of the turbaned head, the bearded face, would have sneered at him from the darkened circular wall, asserted the impossibility of a fair and just dénouement, everyone living happily ever after.

He assumed a foetal position and felt a stone or a snake in his stomach, felt his testicles shrivel and contract, grow numb. Then in the half-light before dawn, another face, ancient and modern, lined like a map, an unknown woman with her fingers pressed to the cracks of her lips and something held high in her other hand. But what was it and what did it mean? he blearily wondered.

The black charger arrives at the foot of the hollowed-out tower and the voice summons, quiet but insistent, almost imploring. There is a constriction in Esteban's throat and his chest hurts. He is wearing a long shirt. He stands and goes to the window. He feels a wound low down in him and as he rises with the golden light on him he tries to speak, and his voice comes out higher-pitched, cracking with emotion. 'Here I am.'

Below stand two masons with hammers to enlarge the window, knowing as they do that another route already lies open. Standing where he does, the boy's face and torso can be seen to just below the waist. He looks different, radiant, yet more unobtainable than ever, as distant as the sun. The men see the ladder will not really reach him.

Unbuttoning the garment, he lets it slip from the shoulders. The nipples are enlarged and two budding breasts push them towards the rising orb. The robe continues to fall to reveal a most slender waist and then burgeoning hips curving out

87

to the edge of the stonework aperture. The pudenda is delicate and coppered by the rays. Its blur points down to the vagina.

Now she stands with her hands behind her head, thrusting the outrage into the light. She twirls her fingers through fine-spun hair and looks to the hills all-knowing, all-encompassing in gaze, stands unmanned, unarmed.

I woke up and banished the ghostly transition. I woke Pablito with a whispered, 'Good morning,' and told him I had a dream in which he was a Turk on a magnificent steed and I was his page, our ages reversed.

He smiled, all-accepting and comprehensive.

Light

ST IDIOTS LIES on the Sept where it slides across the flat-lands like a honey-coloured snake, slithering its way to the Wash. There its mouth gapes as though it would bite the apple-shaped bulge of the north Norfolk coast. Originally there were several outlying villages but relatively recently the town fathers had seen fit to designate the area between them a riverside park and to map out ribbons of tarmac, plant a few trees and build a stately pleasure dome in the form of a public convenience where a local mayor was found in flagrante delicto with a fourteen-year-old boy. He was only saved from that very number of years in gaol because the boy announced from the witness box that he had had over five hundred men since he'd started and that they paid between fifty pence and fifty pounds. The court gulped. The council were inundated with requests to close the offending temple of depravity from people who did not realise that, like a nomad's tent, it would set itself up elsewhere in the blink of an eye. The snake as though shedding its skin swamped the grassland, laving the foundation stones of the modern monstrosity. The pleasure-seekers had to paddle across the car park in the hope that the show would go on despite the interruption.

By advertising its other amenities, the town succeeded in expunging the stain left on its ancient name, a corruption of St Aydot, the fourth-century Dorset giant whose disciples founded a nunnery on the south bank of the stream some seven hundred years later. Why nuns should have an over-grown man as their patron is one of the mysteries of the early church, but it seems that there have always been more male saints than female ones, either because men had fewer ties and more time to be able to devote themselves to asceticism and flagellation, or because the male-dominated clergy were more willing to accredit members of their own sex with miracles and to canonise accordingly. Aydot was, however, pretty obscure as saints go and not a martyr. He was a Benedictine. He is said to have made a pilgrimage to Santiago de Compostela. He vanished from his deathbed rather than be buried, or so legend would have it. Doubtful. He is seen more as a hermit than as a miracle-worker, but then these feats are sometimes rather private, small in scale, unannounced, unproclaimed. The one instance of exorcism ascribed to him is very tentative, a probable later addition to the story. He is said to have rid some boy of some devil. That is all there is to know about him.

The vast majority of the boys and girls growing up locally would find their way into the factories in town. Its main industry was meat – ham, to be specific. There was an abattoir, but most of the plants and dispatching firms had the pigs' legs delivered at their door to be processed: butchered, salted, tenderised, put in pots and steamed in vast ovens. The bones would be collected by the bone man, the skin and fat chopped and made into garlic sausage. The blood would be mixed with meal and made into black pudding, the remains of the meat pulped into pâté. They made York ham and Windsor ham and honey-roast ham. The last-named ham made a sublime smell that would pervade the whole place. Everything knocked out of the pots had to be cut to standard shapes, enfolded in heavy-duty plastic and shrink-wrapped on the Cry-o-vac, which dipped the parcels into boiling water. The cubes of cooked flesh would then be trayed up and carted on the Collis into walk-in fridges. The staff all wore green wellies, white boiler suits with poppers down the front and white cloth hats with hairnets at the back to catch up the bob or the bun. They couldn't wear pendant earrings or nail varnish and the women all got paid less than the men because the union was a weak force, and all were desperate to keep their jobs and didn't protest to change the situation. Radio One would blare most of the day until one of the old-timers would insist on Radio Two for a while. In winter the warmth was a glow, in summer the boys would wear only boxers under the cotton overalls, leaving themselves vulnerable to the attentions of the resident nymphomaniacs who'd corner some youngster in the cold-room and go to it, while the rest of the workforce egged them on from the door. The boy would grow erect and compound his embarrassment, but would nonetheless feel better liked after he'd completed the initiation. The others slapped him on the back and said he'd proved he was a big boy in the end. In the quiet moments in the storeroom or in the lav for an unofficial ciggy, some of the butchers would do the same as the sex-craving women. The boys would not be embarrassed, but thrust their hips forward and smile when the phrase 'fag break' got mentioned. At the end of the week, when the wages came in, most of the young single men would be off into town, flying down to the Eagle or the Bat. And on Monday morning they'd crow of their exploits with some tart or other. They almost believed it themselves: that they'd managed a hard-on and a good time instead of getting brewer's droop and scornful dismissal. Year in, year out the same, and marriage and kids and council houses by the railway besides.

One of those destined for the grinders of the meat industry was called Kay. He hated his fucking name 'cos it was like a pissing girlie's, but he did karate and was gifted with wall-to-wall chest muscles so wasn't too worried about it. He inherited them from his long-absent Scandinavian father. He filled a vacancy in the most prestigious processing plant on the industrial estate at the edge of the new housing area, the one that had the saint as its trademark – a shame the money wasn't saintly, more like alms for the poor. He'd had the ordeal-by-marauding-mermaid on his arrival and witnessed one of the send-off ceremonies shortly after. They got the unfortunate, pinned him down, tore open his work clothes, grabbed at his briefs and pulled out his cock. Then slapped the dye used to colour black-pudding skins all over it. Like potassium permanganate at school, the purple-brown colour would not wash away, only wear off with time. The

91

kid had screamed and begged, but that whipped up the excitement further. Kay didn't think he'd ever leave, but if he did he'd lay the bastards out first, or take them one by one on the way home afterwards. He had laughed along with the crowd and been disgusted at his own enjoyment, the sadness and guilt akin to that following sexual gratification.

He had earned the nickname 'Snowy' or simply 'Snow'. Not because he was blond, which he was, not because his surname sounded Arctic in origin, but because at infants' school, when the teacher read 'The Snow Queen', most of the children assumed that it was about him: a reasonable assumption when you looked at his stern, cold face, and when you saw how he kept himself aloof and alone, even if that was prompted by the disappearance of his father, not by his natural disposition.

When he was still at school, the teachers thought Kay was a model pupil because he usually got his homework done, though he didn't appear especially gifted, except at technical drawing and English. His maths let him down and there was a general consensus in the staff room that he'd make an excellent designer, but that he would not get into tech without passing the maths exam. When it came to it, he did well above average for his year, getting the only grade 1 in English literature in the school. He also got a 1 in English language and in technical drawing, woodwork and metalwork. He failed to get a grade in maths. The head of year expressed regret to his mother and suggested he go to evening classes. She let the ash fall from her cigarette into the palm of her hand and said, 'Oh!'

As the fourth and fifth form had passed, the goings-on of the rest of the crowd didn't seem to communicate themselves to him. He went drinking in the kindergarten pubs that served the obviously illegal prepubescents. He sat and talked to the girls and bought them Archers or Malibu or Martini when they asked, but never took any of them home and only once let Marjorie Proud wrap her octopus-like limbs around him at a debauched party. She was anything but proud by nature, and he was anything but activated. He disentangled himself, lurched into the garden and pebble-dashed the path.

The gossip was he'd swallowed her chewing gum as she tried to perform an oral tonsillectomy. She couldn't be a nice girl if she threw herself at such a noble and refined young man as Kay, they all screeched in the loo. They called Miss Proud an old slag to her face, though she'd heard it all before and at least she'd kissed him, so there. The information had filtered through from the boys that he was hung like a stallion and she was interested in verifying that particular fact.

The electrification of the main line has reached sufficiently far north for the town to become a commuter dormitory, and the incipiently economically successful have demanded the building of an indoor heated pool, a sports centre and better shopping facilities. Before the invasion it was more a half-horse than a one-horse town, though it was quite difficult to establish whether it was the front or the rear half that was involved. Apart from the emporium of fellatio and sodomy in the middle of the bog, there were the pubs and the riverside hall, also known as Idiot's Elephant because the twin concrete canopies at the entrance and the oast house that had been incorporated into the redevelopment looked like a trumpeting head, or more likely because it fell gracelessly between two stools, being too small for large events, too large for small. For a long time the punters stayed away because the beer was outrageously priced, in a bid to recoup the vast expense of building the thing in the first place. Then it became fashionable for the lads to go and line the walls at the disco and watch the bimbettes dance round their handbags. Each youth held his pint in one hand and fag in the other and, as the evening wore on, groups of boys would start eyeing up other groups of boys, as if they'd lost interest in the Tammies and Barbaras and in buying them Cinzano and lemonade in the hope of a snog and a grope. They could pick on the few lads who dared to dance – 'cos they were bound to be poofs, weren't they? But that soon became a dismal sport and something a little more spectacular was called for.

Often the weekend entertainment was simply a case of going to the Eagle at one end of the market square or the Bat and Ball at the other, getting totally tanked up by eleven, then spilling out into the arena of half-timbered medieval houses and Georgian frontage for a ruck. It was one team against the other, or both teams against the men in blue if they were stupid enough to interfere. It was fairly controlled because, if it threatened to bubble over into more than friendly violence, there were plenty of escape routes, four roads and numerous alleys and arcades. Usually it'd all be over by midnight.

With the opening of the Elephant, outside elements came down the tracks to sort out the Idiots gang. Being confined within walls of brick and glass meant that the fights would continue till a definite victor had emerged. Maybe it was the annoyance at having to pay to get in, having to pay 50 per cent more for the lukewarm beer, having to watch the boring blotchy bitches who danced like cross-threaded puppets, having to leave by twelve o'clock or turn into a pumpkin. Maybe it was the lights, the disco pulse, the oxygen-inhibiting Marlboro smoke strangling the stuffy air. Maybe it was something else entirely, ill-defined, but present all the same.

At work Kay found that the young women all doted on him, not only for his Nordic looks and sculptural physique, but also because the apparent sullenness of his childhood had been replaced by a quiet calm which spoke of reliability and maturity and augured well as far as marriage prospects were concerned. Most of the working girls were looking forward to their 2.4 kids and colour telly, even when the statistic would almost certainly be tipped towards 3.7 or more as time progressed. They'd smack the children and their men would smack them and be unfaithful, drunken sots just as their fathers had been to their mothers before them. But Kay might not, or so they thought.

He got himself a moped and wanted a car. He saved some of his wages every week, gave his mother a third and spent the rest on alcohol and chips on a Friday or Saturday night. His mother kept his first fiver, swearing never to spend it. She saw her absent husband in him more and more each day. When his mates started buying dope, he refused to indulge or even try it. No one argued or took the piss. He started an evening class on Thursday nights and the young teacher spent extra time on him because she had fallen in love with him almost instantly. They went out for drinks with the other students after the evening struggle was over. She always wanted to sit near him, but calculated the frequency with which she could without the probability of her interest being noticed exceeding a one in ten chance.

One night she took him back to her flat and without any fuss he let her take off his shirt and kneel to undo his shoes. He undid her blouse. She undid her bra. He buried his face in her breasts and kissed them. She led him into the bedroom. She took off his trousers. He took off her skirt. She took off her panties. He took off his briefs. The door was open and the light streamed in from the living room. They lay on the bed, she guided him into her and gasped at the size of him as he slowly entered her. She bit his shoulder. He was much taller than her. He slid back and forth, pressing his face into her hair. He began to buck and she felt the climax both inside her and outside, as his body juddered to a collapse, drenched in sweat. He rolled to one side and she reached down between her legs to help ease him out. He lay on his side and tears began to fall down his cheeks. He shook with sobs and she wasn't sure whether or not to touch him. When she did, he curled up into a ball and screwed up his eyes and pressed his fist into his mouth as though he were sucking his thumb. She pulled the sheet over him and went into the kitchen to make some coffee. She put a shot of brandy in it and when she went back into the living room he was coming out of the bedroom, pushing his shirt into his trousers. His face still looked streaked and his hair was dishevelled. 'Sorry,' he said and took the coffee. He sat and gulped at it. She went and fetched his shoes. She knelt and put them on and tied the laces. He put the coffee cup down beside the settee and got up. She had to get up too and they collided and recoiled, she more than he. He said sorry again and she said it didn't matter. He left and she said, 'See you next week at college.' Only after he'd been gone five minutes did it occur to her that her flat was a long way from his house.

He walked back across the Riverside Park. Needing to go

to the toilet, he entered the public convenience in the centre of the car park. The urinal was an undivided wall of porcelain. He stood and pissed huge quantities. A man came in behind him and stood right next to him even though there was plenty of additional space available. Kay noticed that the man wasn't urinating even though he had got his penis out of his fly. He had it resting in the flat of his hand, not held between his thumb and first two fingers. Kay shook himself and put his prick away. The man said, 'It's a cold night to be out, isn't it?' and then turned towards him a little. He let his hand drop to his side. Kay noticed he had become erect. 'Do you want to touch it, sonny?'

'No, I fucking don't,' he replied.

'Go on. It won't bite.'

Kay grabbed the man by the shoulders and swung him to face him. At that instant the other realised he had been wide of the mark in his desperation. He felt the knee slam up between his legs and the pain shot up inside him. He tried to double up. He felt the nausea surge into his throat and couldn't manage to say, 'No, please don't,' and couldn't crumple as the youth confronting him had his shoulders held in a clamplike grip. Their eyes met and the light in the steely blue pair sparkled like fragments of glass. The right hand released and then, with his stare still held, the fist struck like a hammer. The left released and the homo folded up like a deck chair on to the ground. And like that deck chair in a comedy film, the struts of the legs and arms were all pointing in wrong directions. Kay half kicked, half pushed the man into the trench, still wet with piss. His arms involuntarily closed on the shoe and caught in the lace, which became untied. Kay jerked his foot back and spat on the man, whose face now bled into the trough, blood coming from both his nose and mouth. Kay turned and walked out. 'I'm sorry,' he whispered. The bleeding face didn't hear him. At home, the teacher did, the sounds still echoing.

The following Saturday the whole gang were going to go down to the Idiot Elephant for a session of wall-propping and right-arm exercise. They rendezvoused in the Hare as they knew it'd be relatively quiet and they might get served

96

without having to press up at the bar, like grapes in a bunch about to have their wine squashed out by sweaty feet. The ancient ones, who sat on their benches with their bottles of mild, seemed to come with the furniture. If they were musing on lost comrades or the inanity of war, it did not show. If they were contemplating the prospect of spending next day weeding the allotment, it didn't show. If the image of their dead wife's fanny were haunting their sadness, it didn't show either. The only thing that showed was their irritation at an invasion of alien-looking monsters and the disturbance to their sup. *They* never had green hair, earrings or clothes like Harlequin or Columbine. *They* never made the noise of an enemy bombardment or abused their elders. Was rebellion a new disease?

Kay seemed more animated than usual. He felt a yawning emptiness inside. He had masturbated twice since the double debacle of Thursday night and each time he had caught his semen in his hand and curled up into a ball around his fist, uncoiling as the viscous substance began to become more fluid and trickle between his fingers to drip on the bedclothes or his thigh or belly. He would smear himself with it and lie on his back staring at the ceiling, then drag himself off to shower, certain he had not rid himself of the filthy secretion, the penetrating odour, the stain, the loss.

All that day he had been at war with himself wanting to regain his purity, fighting any spark of libido. He had no focus for desire, but an erection could creep up on him unnoticed: one moment flaccidity, the next turgidity and the pressing need for catharsis. He knew that were it to happen again the relief of previous occasions would not come on the heels of his being spent, would not banish the depression with a slowly infiltrating mellowness, spreading the body's boundaries, the corollas of that inward collapse into the consuming magnesium flare concentrated upon his loins. He had succeeded in preventing the ignition by frantic activity. He had found that immersing himself in maths questions extinguished everything. Previously he had connected the problems with the problem of wanting to see her, wanting her. Now that that link had been broken it was only fractions, subtraction and long division that he saw on the page. He went shopping for his mother, something he hadn't done for a long time. She asked him why, but had to be satisfied with a remark about having the time or something.

He began to drink more heavily than usual and although his frivolity increased it seemed strained. The best of his factory mates suspected it wouldn't last. His name was Jordan, but everyone called him Oxer. A teacher had told him he was as thick as an ox in response to being told that the reindeer was a member of the ox family. It had evolved through Oxo, Oxy, Occy, but had stuck at the present form by popular consent. Oxer had seen Kay pissed only once before and knew he'd peak too early. He tried to extract the truth and as they bounced and cavorted their way down to the social centre, he admitted he'd been propositioned by some fairy in the loos on the Riverside Park.

'He didn't do anything?' Oxer wanted to know.

'No, of course not, but I smashed his 'kin' face in and pushed the cunt into the slash trench.'

Oxer said, 'It's OK. You're all right, aren't you, and the fucker deserved it.'

'I didn't mean to hurt him, though.'

His mate threw his arm round his shoulder, leapt up and ruffled his hair, shouting, 'I love you, man. You just do me in,' as he did so. The equilibrium seemed to have been restored by the time they slipped past the tusks into the grey belly of the architect's brainchild.

More drink and much standing about. There were a lot of outsiders. In a small town where you had to do the same thing every weekend you learned who were the gang from the other comprehensive and found that the limits were blurred as soon as you left school and were working with people you might have wanted to rearrange a week or so before. This lot were out-of-townies, from quite a way away by the looks of it: cropped hair and boots and plenty of piss. Bizarre, though: they danced. Only to certain tracks, stuff no St Idiots native would have asked the DJ to play. They leapt up and down like demons possessed and fell in a heap on a group of the handbag brigade, one of whom tripped in her attempt to retreat and ended sitting on one of the boys' heads. She got up quickly and the seething mass of arms and legs seethed a bit more, laughing and finding it difficult to make the transition back from a platoon of centipedes to a battalion of boys. The young woman, Mandy Mesmer, and her cronies scampered off to the ladies' to discuss the collision of the various parts and parties involved. They emerged fifteen minutes later to see the beginnings of the fight.

Red light, green light, blue light and everyone with at least three shadows. Strobe light holding the action in inaction as the crucial seconds unfold. Kay watched as one of the outsiders ploughed into one of the girls that Oxer had gone to chat up. He was often the first off the mark and, according to the folklore in town, he has lost his virginity at the age of twelve to his aunt, some said with the full knowledge of his mother, some said with the proof of photographs taken by his brother from behind the arras, whatever that was. They said that if Oxer cut a notch in his headboard for every girl he'd been with, he'd have only a pile of sawdust left by now.

The new girl, Eileen something-or-other, catapulted into Kay's best-experienced friend. He made a protective gesture and pushed the girl behind him. The brute had made a simpering imitation of the outstretched arm, then pushed Oxer with the other, but caught hold of his shirt so he couldn't fall backwards. A pause in the light of white magnesium. Next, photo-framed by flashes, the aggressor brought his face close, oh so close, to Oxer's to betray it with a kiss. No words, as lips stopped by a spark pursed forward. Another flash as the guy stepped back to draw his sword. Kay was seen stock still in three places even though the flow of his movement was as swift as a dart in flight. The dirk was out as he positioned himself to catch the statuesque arc of the arm that was held in an explosion of white above Oxer's startled face. His arm jerked up in a couple of snaps, as if he were going to wipe away the imprint of the lips that never actually touched flesh.

The instant Kay caught the weapon-arm in its plunge the strobe was switched off and the flashing colours let the choreography take on a more oily fluidity. The skinhead might have had an expression of surprise if the pulses had synchronised with that split second before the next one came, so full of anger. Kay was considerably taller so the kick, which was probably aimed at his balls, only articulated with his knee, or maybe that was because the other fighter had to step away to swing his leg in a pirouetting fashion. The pain was off-balancing. Kay lurched to the other side to transfer his weight. His arms had slackened during the time it took his body to readjust and override the collapse-and-retire reflex. A blow came up at his chin and he took three dainty steps backward. Oxer helped support him. It had only taken this long for a space to open on the floor, though it had not yet been cordoned off into a strict arena by rival supporters.

Kay recovered enough to ready himself for the next onslaught. He ducked and the air was flailed by a rotating attack. He crashed one fist into the stomach in front of him and as he sprang up the disorientated thug, still turned by the unconnecting move, received a downward chop to his neck and shoulder that brought him to his knees, having combined with the resonating effect of the body blow. Still in motion from the scything action, he then tilted to one side, put out his arm and caught himself in time to prevent a sprawl. By then the circle was lined by watchers. The weapon lay on the floor. Two stepped forward and hauled their champion from the ground. Still the disco thumped. The overhead lights had been switched on by the bar manager and someone had been sent to phone the police.

One of the squires had slipped the hunting knife back into the hand of the rescued knight. It had shrunk with the return of the overhead blaze. He lunged forward and seemed to embrace Kay as if to forgive him. The blade with the serrations down one side plunged into Kay's chest. The music stopped.

A gasp went up from the circle of mouths. In the ensuing silence a slow jagged exhalation escaped Kay. He brought his hands up to the handle and, in a gesture that could have come from a pietà, the fingertips of his cupped, imploring hands brushed the back of the hands of his assailant as they withdrew from the weapon, opening his palms in offering. The two looked at each other and a second sigh issued from the attacker.

They both looked down at their hands, fluttering in limbo between one thing and the next. Kay's eyes closed and he touched the blood on his white shirt where the metal stuck out. He collapsed like a parachutist. Oxer caught him as he crumpled. He went down on his knees at the same time to cradle him. So slow. He prevented his head from banging on the parquet. Kay curled up as if on to the fist that was no longer pressed into his chest. His hands fell into a position of repose, each finger tipped with red, his red.

Pandemonium broke out above him, but Jordan heard nothing but a roaring silence. He thought how light it felt, the head in his lap. Wasn't a dead animal supposed to weigh more than a live one? He knew that the component parts of the carcasses at work weighed a great deal as he humped them off the roller rack on to the stainless-steel table to be deboned. He looked down at his hand stroking the flaxen hair. The roar, the roar.

In the silence that surrounded the fallen boy and his attendant there were whispers mingling with the internal sound of eardrums abuzz. The manager scuttled about, managing nothing. He was looking for a doctor. The police arrived by one door and the invading force left by a fire exit, activating the alarm as they pressed the panic bar. They had to drag the victor with them. He stared at the victim, his arms limply by his side. The police set off in pursuit, but were impeded by the crush of bodies. People were gathering into groups to discuss what had happened, incredulous that they had seen what they had seen, recounting it in order to rewind and review it.

The manager came over and told Jordan that the ambulance had been called, but that it would be a while as it would have to come from twenty miles away. 'Do you know him?' He indicated the curled-up youngster as if he could possibly have been referring to someone else. 'What's his name? Should I call his mother or something?'

A very tall figure stepped out of the crowd and told the manager the boy's name. 'I'm a doctor,' he said and knelt down next to Jordan, who was still stroking Kay's hair. The stranger put his hand on Oxer's wrist to stop him. 'Put his head on the floor and help me uncurl him. He's not breathing. His heart has stopped. We don't have long.' He turned to the beetle to tell him to resume his scuttling and get everybody out into the entrance hall.

The man had olive skin and a black hooded shirt like a monk's. He had a battered white badge in the shape of a shell clipped to his odd attire. His voice seemed to register an authority that could not be disputed. The manager began shepherding everyone outside as Kay was beginning to be straightened between the kneeling pair. His muscles were already tightening and the amount of blood seemed too little, as if the knife had plugged rather than opened the wound.

Unwound. On his back. His arms pushed to his sides but still slightly crooked. He looked very still, like marble, except for the blackish puddle on his chest. Blood covered his hands and the cuffs of his sleeves, as though he had attempted to stop the flow.

The man put his hand round the knife and pulled it out. 'Won't that . . .?' Jordan tried. The man shook his head. No. He put the dagger-like weapon on one side and looked up as the manager returned. Everyone had been ushered out. The door stood open and the bar staff were keeping people from coming back in.

'Take Jordan with you, and go. No one must come in.'

'I want to stay,' said the younger of the two.

The lights from the disco were still blinking and, now that the people were gone, the colours reached across the whole floor even though diluted by the strips high above. The man, who was wearing dark-grey trousers, black shoes and, incongruously, white socks, stretched out his arm towards the sound system and light boxes and closed his eyes before opening them again. If a camera had had the eyelids in sharp focus, the moment one lid had touched the other the disco lights would have been seen to go out on a split screen.

Oxer stood up and began to leave with the manager.

'Lock that door. The key is in your right trouser-pocket. Let no one come in for fifteen minutes. No, the ambulance won't get here for another seventeen because of the chaos in the marketplace and the traffic jam building up across the bridge. Go.'

The key sounded in the lock.

The hooded man bent over Kay and undid his shirt. The unstoppered bottle of his body was leaking clotting darkness on his already crimsoned chest. It continued, trickling in tiger stripes over his ribs.

The hooded man stood above the corpse, placing one foot on either side of Kay's head. Then he stretched his arms out into the shape of a cross and arched his neck up, closing his eyes as he did so. The overhead lighting went out. The bar lights went out. The emergency-exit signs went out. Tiny fragments of orange managed to squeeze through the heavy lined curtains, filtered, turned down, almost off.

The hooded man brought his flat palms to his eyes as he swung his head back to its normal position. He clenched his fists, then took them away from his face. He opened his eyes. Had the camera still been on him, it would have had difficulty adjusting to the cobalt blue that emanated from them. No eyes would have been visible in the dazzle. No pupil, no iris, no sclerotic. He looked down and the light seemed to concentrate into a beam on the dead adolescent. He adjusted his position and sank to his knees, keeping one leg either side of Kay's head, pressed into his neck and shoulders. He brought his still-closed fists to rest on the closed eyelids in front of him for a moment, then stretched his arms out above the holed chest. When they were fully extended he let them relax, opening like night flowers. Blue light streamed from them, downwards, as though from those great dishes studded with bulbs used in operating theatres, but with such a dark colour, the colour of the sky, the sky before the dark takes over.

The hooded man heard the manager stumble in through the bar. Curiosity had got the better of him. Now he gripped the counter and could not believe what he saw. The pyrotechnics began in earnest. White filaments streaked out of open palms and open eyes, falling like the rose of sparks surrounding a welding torch. He could not stop now. The rain of incandescent motes turned to a brighter white, a yellow that shimmers with blue corpuscles in the way the sun does when you stare at it, stare at it through a tiny chink. The sparks seemed to coalesce on the boy's body, though that was now a mere grey outline beyond the black silhouette. The particles seemed to dance and glow even brighter, like a million flashbulbs going off at once. And, as with flashbulbs, the red and green snakes left behind began to twirl. Out of this rondo of light a sea urchin of laser spines. More and more. White at first, then the yellow-blue of the sun again. More and more and more. All forms inside the light vanished, vanished within the white-out.

Then it all collapsed back into Kay's chest. The manager continued to see white, dark white with no modulation. They found him when the ambulancemen came in through the staff entrance. He was staring from white eyes, no pupils, no irises, nothing, hands glued to the copper top. They asked him what had happened and he asked them to turn off the lights. At that point one of the barmen had flicked the master switch and all but the disco lights had come on. The uniformed officers edged the stretcher past him and with a policeman went over to where Kay was lying.

He was breathing very shallowly, but breathing nonetheless. There was a livid purple blotch on his chest, new tissue. There would be no scar. There were no traces of blood on his skin, only on his shirt and the floor. The shirt smelled as if it had been singed while being ironed and there were scorch marks on the wooden blocks, as if a swarm of dogends had been stubbed out in a neat little circle around the boy.

Kay was taken into hospital for checks, as was the manager. The latter was diagnosed as having 100 per cent retinal burns. The conjunctiva had been severely damaged, too. Kay recalled the stabbing, but could not remember anything else. An examination showed no trace of the wound other than the livid colour of the outer layers of the skin. He imagined that he had been recovering in his hospital bed for weeks.

There were a myriad of witnesses who could describe the fight. When they caught the other youth involved, he confessed to police and the knife was covered with his prints and those of the guy who had handed it over, together with Kay's. But there were no others. No one could identify the man who had claimed to be a doctor and no one had seen him leave.

While he remained in the ward for observation, the teacher came to bring Kay a card and a bunch of grapes and a box of chocolates. She had felt very unsure about coming and had asked Oxer if he would ask Kay if she could.

When he got out they continued to see each other and became an item. The following spring he passed his maths exam.

Dark

FOR THOSE THAT are left behind there is only darkness.

One has to go with the flow or constantly battle against the current. The water is sometimes almost too cold to swim in and it is dangerous, so dangerous when the sun's light is fading and the bottom is out of sight.

Adam lived with his mother and stepfather. Perhaps the one had gained the other in a sort of new-lamps-for-old deal? Perhaps. The replacement fulfilled his conjugal duties as part of the agreed barter and in due course Adam and full brother Maxwell were presented with a pair of half-brothers. Inadequate-sounding, diminished in kinship and reduced in stature, one might imagine. But diminished or not, they had lavished on them the care that all infants demand but never recall, and it seemed greater to the older boys because of their lack of memory of the time when they had been total dependants themselves. Resentment began to smoulder.

Max-for-short and then Adam initiated a campaign of stubborn resistance. The new lamp kept a low profile and didn't interfere. Adam, being brighter, foresaw the best mechanisms for parent-terrorism and also for teacher-annihilation, and set about systematising their usage. He was guaranteed to attract the best-intentioned attentions of the educational psychologists and possibly the local welfare officer as well. He constructed a wall around himself to keep the bad things out. He further fortified the bastions, mined the approaches and set a watch on top of the barbican.

When he laid his plans, Adam hadn't realised he would live in splendid isolation within the castle's precincts. When he began he couldn't have foreseen the desperate need for

106

escape from the fortress he himself had built, but see it he did and then he discovered that even his brother was denied easy access to the ward. The curtain walls were many feet thick and when the rain began to fall he saw the baileys flood and knew he'd have to retreat to the keep and then, if the deluge continued unabated, become a prisoner in his own tower, moated to a greater depth.

He watched the rising waters, a frown upon his face, declaring his wish to reverse the process, to breach the bulwarks and buttressed defences, to crumble the crenellations, to let out the lake. He wondered if the rush of water would knock him against the masonry and put an end to him rather than save his life.

Max-for-short had opted out of school as soon as, if not sooner than, he could. He had found that certain legal and illegal things generally available through the black market could supply a moment's euphoria if he simply inhaled them or swallowed. He became trapped by the laws of commerce and then by the laws of the land. He realised the strength of the need to steal-to-sell-to-buy-to-inhale-to-escape. Had he been gifted with a few more brain cells and been a little more connected to the society which instigated this combine, perhaps he might have become an economic forecaster for a national bank or a left-wing, right-on, liberal-intellectual socialite lecturing to the converted in Neo-Gothic halls in a provincial enclave of university education. He relieved large corporates of a sliver of their large profits and then exchanged his ill-gotten gains for tiny cardboard squares, a drop of man-manufactured ecstasy on each. Finally he was caught running from one of the outlets of the largest retailing conglomerate in the country. He ran into the arms of an ex-army security guard. He was frogmarched back into the office and interrogated.

Together with the pale flicker, his mother wondered what to do. She sometimes appeared unconcerned for the two boys. Her second family demanded, and got, more of her attention, but on one occasion she had crashed the car into a tree while out searching for the errant Adam. She was and, I dare say, will remain a large lady, who once arrived at the house of one of the boys' older friends to recapture the younger of the two. He was having his hair cut by an inexperienced barber because he'd spent the cash she'd given him down the pub. David, the guy doing the job of reshaping the shock of fine, highlighted hair, was gay and Max had warned his mother that some misadventure was bound to be taking place then and there. Wrongly. But nonetheless she rescued him and told him off about the money, and more so about the company.

Adam frequently slept huge chunks of his life away, as many adolescents do, especially when they can lie in bed uninterrupted. He found it even easier when narcotic fumes and alcoholic residues stilled the stormy seas of his body. His mother, in an attempt to appease and to get him out from under her feet, relented and allowed him back to the apprentice stylist's house. In the meantime the teachers, aware that he was hibernating his life away, finally got their way and found Adam a shrink and set about his shrinking, his reconditioning, though it was fairly likely that the hard-stretched department was aiming for minor cosmetic cerebral surgery only. There were more cases jamming up the conveyor belt, carrying the dispossessed kids on to unfulfilling positions in jobs devoid of satisfaction and relationships bereft of love. Get him in, get it over, get him out; dull his glittering eyes, quiet his pounding heart, drown him.

He went round to visit his friend. Floating in a drug-induced stupor, he smiled up at David. The stereo pulsed with a rhythm to dance to. They lay curled like this, laughing at unfunny things from time to time, and then Adam begged to be given a tab of acid, knowing full well that David would refuse, just as his full brother had done, but he wanted to carry the emulation of Max beyond the mere stealing of unstealable things. Max-for-short now had a criminal record and it wouldn't be long before he'd be put behind bars, where the wolves would come after the cub and force him to give head, and maybe sodomise him just for fun, until the taste of roughness had been inculcated into him and he'd seek it out for himself. Or maybe he'd flee to the City of Gold in search of freedom, and end on the streets, tricking to keep himself in money to get out of it, and find he needed harder and harder stuff, and find the lack of food running him down until one day his mother'd come down to the Smoke at one in the morning in a car with a dented bumper to identify the punctured body. Adam would come with her to see his beloved brother one more time, naked, draped with a sheet, his face a strange, Christ-like colour, transformed into the shape of a mask, cheeks hollow and lips blue as if he'd been drowned, dredged up from a riverboat disaster or washed up on the shore; looking as though he'd been trying to reach the acid-island he could see on the drug-busted horizon; his shoulder clammy as if still wet from the sea, but moist merely because of the condensation of his refrigerated skin. Maybe that ending would stop Adam in his tracks, maybe push him further into the maelstrom. But it will not happen. It is too brutal.

Once upon a time two men lay on the floral-design carpet in a cannabis dream, one laying his head in the lap of the other, various other acolytes sitting around following their own heavenly labyrinths in the orange and brown nap, unconcerned, as the cross-legged played with the short dark hair of the supine, caressing his temples languidly, stroking his neck, almost absent-minded. 'What do you think now then, Max-for-short?' David asked.

'I like it like that!' Max slurred. 'You've got such soft hands. Like the woman in the Fairy advert!'

Giggles. 'Not that, you idiot. Your little brother.'

Slight wrinkling of brow eased by washing-liquid-smooth fingers.

'I mean' – pause – 'do you *still* think I'd touch him up?'

Max's huge-huge pupils stared up like twin cenotes awaiting *dorado* victims, sacrifices.

'Well, you *were* the one who warned your mother that I had fangs and wings and talons and claws and a slavering forked tongue and a constricting grip and a voracious appetite and a burning-bush desire, unquenched, unquenchable, a man a gulf a gap, wanting to swallow any innocent lamb passing within reach of my lion's grip.'

The limpid black pools rippled. An abyss-dwelling dragon had moved out of its millennial slime. 'How can you?'

David's fingers pressed into the hollows below the clavicles. 'All right, Sunshine. I'm sorry.'

The congregation remained lost in their respective mazes. Max gathered himself out of the torpor and delivered the message, before plunging back into wilful forgetfulness. 'He loves you. He needs you 'cos you listen and don't treat him like a child like my mum and me do. He keeps telling me he wants to trip with you. Let him. He'll be OK!'

So they did, but that's another story, or could be, or is simply what goes on around here all the time.

Because of the things the boy told him, the hard-pressed psychoanalyst decided that David *in loco parentis* should continue to be in receipt of his confidences, and that he himself should wash his hands of the affair as the youngster was already increasing his rate of class attendance independent of any engineered shrinkage. Almost reversing the mother's judgement a second time, the man had forbidden the youth to come round unless he could prove he had done his homework. He changed his job and got home at 3.30, knowing it would be only a short while before Adam arrived. He got plenty of help, without David's actually doing the work. His marks steadily improved until he was almost predicted straight A's for the exams that would follow in summer. Afterwards Adam would go home for tea and they'd both be down the pub by dark, with the rest of the sect, celebrating another communion paid for in the most part by David the hierophant.

In January it was David's birthday. Christmas had been relatively frugal for both. David endured another tense return to the family fold and only spent a fair amount on presents for Adam, instead of the king's ransom he wanted to bestow. The latter scraped enough together to provide a record of music David would find difficult to listen to, but impossible not to play. Adam turned up on the doorstep on the eve of the unnecessary anniversary loaded down with gift-wrapped parcels. 'I wanted to get you one for each year, but you're too old.' Smile and eye-flutter.

110

'You little sod!' David said. 'Come in.'

There was a box of Belgian chocolates, a badge with a rude slogan, a pair of boxer shorts with an explosive motif, an overbright T-shirt and the inevitable joke presents, along with a book by Carlos Castañeda, though not the first of the set. When they were opened, the one that most impressed was this last, because of the dedication scrawled inside the front cover: *To David from Adam on his One Hundredth birthday to say Thanks for getting me out of the rut.* Even as David was ruffling the kid's hair, even as he was slipping the ribbon off the calorific time bomb, he wondered where Adam had got the money for so many trifles. He desperately fought against the fear that they had been appropriated improperly, purchased with stolen credit or stolen cash. I must continue to trust him, he thought, and did.

In collusion with Max-for-short the higher-priced items had indeed been borrowed, never to be returned. Adam lay in another drugged haze with David on the bed one early evening in February and sadly confessed. The spirits in the resin were all of an evil genius that night, determined to entrap the boy who couldn't bear to deceive, but had to fight to undeceive. He knew there'd be conflict but the sprites of swirling smoke sapped his energy to compete, to struggle. He wanted to surrender. The castle walls had been thus breached and the flood had subsided, but still he stood stock still at the top of the topmost turret, looking down, wondering if he would have to endure the state of siege for ever? In his dreams, the attacking armies of educationalists unfurled pennants from lances and wielded massive shields displaying bold achievements showing lions rampant or passant regardant, clenched fists and bends sinister. They had failed in their bid to overrun the castle or even bridge the moat during their past sorties and skirmishes while David had walked in under the malefic portcullis, the smell of bubbling oil wafting down into his nostrils from high machicolations.

No defence by offence, no attack met by counterattack. Lying beside the boy on the mound of the bedclothes, he felt that the whole adventure had been a disaster and he should have been out campaigning elsewhere. It was as if he had

111

fallen from the drawbridge in full armour and the stagnant green ooze was now filtering through the visor, tarnishing the metal, vanquishing the supposed victor; turning his panache to sodden weed. He waited for the water of disillusionment to fill his lungs and for it to be all over. He had often scrapped with Adam in the playground between the church and the factory and had finished with grazes and bruises everywhere before they had crumpled into a heap together, arms splayed, looking up at an ocean of sky scattered with breaking cloud, trying to get their breath back and laugh at the same time. Now he wanted to strike the boy, to actually bodily harm him; he wanted to bounce him off the wall, smash his fist into his face and watch it bleed. His limbs were limp from the dope, but he could feel the violence gather and blot all that was calm. 'Why?' he groaned, as he flipped the child over and pinned him down, his knee on his chest, hands holding wrists like vices, crushingly. Adam had expected this treachery from within his court, but not with such severity. Why? Why? Why? A repeated plaint. 'Tell me, damn you, you little shit! What do you want to spoil it for?'

Fear had made the vaporous wraiths flee and only hopeless remorse filled the void. The physical pain was nothing beside the black slime flowing into Adam's stomach, building to choke him. The reflex was to flail his arms as the tide covered him, but he couldn't. He could not twist free, he did not want to. He wanted to feel himself sink without trace. The water was in his eyes and he could not see.

'I'm sorry,' he wailed as the river began to overflow. His voice cracked, but David resolutely refused to react to the emotion in it.

'Why?' Again and again. 'Why?' Head brought nearer to blast the siren sound and a wrenching of each arm.

'Because I didn't have the money,' chin quivering.

'Because I didn't have the money.' Mimicked. 'You could have asked me for some, couldn't you?' Venomous. 'I thought you thought I was worth a bit more than this. You can take your fucking filthy presents and take them back to where you fucking got them from. And I don't want you round here any more. Got it? You worthless little bastard!'

112

The boy was gasping and shaking his head from side to side, grimacing. 'Noooo! God, no! Please don't!'

David bounced him against the wall and he curled up into a ball. Standing above him, David commanded, 'Get up, get out and take this rubbish with you. Go on, get!' He picked up the things still in reach, the book, the boxers and the badge.

Adam was shivering all over, blubbering into the pillow. There was a moment's silence as he gulped down air. David glowered. They were in the eye of the hurricane. Into this moment's calm the storm came crashing. Adam, chest heaving, stage-whispered, 'Don't send me away. I need you.' David reached down and swung the clenched fist of Adam's body round to face him. A red blotch glowed on his cheek. It would become a nasty bruise.

'Yeah, I'm sure you do. And you need your teddy bear about as much!' Melting, however.

'No, I mean I love you, I want to be with you all the time, even at night.' The wave broke and the temperature changed to chill and the roar of the explosion and collapse of succeeding waves rang in both their ears.

The tears had dried and the quake subsided, the tsunami had passed, receded. David bent down and kissed the unblemished cheek and stroked the hair. Adam stretched. David lay down beside him. They wrapped their arms round each other. David felt Adam's tumescence through his jeans, pressed into the fold of his hip. Only then did he become vaguely erect. His mind was a jumble sale of thoughts, pawed and sorted and sifted through by the returning miscreant hands of herbal numina; discarded, re-sorted, thrown into heaps without order or sense, some two a penny, some without a possible buyer, some valuable beyond price but unrecognised.

'It won't work, you know,' almost to himself. 'I have to have time to think about this. I won't, can't, daren't take you to bed. I don't believe you want that. I don't believe you know what you want. I don't believe I know what I want. Go now and let me think. I need time.'

Reluctantly the youth disengaged himself and left without

a word, the feeling that he was about to be rejected, abandoned, growing inside him. He felt the thefts to have been a mistake. He felt the mistake a theft, taken from him by a malicious god determined to see his undoing. He left the things where they lay gathered for his disposal.

David avoided seeing him for a week and then wrote him a note to say that he was off on a combined business-and-pleasure trip to Derbyshire. Adam could see no reason for business concerning David in that part of the country, all national park and mills, derelict textile industry. The refusal to see him seemed like a total denial of everything he wanted or had had. No signing of a trade agreement, no strategic arms limitations, instead a new Berlin.

David returned from a brief weekend resolved to end it. The hills had told him not to but he was determined to ignore their counsel.

He saw Adam in the pub and said that he thought he'd be going away for a lot longer next time, shortly. A lie and obviously a prelude to severing all bonds between them.

School had started back after the holidays and the boy was truanting again. Eventually, after a fortnight in fact, the fully accoutred knight from the education department rode after him and demanded that he explain. They sat in the secretary's office. The brave soldier was amazed at the violence his enquiry engendered. The boy became hysterical and overturned two filing cabinets, a giant toppling siege towers. He hurled the swivel chair through the window like a trebuchet launching its load, frightened the horses. Then he crammed himself foetally into a corner in a silence close to that of deep space, a vacuum.

That same day David packed and was heading for his mother's in south London. His provisional escape plan included a return to the city in another fortnight to secretly find other accommodation away from Adam, to move as though to a monastery and lie low in a penitential cell till he imagined it safe to venture out. The unravelled reasoning for the flight still made no sense, but all he sought, all he craved, was the possibility of not thinking about it any more. The jumble sale had become a fund-raising marathon, but the bring-and-buy had not yet been opened to the public with its bargain-scrabbling instincts. He wrote a second note and slid it into the letter box before running for cover, scurrying off to his hole. The note was awful, but he knew he couldn't write a better one, one more opaque to hide his crystal clear intentions: *My dear Adam, Unfortunately commitments elsewhere mean that I shan't be around for a good while. Thank you for your kindness. I hope to see you some time. I will write. David.* No 'with love', no 'kind regards', no hearts and flowers. Thinly veiled cowardice and no excuse.

The deputy head brought Adam back in the early afternoon, tethering his charger in front of an empty house. The child, looking oh so very childlike but not so very childish, quietly assured the force of reaction that he'd be all right and said he was sorry about the mess. He picked the hand-delivered note out of its metal cage and went upstairs.

Late afternoon. David was finished packing. Adam's mother returned none the wiser and assumed her son to be still at school.

Early evening. David rang his mother to confirm timetables and give her a more accurate ETA, then he ordered the taxi. Adam's mother had been out to the shops. She came in with the smaller brood, collected from the child-minder. She began to prepare tea. Just-Max came in and sat in front of the box. He had been on a trip the night before and now slumped in a recovery position on the sofa. His mother climbed the stairs to see if the younger of her first set of children had come in while she was out. She was thinking about the new additions and failed to register anything other than absence. A note on the bed went unseen, unnoticed, unread. She didn't even realise the bed was neatly smoothed flat instead of crumpled into a schematic orogeny as usual.

Mid-evening. David was almost ready, almost gone. Tea was on the table and Max was picking at it and Adam wasn't back, but there had been a call from one of the teachers explaining the damage to his mother as she was trying to settle the brats down to eat. She had gone upstairs once more. She came down from Adam's room with the

115

piece of paper in her hand as Max-for-short involuted into the cushions, food abandoned. She read:

Dear Mum, I am sorry about this but I don't think you'll see me again. I love you very much. I love my brother very much. My stepdad's OK and I was even getting used to having the halves around. But I love David lots more and can't go on without him to help me. I don't think he wants me though so I can't bear it any longer. I am really sorry this will cause you pain. Imagine that this way I will be happier. Goodbye. Forgive me and don't blame David for this either. I think that he loves me really but just can't let it show. Well, he promised you he wouldn't. I can't wait for things to change. Adam.

She phoned David. The taxi had arrived. He was down in the hall and wondered if he should climb back up the stairs to answer it. It could wait. If it was important they'd ring back. Adam slipped the tab of acid into his mouth and took a gulp of vodka, knotted the rope into a noose and placed the razor blade on the concrete in front of him. He looked at it. David picked up the receiver. The voice was unexpected and icy calm. 'Where is he?'

'I don't know.'

'He's gone to kill himself, I know he has.'

'I'll be there in a second.' David left the cases, got into the taxi and directed the driver the short distance to the boy's house, apologising profusely on autopilot for the alteration in destination and giving a large tip.

Late evening. Just-Max was pulling himself together because the overriding urgency in his mother's voice was something totally different from her usual nag-nag-nag, and David's arrival was unprecedented. He had never, ever been invited in before. This was like a hallucination. Stepfather subdued, with subdued offspring on couch. The three more active elements debated where the runaway might have gone and what he might be doing.

Adam took off his clothes and climbed the ladder, attached the rope to the top rung and stood on the plank with the bottle of firewater in his hands. The perspectives began to go akilter. He hunkered down and tied the two bricks around

116

his ankles with the cord threaded through the holes in the middle of them.

David suggested either the pillbox along the river or the swimming pool on the green. He said it was possible to get to the first by the track from the village north of the town. The two adults got into the car with the dented bumper and left Max-for-short to guard the house in case of his return, as if the other three had ceased their involvement in the play altogether. Before the departure of the crusaders, David phoned his mother to say he was delayed and the woman rang the police to see if the boy had been detained. She explained the problem briefly, but they showed no concern. They needed no description of the incipient delinquent and assumed he hadn't gone far, but if he had he'd be up to no good.

The car raced to the field by the river. David sprinted across it, stumbling over furrows and calling the boy's name, desperate. Adam sat on the edge of the board swigging from the dwindling supply, till he emptied it and plopped the bottle into the glitter below. Slow-motion splash. He held the blade to his wrist and began to make a precise incision. No pain. The pins and needles from the drug spared him that. He felt strangely calm as if a bad trip were not to be expected even out of this eternal night. Everything was turning black and his blood glowed. It contained sperm-shaped worms. He cut deeper to let them out. The pillbox was empty. No sign. Back across the benighted mountain range of turned earth to the twin blaze of headlights. Reverse-skid-speed-forward-geargrind-lurch.

The other wrist was open. The flashes of golden-ochre streetlamp glare reflected on the deep turquoise and transformed into lampreys with gaping jaws. 'Soon,' he said and slipped the yoke of fraying rope around his neck. He had climbed up wearing his trainers, then taken them off to attach his boots of clay. How he dropped them over the edge into the sea and two fantastic snake-fishes leapt in brilliant delight. He looked across the ocean of chlorinated waste, and through the palisade of chain-link fencing. Miles away his mother and his dead lover moon-walked towards him.

He pressed his dripping hands against the plastic trim of the plank and teetered on the brink.

Night. His heart was pounding. Her heart was pounding. 'Noooo! God! No!' he screamed. Adam slid off the precipice. The film ran fast through the camera to catch the action. He spread his arms and plummeted a second at a time towards the screeching, swimming demons, fire-coloured, the shape of severed penises, each cut end forming a jagged mouth. Punctured stone hung over the edge, the weight making his legs feel longer. David, ahead of the woman, reached the fence and vaulted over, fell, stood, ran to the poolside. The rope grew taut and the brick footwear came down to meet the surface of the boiling pond. The blood dripped around the depending figure and the water began to redden. The terracotta scraped the skin of the pond and jasper formed under his heels and streaked over the spaghetti of reflections, each strand becoming a vein in a solid slab of marble. David had been struggling out of his clothes as he staggered the short distance to the edge of the crystalline lake. He paused and then ran on across the polished plane. Adam's mother watched through the diamonds, but couldn't climb over. Blue iridescence shot up the boy's legs and his body began to glimmer with its own light. The wounds dried, his hair blazed and from his shoulders a fan of feathers sprouted in profusion, then ordered themselves into a pair of huge wings. The drug and the alcohol left him and his eyes opened in most outrageous clarity. They took in the man sliding across the sea of stone straight to him and he extended his arms to greet him. The rope had vanished, flared into darkness. David gripped Adam and the hard surface began to ripple. David grew his own wings. Their bodies began to sink into the reliquefying elements, but the winged images remained on the mobile surface. The spray rocketed upwards a shower of sparks. The two forms merged and became a single flame that shot up into the blackness above.

Very early morning. The police arrived to recover the two naked bodies, the rope, the bottle, the razor blade, David's clothes, Adam's clothes. The boy's mother told the officer that David had tried to swim out to reach her son, that the rope had snapped but the water had done its work. 'He couldn't swim like that,' she said. She handed over the notes written by Adam and David, and the doctor who had been called gave her a tranquilliser and the constable took her home. The little children were in bed. Max-for-short was waiting, as was the new lamp, a little dim.

Darkness, darkness, darkness.

Panic

Tom, Tom, the Piper's son,
Stole my heart and away did run.

HAVING THIS TATTERDEMALION dandelion of a man sat
in my office must be the last resort, the furniture man
thought. The strain of becoming divorced and becoming
infested. The lack of help from the authorities and the inad-
equacy of self-styled reliable pest-control agencies. Now, in
answer to the flyer that had popped through the door, the
merchant of the antique and the antiqued had in his show-
rooms a character straight out of the rhyme about Hamelyn,
particoloured hat and eponymous instrument included. He
looked out through the blinds at the aprons of tarmac regulated with a regiment of parking spaces, and at the swathe
of green separating the development from the New Jersey
turnpike in the distance. It had been a week since the decree
nisi, but the legal wranglings had stretched back much
further. The incursions of the various colonisers had not
gone unnoticed exactly, but unchecked, in both senses, for a
considerable period and now the wood wasps, wood ants,
wood mites and woodworms had established their microscopic conurbations about the warehouse like a wave of
marauding barbarians, feigning the ways of civilisation and
setting up cities in the manner of the natives they were in
the process of dispossessing. Why they hadn't chosen the
farm buildings a few fields away, he couldn't imagine. Perhaps this spell of warm winters had infected the whole district. Should he ask, organise a committee and demand group
rates?

The ragged patchwork in front of him had guaranteed the sonic methods were a sound means to rid the customer of the most intransigent and belligerent of visitors. The voice was heavily accented and prone to the inclusion of words from his original language as he attempted to emphasise the validity of that claim, accompanied by wild gesticulation and danced mimes of the ridding process. 'You mind I ask in my son come from school explain better he can? He in gym clothes sweaty bit mind.' The slur of this last remark distorted it into a description of the boy's Indian ancestry and rudimentary intelligence, or so the apparent words 'injun', 'close' and 'behind' seemed to suggest, words that weren't there. The dealer in davenports and tallboys opened his hands in desperation, but it was taken for acceptance.

The piper stalked out of the room, boots flapping, to return with a boy in boxing kit, his hands still bandaged, gloves slung over his shoulder as though over a clothes peg. He wore high-waisted long shorts of a satinate material and a vest that seemed the by-product of space research, obviously weighing less than a baby wren, marked with enough sweat to double that total. Black, long-laced boots, a sweatband round the head. Looking at the youth, Honest Harry, the host to Hepplewhite, Chippendale and hundreds of others, assumed he had either died from an unannounced coronary infarction or quietly gone completely insane, a fact presaged by the slogans on the leaflet and the appearance of the father of this god of gods. A fact that would make Helen of Troy pale, the Mona Lisa stop smiling, the beaming air hostesses of countless TV encounters spontaneously combust, resulting in cabin decompression, loss of altitude and expensive reshooting of the numerous scenes whose first takes would end on the cutting-room floor until multiple-disaster movies became the rage again. This was a weapon in the arsenal of the con-trickster. He knew of Honest Harry's trips to the pleasure dome in Scranton, where he'd indulge with kidnapped youngsters, compliant not only because of the huge sums offered, but because of the soporifics and relaxants stabbed into their unsuspecting bloodstreams just before the arrival of the client. That must be it, a blackmail ring, a

121

demand for cash for legitimised services, receipted and documented but useless and imaginary: the removal of insects by way of a charmed pipe, a magical tune. Paranoia might suggest the pests had been encouraged to build nests there specifically for this exotic scam.

'Hi, sir. I'm Tom. Perhaps I can help explain things to my father and tell you what he says?'

'Whatever he wants I will pay. Just ask him what else he wants.'

A conversation ensued in a language that Honest Harry, baptised Ezekiel years and years ago, could not identify: it was not Russian, Czech or either of the Finno-Ugric pair, neither was it Greek, Turkish or Arabic. It overflowed with sibilants and trills, tongue-clicking, even grunts and little yelps. This parody of verbal intercourse must have originated in one of those drama workshops where you use different modes of grunting to convey first love, then hate, then fear, then anger, to one another. These two must have moved on to the advanced course: pretend to come from a mythical land by producing a quasi-language with interrogative intonation and expostulations conveying surprise, concern or indignation. *El chilango habla cantando*, they say. This little papagayo talked with the greatest convocation of avian choirs tripping from his lips, shaming the angels as well as the paradisiac parrots, their plumage a dull grey besides this exponential beauty, their song the inchoate moan of the hurricane. Zeke could honestly smell the youth's sweat. It was sweet, not the acrid tang of an adult, the odour that, stale on clothes, would be likely to emanate from the anachronism pretending price negotiation at that very moment. He could have asked for the world and got it, but terms were more than reasonable.

Then they were gone, promising to come the following Sunday when the shop would be shut, so as to persuade the misinformed insects that better housing could be found elsewhere, in the hills to the west, for example. Perhaps the piper'd explain his message in his bird-call speech rather than by using his recorder or whatever kind of flute that was? Why hadn't they stung him, put their cards on the table and shown him the compromising photographs? Perhaps those secret midnight hauntings were part of the madness, part of the improvisation?

The story of this Ezekiel's escalating penchant for the illicitly perverse reads like a perfectly logical progression, but at home on his own he wouldn't be able to rid himself of the shape of the vision he'd seen that afternoon. He'd even manage to recreate that olfactory miracle, that velvet hand in the iron glove, tickling his nostrils like a narcotic. He knew that the route to Sunday would be a routine of destroying monotony. The papery nests, the boreholes, the powder on the inside of the drawers, all were like signs of impending heaven. He could see himself as a hornet dragged from the hive, following a mysterious scent, or a locust stridulating reflexively to the all-persuasive vibration of the magician's music.

Zeke interrupted his thoughts to think about his seventeen-year-old son. He'd walked in on him months back while he was masturbating. He'd barged blindly into the room and confronted a bed on which his only child lay splay-legged, holding his huge dick between thumb and two fingers like a delicate bloom. Even as he stared, the innocence-losing youth moved his hand nonchalantly up and down, looking at the porn mag he held above his face with the other hand. 'As you see, Dad, it's a bit inconvenient at the moment.'

'I'll come again in a minute,' he said as he left.

'So will I,' the boy intoned. Cheeky little bastard, his father thought, spoilt brat. I knew I should have insisted he stay home in England, in boarding school.

A week later the pair of them had been to the pool and were showering together. It was so open, so Roman, he remembered. Jake had actually asked, 'Do you think I'm sexy, then?'

'With a cock that big the girls are bound to come to you like birds to a ploughed field in search of worms. God knows where you got one that size from.'

'I certainly didn't inherit it from you.'

'Well, you certainly didn't get it from Mom!'

Modern kids just had too much cheek, too much spunk,

as they said this side of the pond. It had been light-hearted enough, but what was the message, what was he trying to make his old man think?

Then Valerie had up and left him, for no apparent reason. He had found his way to that bordello with a client of his. Told him to come along just for the ride. Exotic dancers for all tastes, the guy leered. In a drunken stupor, he'd asked for a boy. He'd stumbled over the word 'beautiful' and it bubbled out like part of a conspiracy, a confession extracted under truth-drug stimulation. He'd gone many times after that and as he lay with the doped deadheads from the poor neighbourhoods, that odd admix of violence and vulnerability on their sleepy faces, he'd found himself always thinking about Jake and the provocative exchange in the changing room. He'd never done this before, had these cravings, then all of a sudden he was addicted to this ridiculously expensive pastime. He never did anything, just curled up with them as though he himself was as doped as the purveyors of the high-priced passion. Now he desired the piper's son in a way he wouldn't be able to describe, let alone justify.

Duly on Sunday the strange pair arrived. Tom wore a tracksuit made of crumply polymer with the logo City of Gold blazed across the back of the jacket and Team Strip down the outside leg of the pants. 'My father will play to the animals and they will go away. All of them. And then he will play for you and your troubles will be gone. He says you should not look at me with lust in your heart, for it is not me you seek but the image of yourself, your former self.'

Ezekiel was definitely mad. The blunt warning could only be delivered by a figment of his imagination. When Tom unzipped his top to reveal he wasn't wearing a shirt underneath, the poor salesman thought he was about to lose all sense of reality, all control over a disintegrating world.

Then the boy darted into the unlit storeroom as the sound of the pipe began to weave its dangerous melody. The notes disentangled themselves from the staves of the air to become a skein of birdlike words, an aria warbling along to the ululation in the dark, a libretto in the weird language the imposters feigned, but readily decipherable to the intent listener. It bade him enter the mountain where all the children had gone, promising that only the boys had been taken, that the poem was wrong and the impoverished of Hamelyn mourned only the loss of their male heirs, not the disappearance of every kid in town. Time had hidden the truth, made a mockery of the specifics of the tragedy. 'Come now and see what you want to see. Tom, Tom, the Piper's son, will guide you. That is the price of ridding you of your insect horde.'

The gloom that was the hangarlike part of the showroom's interior gaped like the entrance to a catacomb. He hesitated, but when he saw the back of the tempter uncovered in the shadows as he slipped out of the dark jacket, he felt impelled to follow. Where the chequerboard tiling should have been, there was a shelf of calcareous Permian limestone, blackish rather than white, scraped smooth by the high-pressure water etching out coralline fossilised remains. To his right he heard the splashing of a rapid watercourse, a xylophone dripping, pitter-pattering an irregular rhythm in the echoing chamber. As his eyes grew accustomed, he saw the devil before him rid himself of his trousers, unzipping ankle zips to extricate his basketball boots. He turned to face the tremulous figure, wearing only a pair of cotton briefs thin enough to indicate a pubic darkness beneath, and tight enough to outline the curve of a penis.

'If you want to see the rest, you'll have to play the doctors-and-nurses game and do the same for me.'

Mechanically the man shed his clothes. He got down to his underpants and stopped. He was wearing a pair of grey midways, neither boxers nor Y-fronts, enough room to form a pouch in the front, but leg-hugging just below. 'Now there's a funny thing,' the youth remarked. 'You insist on buying your *ropa interior* in good old Britain, where you find most of your furniture, don't you, Mr Arthurfields?'

He had changed his name when he became a naturalised Englishman immediately after the war. It had been a Belgian name, but he had dropped the first disyllable as it sounded a sufficient mouthful to be obviously foreign. Then he swapped his other name when he reached the States. No one knew of the alterations, so the reminder was a jolt.

'I see you are shocked. Well, let me give you another surprise. This is a statue factory. If you look over here, you will see what I mean.'

Beyond the scantily clad kid was a receding line of pale shapes. He approached and realised they were men posed in classical attitudes, pressed nose to tail and made of stone. He checked by touching their rough surfaces.

'A new edition is being created for the Post-Modern marketplace, if you'd care to look to the left.'

A dripping carving was being hauled from the stream, heaved out by four naked boys. No, not naked, shrink-wrapped or clingfilmed. They had complete suits of the material used in disposable surgical-glove manufacture. The clothing made crinkly sounds over the noise of the water tumbling from the statuary. The subject was most unusual – a satyric athlete, with arms outstretched in an attitude like a harpist, or possibly a player of some sinuous oboe or hautboy, but what the fingers almost touched was an excessively extended phallus, curving like a bow almost to the stony lips. The workers shoved the grotesquerie into position at the end of the line. They grinned at Mr Field, Honest Harry, until the shock of recognition hit him.

'Yes, the Scranton Brothel creepers. Busy little bees, aren't they? Now, if you'd just care to get into the water, there, where it widens, we can come to some arrangement with you.' He stepped forward and groped the entrepreneur between the legs. 'Not much in your packet, is there? And it's bound to shrivel up a bit in the petrifying river. You better keep your pants on.' A wooden crate splashed into the pool where one of the transparently encased employees threw it. Instead of floating, it went white and sank. 'If you hold on a moment, one of the lads will bind your hands. What we want is for you to sit leaning forward, elbows on knees, looking up as though about to face a final bout in the ring or arena, if you see what I mean. The water will have effect very quickly so get in straight away and take up

126

your position. The masons can carve a bigger bulge when we get you out.'

He walked to the edge and looked in. He looked back at the devilish grin and knew he'd go through with it, even as he began to ruminate about what the contract had said about this bizarre turn of things. He crouched, put one hand on the side and launched into the stream. It was like liquid nitrogen. He completed his intended manoeuvre into the demanded posture, unable to gasp at the horrible pain of the cold as it numbed his legs and thorax and balls. The surface was just below his nose. His mouth was sealed and he could not move his neck to extricate his inoperative body. I am being turned to stone, he thought, but I am helpless to fight it. And all because I wanted to see this creature in the nude.

'Your son is coming. He has just entered the shop. He came over with a friend from Trenton. Before I let on about your predicament, let me tell you a few things about Jake you did not know,' he gloated. 'Because of his pompous British accent, when he arrived here they called him Jerk, deliberately mispronouncing his name. Then he had a tryout for the football team. They mocked him for playing rugby – whatever that is – until they saw his throwing and his kicking. That's when he got the nickname "Javelin" or just "JV" and a lot of respect, too. Then one day, when he was set to train the junior team, one of his senior classmates found him jacking off one of the jocks he was supposed to be in charge of. Call it blackmail, call it what you will, but to keep the crew quiet he had to perform a similar service for the upper grades on demand. So now he gets called "Jack" or "Jacko". But they love the old faggot, say he learned something real good in those two terms back in England. But, before I call him over, I'll give you your prize.' He peeled off his shorts and paraded up to the pool and looked down as though to admire his reflection in the rippling wave.

Looking up with his eyes, the thought struck Mr Arthurfields that the size he thought they were had to be a matter of perspective, for these genitals, thrust forward from the hips, dwarfed the distant chin and nostrils. He noticed something else as he took in the sights. The youth had string tied round each of his limbs and his neck, at the ankles and the wrists, a single strand joined in overelaborate knots, the one pendant from his shoulder nesting in that triangular concavity between the clavicles. He still had his footwear on. Getting his shorts off had been a bit of a struggle because of his boots. Now, he lifted his foot on to Zeke's forehead and tipped him backwards into the ice, where the rest of him froze solid, the water finally slipping into his lungs and crystallising the inside of his mouth, his throat, down to his stomach, as he swallowed involuntarily.

The cellophane gang dragged his statue out. Tom's silhouette blocked the view. When he stepped aside, Jake was standing in front of him. Inevitably he took his clothes off. There were no commands, no requests, just the act. His prick was as hard as a tiny lance. Tom put his hands on Jake's shoulders and moved him sideways till they faced one another directly in front of the unfortunate stone warehouse-owner. Tom's tumescence matched the other's and as they looked down between entwined arms, foreheads locked together like those of bucks in season, they moved until their antler prongs touched, side to side, not tip to tip. Through frosted corneas, the name-changer watched as a silent transformation occurred, to the percussive sounds of falling water. Each penis began to grow and twist, curving round the other, up between the pergola of mirrored images. The double helix spiralled over their shoulders, and as the coils tightened, the two were drawn together till they were pressed inseparably to each other, each head over the opposite shoulder. The convolvulus stem sprouted between them and then unlaced prior to enfolding the two bodies in many loops of shooting flesh. They were bound together into a single mass of tissue combined. Finally the extending organs arrived back at the top of the immobile composition. Simultaneously they opened their mouths as the heads of the penises entered the waiting gulfs. Whether they received their own or each other's was impossible to tell, but the spellbinding was completed the instant the minions came and cast the resulting hybrid gently into the preserving torrent.

The succeeding blackness was filled with a voice and the background noise was of hammering and drilling and obscene shouts.

'This is just what your establishment needs to complete the overall effect. Very Classical. The work is a late-eighteenth or early-nineteenth-century copy of a Roman copy of a Hellenistic original, perhaps by Myron or Praxiteles. Though it is called *The Boxer* because of the bandages round the fingers and wrists, it isn't clear if he is about to fight or has just finished. It seems strangely full of pathos, as though gladiatorial, doomed to die, but maybe he mourns some other loss, or contemplates his impending retirement from the sport. He is very beautifully rendered down to the last detail. Yes, it is believed that the statue's genitals have been exaggerated, but then the Roman audience was less aesthetic, less esoteric, than the Greek, and the Classical Revival artists were glad of an excuse to portray slight lewdness in the name of an uplifting homage to the ancients.'

The Boxer was installed in the changing area of the Sappho Health Spot in Manhattan. The owner, a Miss Belise Honduras, had taken some persuading that the 'in' look required a male addition to the decorative scheme which had cost her almost as much as the rest of the work put together, but now that he sat dolefully at the end of the marbled room, with its barrel vault and 'authentic' pigeonhole lockers, she was more that satisfied with the effect. Her first customers also liked the submissiveness of the copy, as well as its well-endowed exposure. It became a standing joke to 'touch the Boxer's' for luck. Soon the said portion of the effigy acquired a lustrous patina, out of keeping with the paler glitter of the rest of the off-white block. Some of the naked women screeched that his sultriness was because of his impotence to respond.

The stony soul lurking in the forgery had gained an extraordinary form of sight which allowed his blinded eyes to gauge the proximity of these dripping females and to sense their touch as a distant breath on once-real forearms, or whatever else. He hated the skitter of laughter and the maliciousness of whispered gossip, but needed the invisible company all the same.

The insects had marched or flown into the magic mountain in a daze, in balletic formation, undulating lines in the air and curvaceous courses across the plains of the floor. As they came into the aura of the hidden place, they became changed. They grew and paled and their bodies reared up or swung down into the vertical position as they floated to the ground beyond the threshold, putting on flesh and plumping out into little boys and lost adolescents, chattering and slapping each other as the enchantment increased. Were they always boys, transformed into insects, then back to boys?

Now, without their ruling force, they will remain boys, inside the berg of paradise, playing for ever without having to slink back to our side of the stone door, clad in chitin, to build nests in our cellars and burrows in our rafters.

Caleb was simple. That may seem to imply a cretinous or moronic dolt, but really it was a matter of his being uncomplicated, innocent when most people had learned the calculated manipulation of their peers to get just what they want. He had been given a job and a place to stay, a couple of rooms and a private bathroom in the depths of the complex. He was employed as a janitor-caretaker-cum-watchman, with cleaning duties, in the hour between eleven and twelve at night, after the close, and then again from six to seven, prior to opening. He would hand out towels and generally tidy up during the day, catching a nap in the slack part of the afternoon. The proprietress was glad of so reliable a help, and there were clients who were pleased by a reversal of roles that enabled them to fantasise an inverted domination. The owner secretly desired this lithe body, but dared not engineer a seduction. Those eyes would be too accusatory thereafter, when he realised in his methodical way that he had been simply used. Others shared the urge to mother him and a passing Freudian would have incorporated analysis sessions into a recline on the Imperial benches. As for Caleb himself, he was an onanist, and his pleasure was practised in the empty marble halls at night, when he would swim naked in the pool with either only the underwater light on, or the strips in the coving illuminating the false coffering. He'd get out and take a towel into the drying room, where he'd slip into one of the cylindrical innovations which simulated a tornado of desiccating heat. Rubbing himself at the same time always aroused him and he'd step from the gale to spill his seed onto the folded snowy pile. In the morning he returned the soiled item to the alcove and put it with the untouched ones, to hand it out at random to one of the ladies. His deception had not been discovered, but had it been, he would have been discharged immediately. Nonetheless, he indulged his nocturnal habit daily. Variety is the spice of life and consequently his simple mind had begun to map variations on a theme and he systematically spilled himself in each and every corner of the club.

One night it was the statue's turn to receive his attention. He flexed his hips lewdly in front of the impassive countenance and then approached to press one palm to the carved coiffure and his erection, clasped in the other, to the lips of the silent witness. A saline gel clung to the stone, and after a few vigorous strokes his orgasm spattered the face of the sleeper, his forehead, his Homeric eyes, his nose and his mouth. A stone tongue flickered along the line with the sound of a crumpled crisp packet. The drop of moisture penetrated to the core of the statue and cracks shot across the surface, releasing tiny jets of rock dust as the sound grew.

Terrified, Caleb stepped back and plumped down on one of the seats, which, though they looked like stone, were made of thermolytic plastic which warmed instantly to the slap of buttocks and thighs. The towel had slipped partly under him and a glutinous strand trailed from the droop of his tail on to the unstained field. He could not conceive that the sculpture before him was coming to life. Rather he imagined he'd somehow broken it and would be fired as soon as the morning arrived.

The unpetrified Harry stood up slowly, bits of white falling from him, including a large section from between his legs.

131

Caleb swallowed in horror to think a man could lose that part of himself, but then he saw the dark lines of the hairs beneath. The diminutive member looked to be coated in talc. The figure stretched and croaked, 'Water.'

Caleb had been an inmate of an institution for a while, when his parents, and then his guardians, had abandoned him. He came from a large family that couldn't afford to keep a non-worker, so they got rid of him. Not because his learning difficulties were acute, but because there was no one willing to have him. He recognised the plaintive cry and would soon recognise the rambling sincerity this golem would spout once his thirst had been slaked. He looked as if he were the best listener on the planet, so strangers always talked to him. He could read people better than he could read books. The world did not always undermine his security or take advantage of him. His simplicity disarmed everybody.

Once the man inside the hard sheath was there in front of him, he did not worry too greatly about the weirdness of the occurrence. He just smiled and clucked quiet encouragement. Grabbing an elbow, he steered the dusted man to the fountain beside the pool. He drank copiously, the surface tension allowing gemstones of droplets to cascade down the overhanging contours of his chin and chest to rest in the matted thicket below, the glints taking on the quality of diamonds.

The dream creature turned and dived into the turquoise stillness. He emerged almost free of marmoreal debris, except in parts of his hair, shedding his dreamer's costume. Caleb asked him who he was and then if he'd take him away, because the finding of the shattered remains in the changing room would spell his dismissal anyway.

'I haven't got any clothes,' he said. 'Or any money.'

Cable supplied both, though his build meant that the boxers fitted like briefs and the tracksuit like a wetsuit. They went down to the Port Authority Terminal and boarded a late – or was it early? – Greyhound that deposited the pair outside the former emporium opposite the new mall.

It now displayed modern rather than antique stock and the name above the shop frontage had been changed. They went in and asked to see the manager. Harry's former deputy greeted them with incredulity and a fraction of fear. The explanation of the passage of time seemed not unbelievable, but sad in its glibness. Harry's wife had inherited the business five years ago, though the police were still investigating the disappearance of her husband and son. The assumption at the time had been that he had murdered Jake, hidden the body and run. A motive was not proposed, but insanity was offered as a possible explanation. The friend of long ago had phoned 911 after he'd wandered into the place to hurry Jake up, only to find an empty store with water flowing over the floor. The papers and the TV had had a holiday reporting the mystery, but quickly lost interest when no resolution materialised, and other tragedies caught their prurient eyes.

The new manager handed over the keys of the company car, conned into believing Harry or Ezekiel was off to see his ex-wife and then report in to the nearest station. The two fugitives fled, sold the car and then bought another at another garage, trying to avoid clear connections for the investigators to follow, either journalists or police. They crisscrossed the eastern states not really knowing what they were looking for: Caleb pleased to be travelling with everything organised for him; Zeke, now called Ethan, recalling the shape of the fused statue, unwilling to assume that no similar miraculous liberation had freed the boys from its clutch. They hung around with vagrants and street sweepings, showing the photo of Jake that had popped out of the glove compartment, where it had stayed over the intervening months. (It had also held a 'Wanted for Murder' handbill that Ethan's workmate had obsessively kept all that time, which they naturally discarded as a clue to their old identity.) It ended with Caleb becoming a gigolo, Ethan collecting the fees from sex-starved society wives. They moved often, until they happened into Toledo, Ohio. Bored and dispirited on the first day there, they had chanced into the Museum of Art to shelter from the rain.

At the start of their flight, Harry or Zeke or Ethan had stolen food and books on sculpture in the hope of finding some clue, but none had been forthcoming. Soon it became clear that Caleb's ingenuous gaze would get food and rest quicker than Ethan's guarded bargaining. The latter posed as the former health-club employee's father, himself an expert in Celtic art, travelling about on a research project. The landladies didn't immediately believe it, until the pile of stolen glossy publications hid the top of the bedroom dresser. But none of these expensive tomes had the right photo, though some had similarly massively hewn statuary. A footnote once mentioned a Janus-like Green Man in private hands, but there was no plate, no academic description.

In a reassembled Romanesque cloister the slightly damp twosome found what they were looking for at last. The label read:

Recent Acquisition. The Ashford Effigy.
Provenance: Cong, County Mayo, Irish Republic.
Found during excavations of a canal between loughs Corrib and Mask – ironically this ran dry, after dropping the level of the latter lake by some fifteen feet, the water flowing into the Palaeozoic sedimentary out of which the work is carved. It takes its name from the castle where it stood for many years, the home of the Guinness family. It passed into American ownership when the castle was sold off to become a hotel. It is thought to date from the sixth or seventh century. It is obviously a form of Green Man in that vines spring from both heads' mouths, but the fact that the image is a twinned one relates it to the Janus figure, faces looking in opposite directions, all-seeing but dual in aspect, liable to deceive or betray. The fact that one pair of eyes is shut has suggested to some scholars the idea of light and dark, though others posit a material–spiritual opposition. Dr Cappadocia of San Diego points out that the open eyes are 'blind', not only in fact, but in the staring quality they exhibit. He adds that works of this date normally have a pupil and/or iris carved into the stone of the eye. It has therefore been said that some attribution other than Janus should be given. A comparative study has so far revealed little.
Purchase made possible by a grant from Virtual Reality, Inc.

The plan to steal the falsified relic took a while to organise, but proved one of the most celebrated artwork heists after its carrying-out. Caleb became a museum guard and Ethan

134

got a job in a laundry which supplied the establishment with towels and linen for the coffee shop. There was a group of five night watchmen who rotated so that there would be three on at a time. When one of them was on holiday and two were ill with food poisoning, Caleb was allowed to fill the gap in the shift. Ethan hid in one of the washrooms, guaranteed that his companion would not see him during his patrol of the premises. The statue was affixed with four metal rods bent over to position rather than anchor the huge hunk of chalky rock. Once out of his hiding place, Ethan sliced through the steel using a cordless powered saw. The conspirators tilted the bulky weight on to a trolley, readied and padded, which they then removed to the storeroom where the napkins and hand towels were kept. There they transferred the stone duo to a very large wickerwork basket. This had a false bottom, and was slipped over the stolen item until the sprung, flexible portions clasped the statue in an attempt to return to their original position. The bed of the trolley was the exact size to enable the palisade of woven laths to disguise the hidden treasure. The basket stayed in the store till the investigation was being wound down. A cursory search of the building had left the officer in charge in no doubt whatsoever that the theft had been successful. The locks on one of the side doors had been tampered with sufficiently to make it look like there'd been some kind of forced entry, but the alarm had not been triggered. The means to override that particular circuit proved the biggest puzzle for the duped criminologists.

Caleb had, of course, been interviewed, as had the two other guards on that rota. All staff had been asked if they'd noticed anything suspicious during the weeks leading up to the mysterious break-in. It was mysterious because there were paintings and *objets d'art* of far greater value that could have been more easily taken. Such a large item would be far more difficult to transport and eventually dispose of. It was assumed that some inside help had been available, but there were no direct leads to the specific individuals.

The soiled linen was prodded by the extra security personnel as it left the premises, but the smell of dirty tablecloths and tea towels was a discouragement to further inquisitiveness. The two men knew their movements would be scrutinised and their bank accounts watched as the motive of the crime was thought to be monetary, but the effigy languished in the old shed behind the frame house that they had rented on the south side of the town. A more astute police department might have taken it upon themselves to be more aggressive in their pursuit of suspects, but in a place prone to more violent occurrences than this, besides all the drug-related incidents, it was relatively soon that the disappearance was relegated to being merely another entry in the unsolved art-robbery files in Washington, where computer experts tried to establish a pattern from the existing data and the routes of distribution within and delivery to and from the US, as well as probing dubious corporations for their involvement in the illegal traffic.

The daring attempt to get his son and the piper's son back paid off for Ethan, but every means they tried to reawaken the boys proved ineffective. Their first assumption had been that the same disgraceful treatment would free the slaves from their bonds, even though the necessary defilement disinclined the theft's mastermind from trying the spattering release. Every combination of spilled seed was tried, to no purpose, and despair soon invaded the father and his friend.

Then one day an advert in the local paper caught Ethan's attention. 'Piper's Pest Prevention presents proved protection from all parasitic problems.' It went on to describe an ultrasonic method of 'persuading insect, rodent and avian infestation to leave *their* homes and *your* home at one fell swoop'. The outmoded language was one clue and, when Ethan phoned the number given, the twittering voice was another.

He arrived this time in a lounge suit. The charming shawm was hidden in a leather travelling case, but it was definitely him, nonetheless. He did not stand on ceremony, but announced, 'Ah, Mr Furniture, you are wanting your son and my son back. You are surprised I could countenance their disappearance, but then my boy is disobedient and he has been gone like this before. So now we must talk a price. Again you are surprised, but your need to have your

136

offspring restored seems greater than mine. I can of course send mine back to bed, to lie down in the earth, but then you it was that desired him in the first place, and maybe it is the same now, no?'

It was true, but Harry-Zeke-Ethan wasn't sure he dared enquire after the price. The price had already been too great, far too great.

'Ask away.'

There was no alternative.

'Caleb comes with us into the magic mountain,' he whispered.

'He isn't mine to barter.'

'You took him from the tepidarium, out of the steam to where the air is clear. He is dependent on you, but now you must choose. My time is precious and business calls.'

'Are all your deals so unfair, so unbalanced?'

'Of course. That is what I am for, what I mean. Now make your decision.'

Ethan looked over to where his companion stood. He had used him in the past as a means to an end, a bargaining chip. 'Yes, I agree.'

'I will play a little tune based round the lyric "My son Tom, your son Jake", a simple enough melody. All you do is convert each letter to its equivalent tonal value as the birds do. Thus Tom is FAF and Jake is CADE.' He fingered the notes, then blew them gently out of the trumpet-ended pipe. ED-EAG-FAF-DAGD-EAG-CADE. He played the simple tune several times. Each time the pale stone seemed to glow with more colour till two naked youths stood out from the mass, their necks craning uncomfortably, vines with emerald leaves binding their bodies together. They pulled themselves apart, bones clicking back into place, the ropelike vegetation turning yellow and brown and falling away into an encircling tangle at their ankles. They stepped out of the hoops that had restrained them, unable to speak. They rubbed their eyes like mirror images and looked around the darkened shed, out of the grimy window and then at the two other people in the space, silently, accusingly.

'I guess you are bound to this new boy now after five

137

suncycles in his arms. You need not reply for the bargain has been struck. Now I will go and take Caleb away with me.' The piper began another flurry of notes. The back of the building gave way to another cavelike hollow and the door opened to admit a mesmerised Caleb. He began to follow the player into the darkness, as though translating the letter-for-note transposition into a message of eternal promise.

At last the others reacted. Tom summoned a feeble voice to hiss, 'No, that's not fair.' Then he picked up the wreath of dried plants at his feet and flung it over the piper's head like a quoit or life belt. As it faltered over the shoulders, it knocked the reed flute from the quick-fingered fiend. Tom scooped it up as it fell and pressed it to his own lips. A dirge in a minor key slowed the passage of time as the magical lianas revivified and grew broad to encase the enchanter. His apprentice played on like Pan, or Marsyas challenging Apollo's superiority on the instrument. The helical growth of greenery enmeshed the screeching sorcerer till he was completely the prisoner of the verdant gaol. It spread out-ward and up to become the shape of a gnarled old cypress beyond the place where the boards of the outhouse used to be. As the funeral plaint ceased, the tenebrous chamber faded and the reality of those planks reasserted itself. The three tumbled out into the light to see the tree rooted to the spot where it had been sown.

The neighbourhood could not understand how so ancient a tree was possibly replanted, nor how the museum guard could afford such an addition to his property, but the police could find no record of any transaction or shipment and installation. The theory of group hysteria seemed the only likely explanation. It was clear the roots were firm, whatever the people around might claim about an overnight miracle. Perhaps it was just neurotic antipathy to non-locals, especially as their ménage seemed somewhat unconventional. As to the arrival of the inconceivably handsome young man, every single woman, every married one and every divorcée yearned for a touch of that hand, a hug from those arms, a kiss from those lips, yet it seemed he was inseparable from that Jake, the son the police had believed murdered. It had taken them a long time to ascertain that fact. The ex-wife had put them on the trail after contacting them to find a certain honest Ethan, whom she had seen in the *Enquirer* as the owner of an overnight burgeoning. She had doubted the caption, but the faces of her ex and her presumed-dead son had precipitated her into action. There was an odd reunion when the explanation of their past whereabouts was as inconclusive as it had been for the department.

The disenchanted night-club owner hadn't even reported the vanishing statue, sure that she'd be laughed at – the debris, the lack of signs of a break-in and when she eventually notified the authorities of the disappearance of Caleb, they hadn't been particularly interested, as he was old enough to do what he wished. The doctor in charge of his case had been a little perturbed and dismissive of the care and concern the woman had shown at the time, but his new situation seemed admirable.

Almost a happy ending. Ethan's ex-wife felt happy finally to marry the modern-furniture warehouseman and maintain the largest interest in the company, which she had allowed to be renamed at the time of the disappearance so as to be shot of the responsibility while still holding on to a major part of the shares. She was a little alarmed at what she surmised her ex-husband's household comprised, and was on the verge of berating him about persuading their son into immoral ways when Tom's beauty hit her between the eyes and she realised she should not interfere in such a thing. Luckily, she did not give credence to the report that had brought her northwards, nor did she probe into Tom's upbringing. He himself remained rather coy about that and would sometimes sit fingering the holes and keys of the ancient instrument, though he never once raised it to his lips to play.

Empedoclean

LIAM, FOURTEEN. FROM somewhere in Northamptonshire. Bulky for his age. Tall. Not particularly handsome, not particularly prone to spots. Needing to shave about once a week, having passed into puberty well in advance of his peers. Somewhat out of step with his contemporaries. Maybe because of the hormonal differences. Maybe because of the tight rein kept on him by his father. Maybe because he doesn't get on with his stepmother. Maybe because of the brutal beatings meted out when his dad has been down the pub for too long. He has been thrashed across his bare backside in the presence of his father's friends. The pain he can stand, it's the humiliation of having to drop his trousers and pants and bend across the chair that he hates. Some visitors attempt to intercede. They are never invited back. He is depressed at home, depressed at school. The teachers put it down to growing up and the impending crucial year of decision and the career lottery that follows. When she bothers to think about it, his stepmother thinks it's school. She has learned not to interest herself in him. He doesn't want it, her husband doesn't want it, and secretly she doesn't want it. She just wants to devote her energies to loving her husband, making love and making babies. Two stepbrothers and a stepsister arrive in quick succession and Liam withdraws further into himself, into his sadness, his aloneness. Soon he'll be old enough to leave home, but he wants to stay, knowing he'll not be able to go on studying if he's forced to give in and get out. Soon he'll be strong enough to strike back at his old man, but he knows that'd be the end of his plans of becoming a teacher. He doesn't want anything to do with the small haulage firm that his father has built up over the years. He expects the new family will inherit it, anyway. Because of his morose behaviour and his gruff, dense accent, his schoolmates think he is thick, and although his marks are consistent, his tutor doesn't think he's destined for anything other than to be a lorry driver for the rest of his life. Going to Scouts gives him an escape. He is made a patrol leader and working for the Chief Scout Award offers him an excuse to stay out on a couple of nights in the week and go off camping at weekends.

Liam is in love with his Scout leader. He does not know he is in love. He cannot articulate it. There is a wriggling worm of worry deep inside his skull. He constantly curries favour with the leader, seeks out his company, brings back presents from the family holiday, covertly, furtively, handing them over looking at the ground, scurrying off before they are unwrapped. Liam goes round for Patrol Leaders' Councils and lingers at the house with another boy. They have long-drawn-out discussions sometimes. Opinions are coaxed out, never derided, but put into a wider context of experience and knowingness. Liam refers to others when referring to himself. The disguise often works. He is not suspected of great depths and if the thoughts seem odd they are more likely to be word-for-word repetition of someone else's. It is easier to withhold names if there are no names. One night he mentions that he has a friend who thinks he is turning gay. The comment elicits a plea for tolerance from the leader, a condemnation from the other lingerer. Liam makes non-committal remarks, but the worm does a little circuitous dance and broadens its burrow into an echoing chamber, resonant, full of foreboding, full of fear. He says his friend says he just has a feeling deep inside that things aren't right. He has never messed about with anyone.

'How could he fancy another bloke?' the other asks.

'He says he doesn't really.'

Pretty inconclusive.

Summer. Glorious summer. Staffordshire. Liam comes top in a general-knowledge competition, getting 49 out of 50. And they thought he was thick. He wins a new sheath knife with the symbol of the site branded into the leather. A photograph of him holding it, beaming. A combined camp with another local troop. The patrols are all mixed up and given new names. They are called Bears, Bullocks, Tits and Cocks. The last summer before dark days. On Thursday the gang go off caving. Piling into the minibus and leaders' cars. Scruff kit, boots, torches. Liam a bit frightened. Exciting fright. Instruction on the surface, then into a shedlike building with a floor sloping into the hillside. Walking upright through a narrow electric-lit passage to a sandy-bottomed bulge with a dark hole beyond. 'If anyone wants to chicken out now, they can.' No one. Into the dark. Out of reach of the lights they huddle together and are told that the first bit is a difficult section to show them what they'll be up against. A climb up a chimney, then a narrow passage to a domed chamber with a metal-runged, chain-link ladder trailing back down to the floor, an awkward lip to negotiate. The younger ones should have greater difficulty as the hand and footholds are further apart for them, but lack of fear and greater agility allow them to quickly scuttle up the vertical shaft after an initial bunk-up from behind, through strata of slippery limestone, like cockroaches up a drainpipe. Their tiny frames are able to slither past the guide and along to the precipice as though they did this every day. Liam finds it more demanding. At one point the leeway is only a fraction of an inch. A couple of the adults have a struggle, too. Swinging around in a foetal curl on your side before you let your legs dangle beside the ladder is peculiar in that it might well happen under a duvet, but here, between sheets of Carboniferous deposits, the covers won't yield, and are cold and clammy instead of warm and dry. Almost womblike, the dark and damp.

Then crawls, scrambles, ducking under projecting rock, the little ones at an advantage until they reach the glassy-smooth gouge made by a high-pressure underground stream, long since fled. V-shaped, plunging a little before climbing and narrowing, twisting off to the right. They are hot from the exertion. The smaller ones have to be manhandled by the strategically placed larger ones till a sandier section is gained.

142

There is a broadening-out and a rock shelf they can all clamber on to for a moment's rest. The guide gets them to turn off their lamps. The dark is denser than anything up above. The bright afterimages soon vanish. Fingers half an inch from the eye no longer exist. Strangely, it's a comforting dark. A moment ago they could see their breath in the moist space; now the space is gone, the breathing interconnected, thunderously noisy when they hush to hear a silence they cannot hope to hear. Inhalation, exhalation, systole, diastole, molecules bombarding tympana, hammer striking anvil, rustle of clothing, hair growing. Liam feels happy.

Lights. Let there be battery light. Explode. And above, thunderheads have built up anvils of their own and Thor and Woden are banging thunderbolts on the steel-topped clouds, raining down torchlike flashes. A torrent of molten metal pours out of the sky. The end of the world. A second instructor catches up just as the group are investigating the underground river. Each one has tasted the ice-cold stream whose clarity is sharper than air, glass, crystal, whose purity is magical, whose sound is joyful as it tumbles over gemstones. Playing follow-my-leader, Liam and his best friend have edged forward, gulping air and holding breath, to pass under an overhang into a wider passage. The older one has got his waterproof torch with him and they chuckle at the reflections on the scalloped ceiling. It looks liquid as the ribbed patterns play over the limestone, as though they were under the sea at the time of its formation. Beyond the obstruction the party is being persuaded to hurry back to the surface. The boys are told that excess water is nothing to worry about, but better to be safe than sorry. An adult reinvention of language.

They have already reached the fluvially eroded slide before someone realises that they are missing two. There is a large pool of cloudy water at the bottom of glistening rocks and they all slide down into it. A note of panic communicates itself. The guide reverses his tracks to pursue the errant leader and his apostle, after a clipped conversation with the second potholer, who had brought the weather update, about calling a rescue team.

143

Rain-grey water. When the guide reaches the reported last sighting, he slips under the silty stream and into the hole beyond. Clearly they are on the point of coming back. Unwisely, he rolls off his concern and his urgency. He turns and vanishes. Liam follows, and halfway through the water-filled sump, in the dark, the cold, in the muddy flow, he twists sideways and his hips jam into the floor and ceiling of the tunnel. Opening his eyes in alarm, he sees he is still below the surface, glimmers coming through a fog. He uses his hands and levers himself into the air, head clear. He is stuck fast and even through the freezing he feels a burning pain in his side. He explains his predicament and the guide writes on a piece of Perspex with a chinograph that the boy is stuck. There is room to pass it back and the hand of the leader, trying to ease him forwards, persuade him to move, soon latches on to it. 'We'll get you out shortly. Don't worry,' he tells the boy. He stays and chats, knowing how bad the storm is by the water's colour and the rate of its rise. It is also getting warmer. He lies that it would only have been a precaution to get everyone out so quick. The lower levels would have to become totally flooded before any real danger could occur.

The weather hampers the rescuers, but being local they are on their way down into the caves shortly after the party of Scouts is out. An advance group reaches Liam and the guide by swimming through the inundated stream channel. The breathing apparatus and the stretcher, even in its compact, collapsed state, are difficult to manoeuvre. Liam's mouth is under the warm sea by now. He breathes through his nose. A cord had been passed to the one behind him and laconic phrases are dragged back and forth. ALL RIGHT. LIGHT FADING. He has enough air but the level has made it a fish's lifeline rather than an inexhaustible supply.

Liam is mute as the two people in front of him discuss strategy. Time is mentioned more than once, each period seemingly diminished as they think about it. The breathing equipment arrives. The mouthpiece and rubber tube of an emergency aqualung are threaded into the space beyond and Liam is attached to a larger bottle with instructions to try to breathe as if he were going to sleep. The doctor in the team explains that he is going to give him an injection, part painkiller, part muscle relaxant. Frightened people's muscles harden, and they need to be relaxed and compressed, so he can be manipulated out of the tight squeeze.

The greyness has reached the top of the nose clip and Liam keeps blinking the water out of his eyes, but soon has to shut his eyes and let the ocean cover his face. 'We're going to push you back, then twist, then pull you forward.' To no avail. He feels the intermittent touch on his legs behind him. The sounds become strange as his ears are topped by the tide. He can still see the negative shadow of the lights on the rescue team's helmets playing across the steel-coloured wash.

A diver has pushed under the rocks beside him and he feels the padded mitt like a lover's stroke. He begins to think back to the days when his real mother was still alive. She would tell him a story, brush his blond hair from his forehead and tickle him through the blankets. This time it was a story of a boy who had eaten apple pips after being warned not to because a tree would grow inside him. A sapling sprouted and he began to grow a skin of bark, and his hair turned to a mass of twigs, and leaves developed on his fingertips and he began to root in the back garden. He became totally stiff and doubled his height in a fortnight. Birds came to nest in his arms and he felt the movements of beetles and caterpillars all over him. He could still speak, but one day his family found his face turned into one of those knotted bumps that scare little boys out of their wits if they are out after bedtime. 'Yes, of course it's a true story, darling. Now, say good night and I'll put the light out.' She kisses him and he snuggles down. She goes to the door and switches the lights off on the bright-yellow helmets and closes the door. A thin crack remains under the door, on the surface of the water and the surface of the rock where they kissed. The reflections of the men's hand-held lamps ricochet imperfectly back through the passage.

Liam slipped into deep, deep sleep, and into dream. The oxygen ran down and his muscles went slack. He felt himself floating. He opened his eyes to see two marvellous creatures beside him. Vermilion, scarlet, orange, deep cadmium yellow, clothing the two naked men with huge feathers that undulated and glowed like flame. Their hair rose in spikes, branching swirls, a halo. Their eyes were blind, no dark centre. The skin on their faces had tiger stripes of deep crimson over lemon zest. They danced round him and without words invited him to join their fun. He joined in. The dance went on for days.

He woke from his coma and told the doctors about the fire demons who had fed him and played with him in the cave. Post-traumatic delirium. He was lucky to be alive. When his father broke the news that the leader had not survived, they had to tranquillise him with five times the normal dose. Thus began the darkness.

Ixta. Fourteen-year-old Quechua boy. Somewhere in the fortress of the Andes long ago. Small, squat, round-faced, blue-black hair and brows, near-blue-black eyes, gleaming white teeth. Skin the colour of mahogany, or of conkers just as the green sheath splits its spikes apart, almost. Searing vertical sun boiling the air in the saucepan of the valley. Still snow on high peaks. Arid, but jungle beyond. Today limestone cisterns dot the landscape. Bottomless. Indians hurled things into the water from the lip to placate whatever spirit slumbered there. One of the ancestors, one of the offspring of those that crawled from Paccari-tambo, the place of the hole. Human in shape, but blue like the sky, a sidereal fragment plummeted to earth, punching a pockmark into its skin. Lonely ghost, hungry, demanding, unseen, but ever present in Inca thoughts. The craftsmen of the towns nearby worked hard-won gold into amulets and votive figures in the shape of these shards of empyrean night, the yellow metal reflecting the blue from all its finely wrought surfaces. The local potters modelled their stirrup-handled ceramics into scenes of every day, or rather of every night. Explicit depiction of intercourse and fellatio. Portrait heads, slightly shrunken, as vessels for wine and water. Grave goods.

146

Every year at the turning of spring to summer a sacrifice would be made, a human offering, a virgin child unsullied, about to embark upon his own summer, to be stopped for ever, converted to magical matter, particles of solar dust, shimmering, eternal. At the same time circumcision rites would be performed, which the boy selected for the greatest of missions would not have to undergo. He would spend a month apart, learning the mysteries from the priests before being dispatched to their heaven, bearing messages of greeting and renewed faith to the arrayed ranks of gods waiting to welcome him. The boys of the tribe would compete to win the honour of being chosen. There would be contests of strength, of skill and purity. The chief priest would become entranced in an effort to gain an insight from the beyond into the hearts of each of them. There would be a hunt for boar or deer and the one shooting the prey with his arrow would be deemed most worthy. They would have to endure the privation of a week in the mountains tracking the puma, or the discomfort of a descent into the jungle in search of snakeskins. Both animals were sacred to the people of the Altiplano and only proof of contact was needed to show how favoured the boy was in the eyes of the watchers above. To kill one, in panic perhaps, would proclaim the opposite.

Down into the immensity of the selva went Ixta, on a quest after the jungle jaguar, the dangerously invisible, the unknowable, emblem of fearlessness and invincibility, protector of the clan, spotted spectre, with the ability and speed to be in two places at once, undetected. The boy was gone for over a fortnight. The people of the high planes assumed him killed, a poisoned dart in his flank, roasted over a fire while still alive, his head chopped off at the moment of expiry, to be shrunk to the size of an apple. Forest food was plentiful. He journeyed further than any before him, into the territory of the *huasca*-drinkers, in search of signs of the four-limbed beast. He knew in which direction he was travelling because of the sun, reddish glimpses between the trees, but as the canopy thickened, so his senses became clouded, the blue chips of the sky quickly replaced by a jadeite shroud. He could hear the thunder in the early afternoon and the darkness made him pause before going on. It was as if each day contained two days.

He found tracks on the fourth, or was it the eighth? Judging by its paw prints and the span of its stride as it loped ahead at an easy run, the wild cat he was following was huge. Sometimes the tracks would grow unclear, but he recovered them after scouting around in careful circles. It appeared that the stipple-camouflaged creature stopped every time he did or else the distance of the quarry would have grown. As though aware of him, as though leading him on into the impenetrable maze of the upper reaches of the Amazonian rainforest.

When he began to dream in green instead of blue, he decided that it was time to return. He had found a massive anaconda's cast-off skin and felt it sufficient proof of his valour. He put it in his pouch to show on his return. He halted at dusk and made a shelter in the bole of a tree to avoid the crawlers of the forest floor. He was covered in insect bites and felt feverish. As he wavered on the brink of nocturnal oblivion, he heard a growl in the darkness a long way off. He was beginning to drift back into sleep when he heard it a second time. Within a sling-shot rather than an arrow's flight. He stared into the black, the green-black nothing. Then a flash of orange, a flash of red. Bobbing about between the trunks. He got down from his perch, slung his bow over his shoulder, and stepped forward with one hand stretched out in front of him. The humus beneath his bare feet seemed to seethe, crackling like burning twigs, shifting like sand. The red again. He followed.

Perhaps this is a dream hunt, he thought. Perhaps I am dead already. But there was no blue. He trailed the luminous will-o'-the-wisp till dawn. Then he lay down against a buttress root and slept. He was awakened by a hot breeze in his face. As he opened his eyes he saw them reflected in the amber irises of the big cat, purring a hand's breadth from his nose. 'Little Indian from the mountains, why do you pursue me?' The animal's lips curled, its whiskers twitched. The voice in his head continued. 'Your coming here is pointless. You cannot take me back and not even your high priest will believe I spoke to you. You are far from your loved ones, the ones who will not follow, who dare not. I could eat you up, little one, *chiquitito*. I could play with you for hours until you finally bleed to death. But that is the fate of those who come after the end of those that shall forget me, the pale ones that come from across the great water and from the white, white north. If you can stand and face me without trembling, I will make you my own, but if you tremble, the blow of my claws will not scrape your chest alone, but cut into your heart, and you will descend into a hotter, greener inferno than this. If you withstand the blow, the red guardians you followed to find me will lead you back, and your fathers will receive you in wonder and you shall be the Chosen One and you shall open your eyes a second time on my countenance.'

The boy stood as the spotted magnificence withdrew. He closed his eyes a moment to steady himself and as he did so the four sickles sliced into his body. The pain was awful. He blacked out, crumpling into a heap. When he came to he could hardly move. At first he felt as though he'd been exposed on the peak, in a snowfield, and as he stretched the burning slashes across his body flared, and the warmth spread to all of him and he wished he was on the icy wastes above his village, high above his birthplace, high above the high place.

He returned home, waking each night at evenfall and from each overcast storm to see the red glow in the confusion of verticals. He slept during the lighter part of the day, glad to blot out the emerald envelopment. When he stumbled into the settlement, the choice of Messenger to the Gods was clear, for all to see unquestionable.

And so it was that for a month Ixta learned the language and ways of the fanged ones. 'The black cat stalks at night and so becomes night; the mountain puma climbs the crags the colour of sandstone and so becomes rock; the spotted feline, dappled by the fleck of leaf shadow, becomes tree. We cannot see them, my son, unless we face them at death. You have looked into divine fire, into the striped eye of the jungle lord, his hand caressed you and yet he let you go. Perhaps,

149

Ixtahin, we can tell you nothing of his ways, only load you down with our prayers and supplications.'

The philosopher-priests took him to the mountain, to a cave, and there gave him coca leaves to chew. In the iridescent eternity of his dream, he saw a rainbow sky canopying a white wasteland. All across it the leopards, tigers, pythons and anacondas writhed and bled from the mouth, till ocelot markings spotted the sand. He walked on to the plain. Glancing behind, he saw a stream spring from his heels. As the water touched each dying animal it revived and saluted him, bowing with cat head or coiling with snake eyes. He stood still and the wellspring swallowed him, a huge circular pool. The water rose over his head and he found he could breathe just as easily the water swirling about him. He looked up and saw himself, his twin on the cliff, covered in gold, sky-fracture. His mirror image dived into the pool, broke the surface and came crashing through a white splash towards him. They kissed and merged. Then the images stopped. Five hours later he came out of his trance. The pagan cardinals knew they were right to choose this boy. They were amazed at the description of animals and serpents that they knew were not to be found in this world.

On the eve of his death, they brought the boy to the shrine beside the cenote. The walls had murals of leaping jaguars and a giant celestial serpent wound round the sun, its jaws wide to bite it. Their mottled skins were of the same pattern. On each end wall, a stylised fire demon: red man with cat's eyes, a stream of blood flowing from fiery penises, watering the ground from which sprang saplings, snaking upwards like vines at each corner of the room, spreading brilliant leaves across the four quadrants of the sky-ceiling.

Once more Ixta recited the greetings he had learned by heart. Satisfied, the clergy became his attendants. They cooked him special food and gave him drink which they all tasted in turn before him. Thus was he to take some of their essence with him and thereby some of the love of the tribe for their gods. Again the drug-bearing fronds. As he began to get high, they gave him things to delay the onset of trance.

150

They tied his wrists and attached them to one of the roof's two crossbeams. He stood on tiptoe and was kept still while they coated his whole body with a mixture of resin and plant glue. They applied gold leaf to every portion of him, dusting him with powdered rock. The fuzz of his pubic hair glistened like wire, as did the hair under his arms. Before they coated his penis, the chief priest chewed up a small wad of the leaves and pushed it under his foreskin.

Before dawn the villagers all climbed the hill to the sacred pool, some bearing torches to light the way. They were very subdued, only a few whispers were heard. By the time the sun came up, they were circled round the edge of the wide, chalky cauldron. As the first rays shot on to the priest-house they cut Ixta down. At the moment he stepped out into a furnace of sunlight, he opened his eyes, as he had been told he must. He walked to the projecting knoll directly in front of him and stepped on to the millstone. A priest attached the ropes to his ankles. They were golden too, and the rock glittered with the dust. Normally, a heavy collar would have been placed about his neck, but this time it was special. The officiants had consulted for many hours, divining various signs, interpreting their own dreamtime imaginings. They gave Ixta obsidian axes to hold in each hand, decorated with gold and turquoise along their handles. Words were shouted at the crowd, but they remained silent until the sun had risen enough to illuminate almost the whole of the boy's gilded body. Then they began to murmur. The high priest stepped forward and took a knife of volcanic glass from his tunic. He bent down and slit Ixta's penis along its length. The crowd roared, and as the blood dripped on to the stone and the sun lit up the magic markings carved into its surface, the boy tipped himself forward. He flung out his arms and, in the aureole dazzle that reflected from his gilding, it appeared that there were three of him. The priests did not see this as the sun shone in their eyes. Others said that two figures on fire appeared either side of him and held him up. His descent to the water seemed slow, like a very distant movement, that of a landslide which looks slow because of the enormous background it is set against, even though it may take mere seconds to cascade down a two-thousand-foot slope.

He kissed his reflection and the whole surface of the water burst into phantom flames. The boys danced and the fire demons escorted them to heaven.

Memo short for Guillermo. Fourteen. Rent boy. From one of the blight of *favelas*, shanties, ringing Mexico City. Short, slight, hard-set jaw, penetrating, distrustful eyes. Beautiful. A fragile beauty like that of the city, clogged with traffic, choking on its own pollution. How long before some street gang or other shoots or maims him? How long before he catches a fatal dose of venereal disease, or gets HIV? One of *los escombros*, the sweepings of the street, the dross, one of perhaps three million homeless in the largest single concentration of humankind on the surface of the planet. The factories belch sulphurous emissions, the cars fart exhaust fumes, the poison cannot escape as the town lies in the broad basin that once held the lake where an eagle with a snake in its beak landed on a cactus. Once there were a cruel people here, who practised slavery and human sacrifices to barbaric deities. Once a people came with six legs and hair all over them, who replaced the barbaric deities with an omnipotent divinity that promised liberation from servitude, cunningly, in the life to come. Meanwhile the whole nation became slaves. Once, a second invasion brought white merchants who enshrined the god of money and stripped the country of its wealth. Revolution and Independence. The caciques were replaced, the haciendas broken up and the politicos and peasant-stock reformers assumed power and wealth and dominion and the tools of oppression. The debt to the imperialist federation to the north became immense and the struggle to renew was finally abandoned. Boys came from the poor rural hinterland, found wives and bred, and threw their sons on to the street, unable to feed or clothe them.

Everybody called him Bicho. He eventually picked up an amazing command of English, his accent that of Texas. He began with 'suck' and 'fuck' and graduated to obscure Yankee usage, euphemisms, words for the sacrifice to the gods of filth and lucre, the tally of dollars and depravity. When, at the age of eleven, he had been thrown out of the house by his parents, he had walked into the centre of the town and been befriended in the Zócalo by a boy he discovered was called Don Nadie, Mr Nobody. His plainness allowed him to blend, to vanish. It was said that at twelve he still hadn't gone all the way, that he persuaded the punters to pay first and, having aroused them, disappeared into the crowd, walked away through walls. He took Memo to his hide-out a bus ride away, paying the fare for him. The gang assembled. Too late he realised the imminence of something dreadful. His desperation had combined with relative naivety to make him blind.

They stripped him. The seventeen-year-old boss got his dick out and made him suck it. 'Don't just let it sit there. Imagine it's a strawberry ice. Leave it there till I come and swallow. This is what you've got to get used to.' A fifteen-year-old, at a sign from the commander, came up behind the boy and attempted to sodomise him. He took the prick out of his mouth and begged them not to. His hair was yanked backwards and the boss spat in his face. 'Get used to it, I said, shithead, or it'll be worse. We've all had this. You'll get to like it after a while.'

The penetration was excruciating, the thrust forcing him on to the cock in front of him. It exploded and he wanted to howl, to vomit, to bite. A blow to the head as his tiny teeth began to close. The boy pulled out and Memo swallowed because of the pain in his temple. Without the support of the boss's body he started to pull forward. The other boys grabbed his arms. 'Oh, please don't.' The rhythmic bucking became frantic, then stuttered to a close, not before he'd been scratched all over his back and sides.

'Arrgh,' the boy behind yelped, as though in triumph.

Memo fell to the floor and drew his legs up. He wanted to curl into a ball and die. He felt himself bundled on to a table, face up, his legs still drawn up protectively. They spread his arms and pinioned them. 'You better uncoil, little

153

brother.' Two boys with cigarettes, thirteen and ten, approached and put the glowing tips near his eyes, another held his head still. 'Do it, or you won't even see what we're going to do next.' He let them stretch him, open him, legs wide. Muscles remained knotted with tension. They took a bottle of chilli sauce and one of their number splashed it into his hands before wiping it all over his genitals, anointing the end to make sure the liquid went under the skin. At first it was cool, and then the pain became unbearable, as though his penis were being sliced with glass slivers or burnt with cigarillos. He screamed. 'Let it out, *chamaco*, let it out.' He quaked and writhed, the parody of a man during intercourse. The gang laughed and one pointed to the mole on the inside of his left thigh. Almost black, about two centimetres long, several dark hairs sprouting from it. A beetle making its way up towards its nest. *Bicho* means bug.

It must be over now, he thought, but then the lieutenant who had fucked him said, 'Now for the second part, Bichito. We are going to burn you and you are going to keep silent. That's what they want. You can fake the pleasure later. If you make a sound we will fill your mouth with dog shit and you will eat it, then we'll cut your *pito* off and you'll be no use to no one, and you'll bleed slowly to death.'

His eyes opened pleadingly and tears slid down his face. He knew any pleas would go unanswered. He prayed to the Virgin of Guadalupe for help, as his mother had taught him. Nothing. No answer.

The first cigarette was stubbed out just below the intersection of his collarbones. He tried to push backwards through the table. His aching muscles contracted further, and went limp as he felt the pressure stop. His head shook from side to side. The pain was much worse than that in his penis. Five searing marks down to his navel. He had made a few involuntary moans, not at the moment of attack, but rather as the dog-end was taken away. 'Just three more, little insect.' He calculated the spaces in his head. He could see the gap between his bellybutton and his willy. Not enough. Oh, God! Not enough. They'll burn me after all. It felt as though an incision had been made along his chest and belly as the individual pains joined, a martyring chainsaw. He counted the next two, then fainted as he felt someone take hold of him between the legs again. He couldn't see through the tears, the smoke, the shadows. Then he couldn't see.

The relevant agencies say that boys as young as six have been known to be used as prostitutes. Often these are actually for the gratification of the gang members, rather than out on the street. Many are dead by the time they are twenty or end up in the few hostels for drug addicts that there are in the city. Some of the luckier ones are taken over by organised crime to be supplied as catamites to ridiculously wealthy businessmen or criminals in Coyoacán or Cuernavaca. They are well clothed, well fed, screened for disease on a regular basis, given a place to live, an almost palatial place to live, a place to rest between appointments. Or taken into one of the brothels visited by deputies and foreign diplomats. For the rest the shared needles add to the problem of infection. Those who still exhibit the mismatch of childhood and cynical old age play on the dumps and splash through fountains used as urinals, a moment's release from the rounds of sleeping the mornings away and walking the Alameda or that special stretch of Insurgentes Sur at night.

A series of bizarre murders. The press reported that the bodies of three boys had been found at the top of the Pyramid of the Sun at Teotihuacán with their hearts removed; one on each full moon over the past three months. They did not report the profession of the victims. Indeed, it had taken quite a while to identify the corpses as the urchins spread throughout the inner city and the members of the gangs were very secretive, and getting one boy to come forward and identify another was very difficult. The organisers of organised crime did not wish for too public an investigation, and anyway, what was the loss of one or two fifteen- or sixteen-year-olds who'd probably not have made it beyond twenty?

As soon as the superhuman powers of deduction of the corrupt police had been put into working order and a pattern worked out from the evidence, guards were placed at the edge of the compound where once warriors had become gods. On the night of the next full moon a fourth killing took place. Again the heart was taken, blood flowing down the steep steps from the cavity in the chest of the naked boy. There had been no sexual assault, according to the pathologist, though a body so used to such abuse displays fairly inconclusive signs. At least no trace of semen was found and no fresh bruises or contusions on the buttocks or upper legs. Rope had been tied around the wrists and the arms held behind his back. The ankles showed no such marks. It was assumed that the clothes were partially removed before the stabbing and that a knee on either side of the young man's legs, possibly with his trousers half off, would have been sufficient to hold the body still before the *coup de grâce* was administered. The chief wondered if his men were implicated in that the posting of surveillance officers had been in vain.

The normal dress for these boys is a baggy white shirt, a neckerchief to identify the particular gang, loose-fitting jeans. They cut the right-hand pocket lining and tie a sheath knife or a stiletto to their legs, so that while they stand languidly underneath the jacarandas and planes of the parks, hands in pockets, waiting for customers, they can feel secure in the knowledge that some punter with outlandish tastes can be warned off with the quick draw of a blade. The investigating team wondered, therefore, whether the victims had been coaxed to take the one-hour trip north at gunpoint. Unless there were more than one attacker involved?

The fifth full moon. Lookouts with night-sighted rifles were positioned and a number of sub-machine-gun-toting *huaruras* were stationed at the base of the pyramid. At 8.00 a.m. a badly mutilated corpse was found on an altar at Xochicalco, to the south. It appeared that the victim had struggled, even perhaps escaped, before being brought back to the stone. There was a splash of blood a considerable distance from his final resting place. His jaw was broken, two teeth dislodged and a large amount of blood had collected in his mouth. His eyes were open and he had defecated, terrified. His leg was badly gashed and a tendon cut. A slashing stroke snaked across his lower abdomen and down towards his groin but stopped as if prevented from continuing by a

156

sturdy belt. A Nike trainer was found in the tangled undergrowth near the splash of blood, a strip of torn denim covered in blood on the steps. No other clothes. Heart gone. Some tissue was found under his fingernails and the blood group identified as other than his own. The police felt they were getting nearer.

The sixth moon approached. A box arrived at HQ with a knife in it, caked with blood. The blood of the last victim. A note came with the box: *This time it will not be Teotihuacán or Xochicalco*. It was at the Templo Mayor just off the city's main square, next to the cathedral and the parliament building. It was an outrage that such a thing could happen in the very centre of the town, so near the seats of government and ecclesiastical power. The authorities pointed out that the boy, who this time was only twelve or so, had been killed elsewhere, the blood already congealed, before he was laid at the food of the truncated pyramid, beside a row of mummy-like idols. To allay a growing fear among the powerful that their sons could be next, the shameful employ of the children involved was reported for the first time. Boys now waited in pairs, not next to each other, but in clear view so they could see what was happening. If a client arrived, they'd exchange signals that it was OK and then the one left alone would slink off to his lair or find another partner; after all, the Alameda wasn't that large and was fairly well lit. The Rococo excrescence of Bellas Artes stood out at one end and two churches flanked it, and the shell of the Prado Hotel devastated by the earthquake. The annexe of the National Bank was still being constructed opposite and the digital display of the Torre Latin-Americana flashed time and temperature down at the vigilant. Patrolmen walked the perimeter, but refused to go into the park.

Next full moon Bicho and Don Nadie went to the Alameda after smoking a couple of joints. They had a meal in the VIP's overlooking the trees and fountains. Enchiladas, frijoles. *Capirotada*. Coca-Cola, *hecho en México*. They went and sat in the centre, looking at the jets that had been switched off, the leaves tumbling round the circlet like horses at the Hippodrome. Bicho had brought a tiny bottle of *char-*

anda. They downed a couple of swigs each and then took up position. Don Nadie picked up almost immediately: a corpulent, balding letch. Bicho thought that because it was early, he didn't need to find a protecting colleague. He fingered the head of the knife pressed into his hip like someone else's erection. A man approached him from behind the tree he was leaning against. He was startled. The man spoke English, not gringo – European, or pseudo-European. There was something about the precision and softness of the words that seemed to betray some act, some falsehood. 'How much for the works, son?'

'Twenty-five dollars, sir.'

'And in pesos?'

'I'm not interested. You obviously have the dollars.'

'Where can we go?'

'I will hire a room down towards the Academia, sir. It's walking distance.'

'Will you take a ride with me?'

The *charanda* and the *mota* said yes. 'Provided the price is up a bit.'

'Fifty?'

'Sure.'

The man took out a tiny walkie-talkie. In perfect Spanish, he said, 'Jorge, pick me up in front of Bellas Artes in two minutes.' He put the device back in his suit jacket. Then in English, 'I want to take you to a party on the outskirts of town. Beyond Satélite. Is that OK?'

'Yes, sir. Can I have the money first?'

'Only if you let me have that dagger.'

'What dagger?' (Why didn't he say knife or weapon? As a joke?)

'Come on, little boy. I saw you playing with it a moment ago.'

'It's difficult to get out.'

'So there is a blade?'

'Wait a minute.'

Bicho reached into his pocket to release the poppered band holding the knife in place. He had been holding his palm out for the money. His other hand was still in the other pocket. The man grabbed his right wrist, firmly but not hurtfully, and put the other gently between the boy's legs, closing the gap between them, to hide the gesture. 'Want these little meatballs crushed to make gravy?'

No reply. A slight shake of the head.

The man stroked his hand up and undid the clasp of the boy's belt, rather like a Scout buckle, two interlocking plates for quick release. Then the button, then the zip. A practised hand. He let go of the wrist and with both hands eased the trousers open and down, but not far enough to make Bicho take his hand out of his pocket, exposing the top of the knife, the boy's fingers still on it. The man put one hand in between the boy's legs, brushing his balls, but without any apparent interest. He found the leather strap and snapped open the popper. The other took the boy's fingers from the hilt and held on to them as the knife, the sheath and the strap were removed. The boy watched the performance and felt himself becoming hard. There was something comforting in the lack of dithering, of fumbling and fiddling. This man knew what he wanted.

The man tucked the tails of the boy's shirt into each trouser leg, after releasing the hold on his right hand. He did the button up, the buckle, the zipper, without further contact with the boy's privates, leaving Bicho disappointed. He looked at the knife, which had been pushed under the waistband of the man's dark trousers. He transferred it to the inside pocket of his jacket, touched the boy's face and said, 'Sorry. Just a precaution. We don't want you getting the wrong ideas about stealing any more than the price you deserve.' He then took out a wallet and handed over two fifty-dollar bills. 'No hard feelings, eh?'

'No, sir.' The face was like that of one of the Zaga models on the metro. Usually the punters were horrible. This would be almost a pleasure.

When they reached the entrance of the museum, a black Cadillac was waiting. The chauffeur was obviously Mexican, as was the registration plate. There were two other men in the back. One was silent, the other had that same, strangely synthetic accent. There was one of those fold-down seats and Bicho went to sit on it. 'No. Sit between these gentlemen.' They drove off. He was offered a drink from the cocktail cabinet. He chose whisky. There was a television. They watched a *telenovela*. They told him he was beautiful but he was not touched.

By the time they reached Teotihuacán, he was quite drunk. His English got mixed with very low Spanish. The driver pretended not to hear, the men pretended not to understand. The car came to a halt by the restaurant called La Gruta, and they heard the caged parakeets and other exotics. They walked across the gravel and into the compound through a hole in the chain-link fence. They were walking in near darkness. Bicho tripped and laughed. 'Where's this party, then?' His arms were pulled back and handcuffs clipped on tightly. He found it difficult not to laugh some more. They want to play games, he thought. They half marched him, half carried him the rest of the way. He saw that the mountain in front of him was closer than he thought. Its perspective changed too quickly. It had straight stepped sides. He realised. My God, it's the fucking pyramid! 'Oh no, please not here, sir. Please.'

He began to struggle and was punched in the stomach. He was dragged up the steps. There is one point where they become extremely steep. 'You'll have to climb sideways here. If you try to get away you'll fall. You won't die quickly. Then we'll flay you, piece by piece, starting with your balls, and rub chilli into every one of your wounds.' Remembering the initiation ceremony of three years ago, he stood quietly. The silent one went ahead, then reached down, gripped his hair and pulled him up behind him. He remembered the seam of cigarette burns down his belly. They had healed and become a dotted line of only slightly darker flesh, like the perforation on a stamp.

They reached the summit. The man looked at his watch. 'Just in time. Moonrise in four minutes. Look down there. There's a guard.' The other English speaker drew a gun and shot into the dark. There was a groan and a thud. No detonation, no bright flash. Only a sound like a bicycle tyre

160

being punctured. 'Don't worry, sunshine, he's not dead, just drugged. There'll only be one killing tonight.'

'Me?'

A glow showed in the sky between two peaks. The man took out Bicho's knife and cut the shirt from him so as not to get it entangled around the handcuffs. He collapsed on to his knees. 'Please don't. Please.' The three twisted him around and took off his trainers, his white socks, his jeans, his briefs.

They pushed him backwards on to the rough stones. The altar and sanctuary had been removed by the Conquistadores. The man saw the line of burn marks down the boy's chest. His two accomplices pressed down the boy's shoulders and knees. His hips and stomach bulged skywards because of his trapped wrists. The man took Bicho's knife and tickled the point down the row of dots. 'Cut here,' he said. Tears and mumbled supplications. The knife flicked at his genitals. 'Not much use any more, is it?'

'Don't. Please.'

'Do, do. You had your hundred dollars. Now I want what I paid for. It won't hurt. It'll be nice and quick. Lie quiet. Say your prayers.'

Not for three years had he begged anything from Mary or Jesus or God the Father. He screwed up his eyes and implored the Trinity for succour, deliverance, forgiveness, absolution.

'Pray to Coatlicue, goddess of death, she whose garment is made of snakes. Or to Coyolxauhqui, goddess of the moon. She is coming to take you away, ha ha!' He put the blade on the mark made between the boy's collarbones, kneeling beside the quaking form, hands in a position to force the knife down into the flesh that hid his heart, ready to sever the sternum and extract the still-palpitating organ, the pump that should sustain life.

The moon came up as the fire demons soared up the slopes to dance for him. He stopped crying. His heart continued to pound. He drew quick breaths and tried to blot out the moonlight in his mind. He knew that when its full face emerged his life would be ripped from his chest. He saw the

161

flaming guardians. They were just his imagination running away with him, he thought. He was looking up, the others looking down or sideways at the moon.

Flames flicker shadows and brightness across his body and he feels their warmth. The assailant at his head has seen the floating apparition in front of him. 'Look,' he says in Spanish. The moon frees herself from the hills. The man presses down on the knife, but looks at the strange flying figure positioned at the boy's head. *¡Diós mio! ¡Madre Santa! ¡Qué chingado desmadre!'*

A bolt of incandescence surges from the eyes of one of the demons. It hits the dagger and shoots up the man's arm and all over him. His suit and hair catch fire. Smoke streams from his ears and mouth, his eyes shrivel. A charred husk collapses on the sacrificial victim and crumbles. It is hot but blows away like chaff immediately.

The other two stand and turn to face the scarecrow spirits. Blue moon colour spills from their eyes, a torrent of tears which showers the child-catchers. Clothes melt and the remains of the charcoal debris scatter in the breeze. Each fantastic phantom has a priapic erection. They open their arms and embrace the blue-skinned men. They kiss each of them. The panic prong stabs burning into their bellies, their vitals. Two tongues of fire probe two throats of ice. Azure phosphorescence on their skin coalesces into flames. Their heads tip back and their buttocks contract. Their colour shifts through purple violet rose red russet copper. They come apart and, as the two coupling pairs separate, they dance round the boy and jets of supernatural semen spurt across him. It feels like the cigarette again. The handcuffs come undone and he stretches as the four rise into the air and appear to merge. The fireball drifts over the avenue to the Pyramid of the Moon, where it launches itself towards the rising orb at the speed of a comet. Soon it is out of sight.

He puts on his trousers and wipes himself on the remnants of his shirt. The old burn marks have gone. He picks up the knife. The leather and the wood have gone. Only the blade, the crosspiece, the tongue and the knob that adorned the haft remain.

*

The man was covered in recent scars, scabs, weeping sores, contusions, livid bruises, abrasions, blisters, scratches, glistening patches where plasmolysis had taken place, caked blood, burns, needle marks and odd clusters of blemishes like bites made by a small rodent's jaws. He was strapped to the chair by his wrists and ankles and a belt around his chest. The bits of skin unaffected by whatever had happened to him were clean and the white boxer shorts exaggerated the vile condition of the rest of him. His genitalia hurt where the light cotton touched. The fingers without nails throbbed as he delicately placed them on the arms of his throne. The splint and bandage on his broken ankle reminded him of the metal boot they had used to force wedges into till the bone gave. His left eye was reduced to a slit. The missing tooth had left a tender spot. He could taste the blood, smell the blood. He trembled from time to time, even though the soldiers were sweating and his interrogator had rolled up his sleeves. He was sure that San Lorenzo's fire still ran through his body. He felt the crisscross of the grid on his back, on his front, although he had been taken off the apparatus hours, days ago, and the current disconnected.

'Now we have cleaned you up a little, perhaps we can talk more civilly and perhaps you won't wet yourself again. You know how much that hurts. You haven't said anything useful for a long time. We haven't tampered with your tongue.' Must be the only bit. 'We only need a few tiny snippets of information.' I told you I didn't know. 'You know there are worse things. We can have you blinded, gelded. We can cut the whole lot off. Feed it to you. Tie you up till your kidneys rupture. We can peel the skin off your back, roll you in salt or chilli. Make a meal of it.' Very funny, fuckface. 'We can systematically break every bone in your body. We have the time. We can infect you with parasites and wait till they hatch.' Go on, then. 'We admit astonishment at your resistance to the drugs. When we had you sodomised; when we played back your screams; when we nearly drowned you . . .' Try again, Batman, you might succeed this time. There is nothing you can do to me, now. 'We admitted we couldn't easily get hold of your family and that the threat to have them shot in the States would be difficult to prove.' Why don't you believe me? I don't know the answer. 'We almost believe you do not know.' He paused before going on, 'We are planning to force you to question another one of our guests. We thought we'd find a nice young woman and you could experiment probing the cattle goad into her most intimate areas.' My hands free? You must be losing your grip. 'But then by a stroke of incredible luck we think we have found the key.' There's no pissing lock, stupid!

He looked at his reflection in the mirror and at the interviewer who stood behind the chair, occasionally stroking his shoulder. The contact was vile because of its apparent tenderness. Yet this was the hand that had pushed the heated rod up his penis. This was the hand that had punched him in the testicles until he had fainted. This was the hand that had pushed the pins under his toenails, held the blowtorch, wound up the generator. 'All you have to do – ' again that gruesome caress – 'is tell us about the fire demons. Who are they, who controls them? Is their energy electric, nuclear, other? You stay silent. Then let us see what is behind the mirror.'

He had been tortured in this room before, watching what had happened to him as if it were a play, the soldiers doing the damage, their inexpert hands less predictable, while the voice of the bastard who now stood behind him came from a loudspeaker above him. He had suspected a hidden camera. Now the idea of a two-way mirror seemed all too obvious. The lights dimmed and the ones behind the silver came up to reveal an almost identical room. They brought in a boy. He had a hood over his face but he seemed familiar. The man felt his stomach churn. It wasn't possible.

Alexei. Fourteen. American. An internal flight had been hijacked. Cuban authorities had passed their prize to the Chileans. They passed him to the Venezuelans and so on. He had not heard from his father for six months, but messages were coming out of Washington that pointed to the fact that his top-secret research had landed him in trouble with some South American authority. The family had originally thought he was in Zambia.

The boy had been well looked after, even if he'd been kept separated from human contact and blindfolded for much of the journey. At first he had been glad to be alive and then thought the ship they put him on was headed for home, and that the security had to do with politics, quarantine or some odd investigation into the terrorists which demanded that each passenger be kept alone for their own safety. He spoke next to no Spanish, so found it impossible to glean any information from those who fed him. Even in the foreign port, he had assumed some cleverly calculated route home. The guard had let him look out of the Land-Rover between the dock and the airport. He told him in English to say nothing about it. He'd been shown a glimpse of the jungle as they flew south. He began to wonder, the construction of reasonable explanations in his head collapsing in a heap.

'Take your clothes off.'

'What for?'

A knee to the groin and a blow to the back of the head that sent him sprawling. He reached up to take the hood off. The guard stamped on his other hand. He screamed.

'Now listen, Alex, if you don't cooperate with us, it'll be far worse for you. We are going to ask you a few simple questions about your father's work. That's all. Now get up, there's a good boy, and take off your clothes. Perhaps you'd like a hand.'

'No, thank you. I can do it myself.' The microphone distorted his voice but the speech patterns and the name confirmed the prisoner's worst fears. No one called him Alex, but it was him nonetheless.

He sat up, undid his trainers, removed them and then his socks, his jeans and Calvin Klein underpants. He did this on the floor. He felt vulnerable and didn't want to stand.

'Now stand up.' He stood and pulled the T-shirt down over his cock. 'Take that off as well. Actually, I suppose you'll have a problem with that thing on your head. Wait.'

The other guard went over to the boy and tore the T-shirt off. It was reluctant to snap at the neck, eventually tearing

165

below the collar. The shreds came off, leaving the white elasticated ring like a torque below the black cloth of the hood. His head felt hot. He kept his hands over his privates.

'Sit.' He was pushed back into the seat. To balance, he put out his arms. He kicked out as he landed on the chair. A backhander across the face and a boot to the shin. The soldier's watch split the boy's lip. They tied him up, hands behind him and over the back of the chair, ankles to chair legs, and then they took off the hood. A dog collar and a smudge on his lips.

'As you can see, señor, we have your son. Pretty soon his body will look like yours, but watch this first.' One of the guards came and stroked the boy's hair. 'Pretty boy,' he said. He ran his hands across the boy's chest and further on down.

'Leave me alone. Leave me alone, for God's sake.'

'Shut up, pretty boy, or I'll rip this bit off.' He took it between his thumb and forefinger, deliberately standing so the action was clear through the aquarium glass. 'Juicy, juicy little thing. *¡Voy a chuparla, joto jodido!*' He came round in front of the boy and buried his head between his legs.

'Oh, no! Don't, don't, don't.'

He came quickly. The guard stood and spat the semen back in his face. His erection subsided and a dribble of sperm trickled on to the green leather. Tears poured. 'That was disgusting. Whatever for?'

'You enjoyed it really, didn't you? Your dad would have enjoyed watching that.'

'I want to be sick.'

'Do not be sick, little one. Not until you have had some of mine in your mouth.'

Behind the looking glass the empurpled victim reacted. 'All right, all right. Stop, for Christ's sake!' I am playing for time. I can tell them nothing. I hardly know what they are talking about! It's a story. One of Alexei's stories, goddamn it.

The guard had unzipped and was pushing himself towards the boy's face. The interrogator spoke into a microphone. '*¡Párate, mano! Bastante.*' Reluctantly, he put his prick away, glaring into the mirror.

166

'Perhaps the boy would like to see you, to know you saw him.' Inhuman monster.

'No. Let him go and I will tell you all I know.'

'You must think me stupid, señor. We had to go to a stupendous amount of trouble to obtain this prize. And if you cooperate we will release you both.'

'How do I know you won't have us shot? We know about your operation here. We will have the scars to prove it. No. You must let him go.'

'If I say I have let him go, you will only have my word. You have nothing to bargain with. Our trigger-happy friend there will be so happy if I tell him our guest is staying on after all. We could always start sending bits of both of you back to your wife and daughter. Do you think she'd recognise your pricks wrapped in tissue paper? We could always chop the guards' off and send them instead.' I wish you would. 'But surely you don't want to see your son's amputated? No grandchildren! And you don't want him made gay either, do you? He's still young enough to be conditioned. Shame. I'm sure he'd make as good a father as you. But the US is rather full of homosexuals, isn't it? Any training would be difficult to undo.'

'I won't tell you unless you let the boy go.'

'No deal. I will leave you to think about it.' He left the room with his two assistants.

The man watched and screamed for help, as he watched the two guards next door resume their game, nearly ready for climax. One went behind the boy and put his hands round his throat and began to throttle him. He let go and said, 'You take his prick in your mouth and you swallow him or else we kill you.'

Alexei swallowed the first mouthful, but the second he kept in his mouth and spat it out as soon as the two had left. He sat sobbing, his shoulders heaving up and down. 'Why? What have I done?'

Five minutes later the lighting changed and the father became aware that his son could see him. The boy tried to close his legs but it was too difficult. He hung his head. 'Did you see that?' he whispered.

'Yes. Don't worry, it could have been worse. Look at me.'

'Oh, Dad, Dad, what have they done? I'm sorry. They'll make you tell them whatever it is they want to know, now.'

Long pause. Just looking at each other. Managing a smile.

'Will they kill us?'

'I don't know.'

'Did they make you . . . will they make me do it again?'

'I don't know. But believe me, there are worse things.'

'What do they want, anyway?'

'They will be listening to this. They want to know about the fire demons.'

'Aw, Dad, don't be stupid. That's only a story. They don't exist. It's a story.'

'Shhhhh!'

That evening they were put in a cell together, still tied, light left on. They talked. They shared knowledge that seemed so scarce. There was a legend recorded by a Jesuit somewhere in the Andes. Unreliable source. There was a report in a Harvard journal about the delusions of some kid in England who nearly drowned in a cave. Inexplicable cheating of fate. There was a boy in Mexico who had become rich by selling a chunk of gold left behind after an attempted abduction. He was a catamite and a known drug-taker. There was no trace of the serial killer who should have taken him as victim. The time Alexei fell into a coma when he was knocked down by a car. In the absent time, a man who glowed red had led him out of a circular labyrinth on a hill, and told him he'd return in time of trouble. The doctor ascribed the experience as an easily interpreted Jungian dream. Alexei replied that it wasn't a dream. Burns on the palm of his hand seemed to prove that. Friction? Developed a month after the accident? They knew they were being listened to. They didn't care.

In the morning they were thanked for the informative discussion they'd had, and then they were taken back to the mirror-divided rooms. Alexei had his jeans back, his father had been offered a pair but knew they'd be too painful. Alexei was secretly worried that if the fire demons existed, they'd not come, or that they'd save him alone. No adults were involved in the stories and in the Inca myth the boy

168

died, even if his descent was accompanied by two flaming angels.

'Let's make a start, shall we? We have learned already about the old wives' sayings, but what about your work for the government, Mr Zinoviev? Tell us for the sake of your son. Or what seemed like depravity yesterday will be made to seem like a picnic today.'

The crocodile clips, the current and then, when he shat himself, enforced coprophagia. His father said he'd tell them all about his work. He spent the afternoon explaining his role in computing espionage, the planting of viruses or the masking of an override code within the defence systems of unfriendly powers; the hacking into police files in Latin America to detect just who had connection with the drug barons. They kept them awake a further forty-eight hours, flogged the boy a couple of times, and dowsed him alternately with scorching hot and freezing water. Despite the apparent cooperation.

The order of execution must have come in from elsewhere. The interrogator was furious. He was enjoying working on one so young. At least the directive allowed for a slow, painful death for each. He was wondering exactly what method he'd use. He decided on fire. Fit punishment.

In a courtyard of the mountain prison two bonfires were built around the wooden posts used for shootings or dog attacks. There was a heap of faggots to build up around the unfortunates. He'd feed the rest of the inmates roast meat tonight and then tell them what it was they were eating.

They were chained facing each other. Zinoviev implored the man he felt certain must have some shred of decency in him to dispatch his son quickly and then toy with him at his pleasure. 'I will not disappoint you.'

'You certainly won't. Delay the torching of the man until the boy has been well and truly roasted.'

The torch was put to the wood. Alexei felt the heat. His eyes blurred with smoke. He coughed. He saw the approach of the time for dreams again. 'I love you,' he shouted across at his father. 'I damn you,' he shouted to those that looked on. 'I call on the fire demons to destroy this place.'

169

The flames crackled behind him. He felt the bonds give. He felt the hands push the stake away as though it were a cocktail stick. He saw the look of incredulity on all the faces. He stepped out of the burning. He was covered in flames but not consumed; he was untouched. He turned to his benefactor and with a gesture made him withdraw a little. The sprite danced into the air. Machine-gun fire blasted the boy's body. The bullets bounced off the walls behind him. He spun round, pirouetting. A spiral of red whirled out from his heel. Like a ripple, it covered the courtyard and broadened to turn the sandy floor to a lake of molten glass. The guards dropped into it immediately, soundlessly. The torture chief stood on the surface, shouting, 'This is untrue! This is not real! This cannot happen!' Strings of fire surrounded him, sent out from Alexei's hands, eyes, mouth, ears and navel. They formed themselves into the shape of a double egg whisk, an hourglass made from wire. The man inside was unable to touch the bars as they burned so. The cage spun and inverted. The man became wedged in the inverted cone and passed through the vortex into the other chamber. The whole thing sank into the lava. The boy's father stood on an island above the boiling rock. Alexei walked across and touched the pole. The wood stack crumbled and vanished into the patch of mud. The chains evaporated and the stake tumbled into oblivion. Father and son embraced. At the speed of fire, they shot into the sky, arced north and arrived in a field outside the new development where they lived. The boy's wrapping of light fluttered to the ground like the paper covering a parcel undone. He pointed at the grass and two bundles of clothes appeared. They dressed and walked home.

The walls here are a sort of green, as though viewed through a mist, a proto-Impressionist colour. Beyond the windows the expanse of the grounds appears to have been brushed in by Monet. The building we are in is more Barbican than Barbizon. The shade is there to calm us and the guards to prevent us from harming others or ourselves. On rare

170

occasions, when we are very good, we are allowed out into the honeysuckled park. The staff are nice and polite to me, but perhaps that is because their colour scheme has worked wonders and I don't attempt 'anything silly'. They call me 'Spitfire' behind my back, as though my delusional universe were merely that of a pilot *manqué*. They have nicknames for all of us. Some of my fellows have remarked that sometimes at night when I'm awake, I make the paintwork glow a different hue. But one doesn't want to give those old crazies credence. It would go to their heads. They also say that I disappear between the dusk and dawn, as if I were one of their extraterrestrial vampires, the original ones that abducted them, the ones who took their sanity before their abandonment, before they were marooned.

We have all sorts here. There is the man who is convinced that he is an Earth-Eater from Papua New Guinea. He has to be kept away from the flowerbeds. There is the guy who swears he is a merman who has lost his tail, and therefore his ability to swim. He is terrified of the pool. There is the ballerina, ancient now, convinced that she is starring in *Les Sylphides*. She flits around in a comic dance, face as serious as can be, waiting for the approbation of the inmates and the staff. Then there's me.

On the top of my beside cabinet there sits my little collection. Objects from home are considered a good focus for most of us. I add to my trophies sometimes, but the overworked, underpaid, bored care assistants tend not to notice new acquisitions, and if they do, they never tie them in with the *lack* of visitors. 'You must have had a visit, Mr Lawrence,' they simper. I am burning to tell them where I got each one, but they disbelieve everyone else so why not me? There is a sheath for a knife, a pair of handcuffs, a fragment of a carving with wavy lines on it, a small gourd full of lime concretions, a dart, a lump of oolitic limestone, a pinned insect and a golden figurine everyone assumes is gilded lead.

The expert in these things gets me to retell my stories over and over and then asks me if I am able to distinguish the real from the imagined. I reply that I imagined him to be less definitive about definitions. He smiles wryly, as if to say,

'You don't fool me.' I smile back. *Oh, but I do.* He said I should write them down and have them published. 'I leave that to you, professor,' I said.

Fit

α

MAMMALIAN URINE IS the greatest natural source of the auxin indole-acetic acid, the growth hormone without which plants cannot develop. If a healthy specimen is deprived of light it will etiolate, it will become white through lack of chlorophyll, and photosynthesis will be halted, eventually resulting in death. Vegetable matter exhibits positive phototropism in stems and negative phototropism in roots. The meristematic region of most flora is located in the tips of the shoots, but in grasses this growing tissue is at the base, thereby allowing them to be cropped by grazing animals without suffering complete destruction. Trace elements are essential for normal maturation, too. Zinc, magnesium, iron and potassium, for example, are all essential to proper growth. Without them the plant dies.

β

The building is of dark-grey brick. Nonetheless the authorities opt to disguise its blatant function further by girding it about with growing things. The avenue on which it is positioned is lined with horse-chestnut trees which, in the right seasons, are either decked with a profusion of bridal white, or become heavy with spiked fruit, balls of protection, which rain down and split to expose a shiny virgin seed within, old copper visible through the cracking gape. The small plot where the cottage stands is ringed by iron rails, a bailey,

within which jacaranda, laurel, bougainvillaea, ivy and rho-
dodendron sprout. Or so they should, though the patch is
often neglected, weeded. The city's wish is for the sanctuary
to be swallowed up by impenetrable wilderness, its purpose
denied to all but the inquisitive and persistent.

χ

The smell is dank, dreadful, deceitful, chthonic in the
extreme, suggesting the foul underworld, Persephone's
prison, a Hades of perpetual benightedness. Here, the Rivers
of the Dark debouch or have their source. It is unclear
which, for they are forever circulating through the ground,
emerging, vanishing, re-emerging, intermittent. The odour is
of broken sleep, agrypnotic, the waft of stagnation. The
scent of the Damned billows about the vault. Fear can make
the atmosphere bristle. The carnelian tiles of the floor are
spattered by a libation of excess and egress. An undercroft
ringed by a fosse. No parvis, no narthex, no galilee. No
transepts, no chancel, only aisles lined with votary altars.
The plan could be that of a baptistery or a crypt. To one side
thrones where bishops dangle. Sedilia, cathedrae. Lancets do
not disrupt the skin's curtaining. No rood or iconostasis,
no fencing-off of clergy from congregation. No pews, no
hassocks, but kneeling in adoration of the host an integral
part of the ceremony.

δ

White walls of china against which the initiate stand. Hard
glassy surfaces amplify light but not reflection, denying
shadow because of precious shine. The compartments are
like cells in a hive, the imago horizontal in its case, seemingly
dormant, surprisingly awake, ready to burst from its confines. Or are these compartmental partitions the replacement
for choir stalls, where the chorus dallies between perform-
ances? The chorister does not get to chant, lest his tongue

174

be torn out to prevent him squealing. He must keep quiet whatever happens. That is the rule of thumb.

ε

There are more than one type of celebrant here. They divide nicely, but establishing an order is impossible, by virtue of the fact that this is a Trappist sect. No one must speak, mutual transactions must take place mutely tactical. Eye-to-eye contact is minimised, the propitiatory acts normally hurried to conclusion. To sacrifice and to leave, to exit reduced. Many's the married man that marches into the precinct of promiscuity, feigning ignorance or indifference; desperate and determined. And the conjugal bliss of home is not negated, neglected or denied, for this is necessity and the wives never know; till they swell with buboes and skin-burst with scabs. Stigmata for the unfaithful. But within this temple no love is lost, none spilled. Remorse is not for lack of care but for degree of carelessness. The silence of the makeshift sacristy pleases them, replaces a meagre com-munion with an empurpled community, poorly felt, though present nonetheless, partially projected. The lack of speech democratises. Joiner, teacher, prelate, professional, all are one. Masked by lack of mask.

φ

The ugly. This is their fountain, their font, their watering hole; a place where their disfiguration, be it through the ravages of disease or time or birth, is left without, is mean-ingless, becomes currency of a different coin, a different compass. The club-footed can swim, can show off their prowess and strength without exposing their Oedipal appendage. They are free to imagine, as are all comers. That this is somewhere else and something else is part of their imaginative landscape. Here, where all are made up, trans-figured and transubstantiated, to become whole and whole-

175

some, here can be paradise. For the purposes of transaction they are headless, identity-free, limbless, and their hearts are in their hands. The prospector does not look up, he forever holds his eye to the ground. That England should be sprinkled with suites the likes of these!

γ

The adolescent, without his own space to fulfil himself, looks so self-sufficient, self-fecundating, self-fructifying, Ouroboric, self-centred and self-satisfied. Elsewhere he is untouchable, untouched; here touching, breached, persuaded, plucked and harvested. Can the plain depravity appeal? When the time for debauch is upon him, the descent must be gutter-bound, autochthonous but deranging, reordering sense and senses. These are the dangerous ones, the messengers from the world of the pure, the differential, the reverent. Does Gregory's remark hold true of this slave market? Angels with dirty faces, impure thoughts, stains, crumpled wings, strapped to their backs the helicopteral blades of their scapulars. Skin-tight youths clad in unadorned rags, proclaiming the failure of this cohort of decadents to ruffle their composure, to do anything other than temporarily enthral and relieve the burden of libido.

η

Outside the plants cloak the structure, blur it or blot it out, remake a skyline already too low, engulf it in virescent profusion, most often indeciduous, dense and composed, clogging the railinged quadrilateral. Natural chaos clamours for recognition, its victory imminent, tapping at minimal panes, rustling the metal vanes of glossed leaves in mild windless August. There is hidden symbolism in the municipal mind: that laurel denotes triumph and eternity; acacia, the immortality of the soul. The thorns divide: the bush the minor sins conveys, the growing briars proclaim the greater.

176

Along the avenue itself paired planes should stand, for they are for charity, firmness of character and moral superiority. The grass spreads around this unwelcome altar like the sea around an island rock, flat and spotted with a froth of daisy, fascicles of dandelion, clover and plaintain spike. Cows come graze, cluttering the expanse that widens to the river. The purple eye of the *Convolvulus althaeoides* opens with the dawn and closes nastically with the dusk. It is all but scentless. The honeysuckle thickens the air with the pitch of its song. Its starry explosions dot its bush. *Lonicera caprifoliaceæ.*

ι

Our specific transgressor ought to be a nameless one. He could bear the infinitive title Phaskein, but it is of no matter. He wears a pair of T14 2080/3409 WHITE (S); a pair of 940103 T2–0; a pair of W30L30 501 0185; an M 60566 05 04 and a jacket without a serial number. It would be most suited if it were a black leather bomber, with a line of fringing, maybe. As though in his carriage of all these numbers he is offered protection. He crosses the step into the grave basilica; as if this obscure description will prevent anyone else resuscitating his image; as if he himself knows these codes and therefore these peculiar practices.

φ

His eyes will be grey; with a paleness as intense and penetrative as a comet's tail, all bright and polar. His eyes will be open wide, ready to tilt down and look away, to avoid the eyes that seek his body but not his face. He shall be fascinated by the surroundings which have become other than what they were, something different from their design, their daylight usage. The whites of the eyes are large in the innocent and the frightened; he shall be the innocent and the frightened. He scans the crossing and takes in the structures

177

and the structuring, the evident hierarchy but not the operation of that reordering. His gaze dissects the plan of the inner sanctum, and he denies his own trespass.

κ

This is a place where blood has been spilled, a crime for which they invented motive and suspect, but found insufficient proof, managed no confession. Here was the ritualistic slaying done, the regicide rehearsed. Here, the vagrant had the terrible indignity inflicted and self-accommodated violation executed. Where was Gaveston on the night of the killing, the investigator desired to know? Too late and to no avail. The executioner had fetched from an alcove a broom and forced the handle into the waiting asterisk, as the witch-hunted hags of bygone ages similarly applied the paste of *Datura stratonium* to mucosae, close to the running of ancient arteries. This flight ends in death, a panic ride astride a besom, into the underworld as the rod gets rammed home, rupturing the secret contents of the body's cavity, where hides the life force, the animating ghost; where dwells the inner pulse. Flicker brutally extinguished to propitiate a daemon of deep filth and wretched sound, an unnecessary sacrilege.

λ

The avenue meander upon whose bank it stands is named for Nike. It splits a common from a green, and a Wormbridge college stands in front of its gates in *enantiodromia*. The realm of intellect answers that of action; thought versus physicality. Students run down to the quaky spot where their library work suspends. But the boy in this tale is not one of those. His time is his own and his mind, his hand and his wand. He bears a branch of victory, the badge of the postulant noviciate. He demands entry, he requires tuition. Excitement thickens and thins his saline sanguinity, his

178

bodily fluxes. He has come to read the writing on the wall, to translate the cuneiform and pictographic.

μ

The walls are all palimpsestic display, a cartography of messages oblique and obliterate. The words are crude, the writing uniquely unindividualised, as though copied from a specialist primer a new impersonal scripture. Monosyllabic Christian names, more numerals, figures, diagrammatic and diagnostic. Poetry penned by illiterates, anatomies of the aesthetics of reduction or subtraction. Male genitals become little more than two maddeningly circular testes connected by the swoop of a test-tube line, a tau imposed at the tip of the tail. It looks like a face: two eyes and a mouth, though it is that third eye which has become a closed slit, winks. Yet it should show the greatest alertness, the phallic seer, the retina at the snook of the snake, the stub, the snub, the sticky sight, and the origin of the hard, hard stare.

ν

Statuesque male nudes always have fig leaves, diminutive penises or, by supposed accident, impoverished decapitations where the member once had lain. Everything is on display except, paradoxically, the manhood, the virility, the potency or even the potential, for there can be no transition to kinetic, the world of automation and motility. Yet in the cella the phallus protrudes, erect from a covering of clothes that negates the rest of the body, separates off the *membrum virilis*. The colonette rises from the toothed yoni of the zipper's mouth, the apophyge cut off from view by the fibres of cloth and hair. The capital is free; the astragal and echinus conflate beyond the perverse position of the incomplete scotia, below which the entasis bulges, in novel architectural order. It projects towards the blind arcade, a snowy colum-

179

barium. Each of the niches is an aumbry, a recess for sacred vessels.

o

The pedagogue in this conjunction must needs be older, but not by far, just enough of an initiate, a knower, maybe known. Perhaps he will be called Gordon? His clothing will not be wrapped around with numerical law. He will crave indulgence, be seeking some response, definitively other than the usual furtive trickle, the flick of the wrist as the quick brown fox jumps over the lazy dog. He will loathe himself, and denigrate his coming here. In all the world of loneliness, he thinks, why build many mansions more? Is this a humble reproduction of the myth of Babel? He already feels the urge to speak in tongues, to destroy the taboo, clamour lamentable, diatribe and dithyrambic. He spots the signs and studies their analphabet. Graffiti shapes fishes and stars, witches' doodle and imprecise atomies.

π

The peelers put up to effect a closure, to overturn the misappropriation, dress in midnight blue in daylight, but are of another colour nocturnally, dichromic, Protean, false friends to the learners of a second language. They put away their night sticks, peculiar badges of appropriateness, but hide manacles in pockets and can call on backup from their conveyance outside the chapterhouse garderobe. Pity their poor systolic pressure, their refusal to be part of a nation déclassé. And how do they manage to fake the flag of surrender, engender entrapment? Plastic mutability or a relaxation of the rules of Philomela. Accoutred daily with mouthy whistle, chained, and breast-shaped helmet and gleaming buttons. They cannot write while the seductive pleasantries are taking place and post-orgasmically they must suffer the same invasion of sadness as the rest, unless they apprehend before

180

ejaculation. Do they not expose their vulnerability at all, and thereby strain like spare pricks at a country wedding? If not satyric, priapic, lighthouse-keeping, what are they? Which way do the lies point?

θ

If what goes on here, what comes off here, is so dreadfully commonplace, why does the secular authority attempt to diminish the pagan attractiveness? To proscribe these activities irregularly? Half-hearted measures, because the church will move and another mass rock consecrate. This is not the place of a select few, a tribe sheltering from the wilderness, this is a cosmopolitan sub-city, a thriving market where only glances are exchanged. Emblems of this other creed are penned upon the ply. The plain sheet of the wood has messages carved, bustrophedonical, isolates that pinpoint, scribe and scroll. *Mene, mene, tekel, upharsin.*

ρ

It seems strange that many wish the place to be not temenos but abattoir; coliseum rather than agora. Algolagnia involves the psychical as much as the physical. This is a true lyceum, a den of wolves. Here there is omophagy, here prostration. Everyone is alone, though it is the company they seek. The rapacious come from the four corners of the town and beyond. The officiants arrive by car, by bike, by foot. Either way the laity line up to observe the ebb and flow of the entrants before daring to go into the dark to relieve themselves.

σ

Going to such a place for the first time can be hell. You don't know the dance, the steps, you don't know how to

181

stand, where to stand; and before that even, what to wear. If you are there it doesn't necessarily follow that you're there for one thing, does it, officer? The lay-by close at hand is where the coaches pick up and deposit the kids from the main language school in town. Which of the official planners for that limited company decided on so fortuitous a positioning? The boys, the youths, come and go, dreaming of Michelangelo. These Sicilians, Sards, Milanese and Romans should be on a leash, should be prevented from making their casual use. The curious, the unwitting, the unwary make the rhyme and reason more remote or less predictable, unstable, volatile. Good money has been spent for sons to be sent, and not in the expectation of seduction by a foreign cult. Yet they take to the trough like swine to swill, but their svelte, trim forms are too golden for this, Cybele's ground, Selene's court. Numbered, numbered, weighed, divisions.

τ

Maybe the beams of the moon had punctured his brain, maybe the acrid taint of the grotto; perchance it was a chemical slosh within, coupled with the draw of the gravity without. It could have been the malign influence of those that stared through the improvised hagioscope. It might have been impure chance. The darkened boy, his penis still concealed, felt the rush, the surge, the tidal bore. The pavilion of his skull was flooded with whirlpool dynamics. The rose window opened in his head: leaded lattice tessellates of seablues and crimson translucence gyrated; scintilla invaded spinal fluid; he arched his neck and slow-motion fell.

υ

Epilepsy is little understood, but in the time when lunatics were thought of as god-ridden, possessed, enthused, they were not hounded, but given succour and special favour. The fits are unpredictable in their arrival and departure. The

182

spastic movements are accompanied by a clenching of the jaw and a rigidity of other muscles so that the contradiction of static and violent action, and being incommunicado, deaf to all assistance, creates a disturbing barrier. Ecstasy literally. The first slip into this land of hypnagogia may be early in life or late, and it can be induced by external as well as internal events. The Uranian froth flecks at lips as the collapse into the black shell continues and consciousness fades.

ς

The plain and palsied marbled verticals of the pit smoked in a veiling of tears. The dots jazzed in a distant sound, plotting trajectories of subatomics. This was a bubble chamber, pure experiment. The paisley print began to dance with strangeness and with charm: gymnastics and gymnopaedie. The roof lurched back to curl into fernlike filters for lunar lightness. Silver motes cascaded in to make the cavern shift. Creepers crazed the plaster, tendrils draped the barricades. The wild growth hid the bricks, mortared mortar with stems, stolons and some suckers; secreting stalks whose acid organics melted baked clay and turned the chapel to thicket dense. Then burst the buds in embowering profusion and scented moist air with powerful perfume. The forest would house the nests of a myriad species, insects glitter its leaves. Saplings from the concrete floor did sprout and grass grew underfoot. The entrance sealed itself on them that stood inside. They that saw this trick, but were not afraid of it, wished on this sudden change.

ω

From the web of the trees created, the eyes of watchers beam. They have become the wild things, witnesses to stranger combinings. They are hirsute, the pilings of hair around their bodies darkens their colour, dulls their separation from shadow, blurs the contours, marries them to midsummer

183

madness. Their heads are asinine, ears foliate, the murmurs come from throats as moans, a bray among the briars, while avians slumber on. They are enchanted by what they see, but cannot enter the arena, detained by walls of wood, cramped by thorns and stings. In the centre the rites go on and on. Limbs of pewter, gunmetal, clash and slide, skin on skin on skin. Soon the spatter of floury rain. The glade will fill with seeds, the climbers will all blossom, and pollen will gild these iron lilies, and from twin scratches in their backs drops of saffron blood will dowse the gravel and the loam. Sea will coat the sand. Night-scented stocks.

ξ

The boy spoke. Speaking alone drew the eyes of the onlookers to the delicate softness of his illuminated pale and the paradox that was the delineation of features too pure for darkness as for day. By his sentences were enchained all three listeners, surprised by the daring that casts a spell through unexpectedness. Mellifluous sublime mouthing matins in strange vernaculars, an epiphany, something from another age. 'My name is John Edleston. I am fifteen years old. I am frightened. I feel like I am drowning. Save me.' Some of the words could not have been his to use. Their power was invincible increase. Across his cheek a single tear coursed down, diamantine transformed to petrify. While in serge shirts like horsehair itching, midnight-blue prickling thistles at their privates, the overseeing diarchy were as hand-cuffed to one another, arms stretched up the partition between their separate traps, or better: magically connected through Pyramus' chink, not large enough to admit either wristband, but the buckling at that nexus nonetheless. They had been bound to one another for no reason 'cept knavery afoot, apparently. Incapable of decision and intervention, or yet of vocalising their astonishment. Writing on the wall this verse.

After moments the sergeant and the constable were released, with their cocks hanging in their palms like sixth fingers, to emerge from their lairs to glower down at the twinned, twined brothers. And the semen on their impotent hands will drip lamely like slug's slime on to the mess of garments torn off and turned to bedding, a layette now soiled, creased and greased. They are the ones who are arrested, they the depraved, the dangerously losing control. As one they bring their smeared paws to their noses and only then does the odour of the unnatural supersede that of Nature herself, bountiful, metamorphic and metaphorical. They smell their own smell and the psychotic swirl of pattern that is not there vanishes into the blue. Dicks, bobbies, unready and unuseful under cover. Have they indulged themselves? Why did the ritual congress in front of their eyes arouse them to spillage? What can they report about two they came to catch, any two to fill their quota? They had failed to. They would be loath to return to this haunted space, but there would be little option. They had volunteered for the operation out of some deep conviction, but now they were otherwise convinced. They were wise after the event.

ζ

The smell and roar of ocean woke those two. Silence was reimposed. They got up. They grabbed their separated clothes. They carried them out into the dawning day. They fumbled into their disguises to flee. The youth stared at the earth, the man pierced the boy with a look of astonishing vision. What he saw was unclear. Back in their unmarked car as quick as lightning, the accomplice boobies blanked his enquiring glance, blandly, pretending not to be his accessories. These things could not and had not happened. The brain-stormed annunciating Angle had fled. The teacher turned back to see which direction he had gone, but he was not sure which of the wraiths was his in the silk sheet of

185

mist blowing from the river. There were several candidates, pedalling furiously about their business. At this moment they could equally easily be the baker's boy, the butcher, someone off to take charge of a delivery, or the candlestick-maker, going to open up his premises. One swept along the towpath towards the Ferry Bridge; one sped along the tar to gain the crest of the road bridge over the Worm; one, now of indeterminate sex, had made the Non-conformist western façade a backdrop to their flight. The blithe spirit had flown, the bars of the cage snapped back into place at the coming of renewed, imperfect day.

Trees

Canst thou not minister to a mind diseas'd,
Pluck from the memory a rooted sorrow,
Raze out the written troubles of the brain,
And with some sweet oblivious antidote
Cleanse the bosom of that perilous stuff
Which weighs upon the heart?

Macbeth (5, III, 40–44)

SODOMISED BY A ghost. First the poison, then the change.[1] They put the boy in the box in the ground. It was wooden. I saw. Slowly came the transition. Lignification. He was dead; but like a cat in a box. Not a boy. The oak casket in the loam. The flowers. The useless platitudes. The planed and polished boards, dead. The June buds withering in the sun. A wine left too long sours.[2] A body left too long sours. Bright blooms left in improvised vases sour.[3] The seed in the ground sours untended. The boy, a man, sours the lives of those left at the side of the car-park plot. In a land of trees the only begotten son gave up the ghost, but came to me after the interment and lay with me and sweetened my soul with his attentions.[4] The final parting no bitter sorrow, but fondest farewell. The ghost, then the suffering. The quick and the dead. Rheumatics, said the doctor.[5] Tropical eczema the specialist said; *Lignum vitae*, the untutored eye. The carpenter looked at the grain and saw the wood of life, the *bois sacré*. Holy copse, unholy corpse, *âme damnée*, dendritic process. Fibres coalesce, myonemes to cellulose, myth to concrete fact. Feet of clay, putting down roots and reaching for the sky, clawing the clouds with twig-fingers, breeze-

187

shaken, consciousness shrunk for ever yet not gone, lingering. Wouldn't you? Challenge the change, deny the animism, refute the transposition, scream mutely with a sloughing susurrus of laminate cloaks, a leaf shirt lifted over the shoulders to reveal knotty trunk, a torso swathed in gnarled bark, miniature ravines vertically conducting fog-drip and rivulets of dew.[6] Perspiration, respiration, transpiration, expiration.

Daphne and Apollo? Daphne became a laurel and that became Apollo's plant, but there were others who merely entwined and grew for each other's shade and delight. My Apollonian visited me from the grave,[7] his wooden bed, his sheath of varnished finery, the brass handles, the plate, the chamfered joints, the reductio ad absurdum of beauty to a rhombic cipher, a satisfaction for onlookers in its geometric dehumanisation. Yet the ghost kept its shape[8] and came to me, bedded me in an untied cotton shroud on a bone-white tabula rasa, a desert sheet on which to spill sperm, a ghost-white slick, proof of life, proof of death, drying, impotent, dying, a mourning stain, a dire meaning.[9] The mark of his coming, his passing, the covenant signed by a revenant. He was dead, dead and buried, but I bore the mark of him, on the inside, on the out. The bed bore him, showed me no dream, no consequence.[10]

Early summer to late summer and an intervening year, pregnant after his ingress, his resurrection, the rigor mortis of his *membrum virilis*, his turgidity and his flaccidity, there but not there. I held him in my arms. He took me. No cold postmortem golem, no apparition to whom I could wail, 'Come let me clutch thee: I have thee not, and yet I see thee still. Art thou not, fatal vision, sensible to feeling as to sight?'

Skin of silk, disbelievable. Fabric of lies, untrue, illusory. I felt my sanity slip even as I felt his tongue probe me. A kiss, a warmth, no breath, verisimilitude without the life, the animating force, the passion, his joie de vivre, his eyes, his lips, his phallus, a burning hot poker between my fingers, between my legs.[11] Truth is beauty, but here was a lie, lying beside me, within me, juddering to an opening, to a close, nails piercing my body where he gripped, desperate, collapsing, wordless, no sound except gold on silver, hair entangling, electric. Sumatran sun polishing his body, varnishing it, making it gleam. My hyperborean flesh the colour of the moon, a lunar glint; a clash of metals, and his beauty, his beauty, his beauty. Perfection. Love without promises, falsehoods, ideals, praise, deception, duplicity, speechless. Power, strength, contained violence. I contained it. Some men incite violence,[12] demand defilement, beg for subjection, have to have a breaching, a breaking-in, a burglary, a theft. Neither of us thieves, but I a house to be entered, a home to trespass in, a sanctuary to be sought. Aaron back with me, a ghost of his former self, the same in all things, but dead.[13]

Afterwards, he got up to go to the bathroom as spent lovers often do, but I knew he would not return. His warmth had woken me, and the smell of him tainted the bedclothes, perfumed them, freshened them by covering the enzymatic cleanliness. Powders may wash whiter than white, imprint the spring over printed patterning, but who wants floral tributes when the scent of a man can be had? The faintest traces are more evocative than any photograph, more demanding than imprecise memory,[14] the abracadabra required to bring the lost love home to bed. The slight acrid tang of the deceased left behind like a flag, a neon of remembrance. My lover, lost to the Pacific Orient, taken in a flash flood, swept into a cauldron of cold-boiling mud, blood-coloured churning, an angry improbability.[15] And his trying to rescue a goddamned spider monkey, the one he told me he'd tamed, feeding it grapes from the handrail of the verandah. Stupid little monkey.[16] And it climbed over his shoulder and leapt to safety as the bamboos gave and he tipped into the inconsequential stream, a brook gorged to become a man-eater, a land-shark with a billion teeth, lacerating the hillside, taking away the very ground he walked on, the ground I would once have kissed, but now curse, now curse, now curse.

When the curtain-filtered sun that did not shine on Sumatra shone on me, I breathed in the essence of him, the musk, the sponge soaked in vinegar, the ghost of his ghost, and

prayed the dream of his death unreal and the dream of his
return foolproof, confirmed, a phone call away. The other
side of the world, not the other side of things. A wire connecting us, not a notional linkage, a thirst, a hunger, a need,
an unbreakable bond. But I knew the smell of him was all
that he'd left, or almost all. The final gift I did not discover
till the doctors gave up and told me it was a deliberate
mystification on my part, that could not dupe them. How
could I be deforming?[17] Where had the impulse come from
if not from me? A fixation that confused Sumatra with Elys-
ium or Tartarus, a borrowing of the robes of concealment
in an imaginary forest I wished to wage war against:[18] the
perfect disguise for the would-be defoliant, like primitive
peoples said to be able to blend into the jungle, to stand as
still as statues, the colour of bark, the texture of trees. I
smiled and watched as my silver became gold, tan, etched
with sienna, crevices with umber, earth colours creeping up
my paraplegic carcass. I would soon struggle out to a spot
near his grave to plant myself, before the organic process
accelerated me into total immobility.[19]

Adamic, they must have fished you from the subsiding torrent. For that is the meaning of the word: red soil. Maybe
they found you foetally coiled, caked in the rust-coloured
casing like a pond-bound caddis, a mimetic stick-caterpillar.
They will have washed you in clear water, restoring life to
dead earth, ritualistically bathing you, showing due defer-
ence, if only for the difficulty of manoeuvring your dead
weight on the slab, or in the tray, a shallow sink built into
steel. I wonder if even underneath the sun's changes, the
mud's stain, you showed a pale blue, the colour of the
asphyxiated? I cannot give you shades of cobalt or lapis
lazuli, Egyptian inlays; I cannot give you the mosaic suit of
jade tablets the Chinese tried against the escaping essence.
In that land which is an emblem of Paradise Lost, unknowable, for ever out of reach, they will have anointed your
skin, covered you with unguents to stop the rot, stay the
bacterial spread. They will have tied string around your

penis, placed a bung in the most secret place, maybe bound the jaw and splinted limbs to reshape them. I don't know, and do not wish to know, about the sucking implement they introduced to your body cavity just above the navel, to scrape out the internal organs, your heart, your lungs, to return you to me patched up, incomplete, a rag doll in sham Sunday best. If you were horribly bruised they'd have had to use cosmetics, a drag, a second skin, scaly, untrue to your complexion.[20] Did some child discover your mummy and call in its equivalent tongue, 'What bloody man is that?' Surely not, but I in my melodramatic reaction raged, 'O, never Shall sun that morrow see! Your face, my thane, is a book where men May read strange matters.' Drama queen? Not really. What does one say on these occasions that hasn't been said a thousand times? The one who came to tell me, my present amanuensis, all she could say was sorry, and sorry it was her that brought the news and sorry a few more times.

I remember our first ridiculous meeting, at that Post-Modern Reductionist display of fragments in Abercrombie Mews. I had just been looking at a pair of unintentionally monumental Y-fronts soaked in plaster and attached to a square of chipboard with the title 'Stateless' emblazoned in undercoated string. The artist had then glued on a huge crop of his own pubic hair.[21] He explained to a captive audience that it was a piece about the way we assumed sexual roles in the way we change our underpants. He explained that they looked big but were 'Small'. Because they were in an isolated frame, out of context, and also because they were flattened rather than body-hugging, they looked inflated. He told me that some of the other works used other people's body hair.

'That's all right,' I said and walked away: the saline pretzelly things they serve at those dos always make you gulp the plonk, which then makes you quick to heap praise on absolutely anything. I had viewed various of the huge charcoals or pastels of male genitalia, both expressionistic gesture and hyperreal accuracy of delineation at the same time, and

I moved to the next one and exclaimed to the scrutinising onlooker, 'That's a beautiful one, isn't it?'

'It's mine,' you said.[22]

I was trying to untangle whether I meant the drawing or its subject, and the riddle of whether you were the owner of the picture or of the individual part on show made the whole exchange insecure, unstable. We both realised this at the same instant and just smiled by way of an answer. Then we both said, 'Both,' and you extended your hand and said, 'Aaron Something-or-other, but call me Air. Everyone does.'

I turned and caught the exhibit's label: *Aaron's Rod*.

'Not very original, is it? As a title, I mean. This plonk is worse than usual, isn't it?'

'What would you have preferred by way of a title? God said unto Moses, You shall all have round Noses, All except Aaron, 'N' he shall have a square 'un?'

We laughed and I almost added, 'Square peg in a round hole,' but the wine wasn't *that* bad.

You it was that gathered the gold jewellery from the Israelites, melted it and made for me an idol. I was already genuflecting before your brave altar. You claimed you were not gay. You claimed you were celibate. In foreign lands foreign hands will have defiled the Lord's anointed temple, and stole thence the life o' the building! In trying to enliven you they'd bring travesty. I would have felt better had you been clutching your perishing, precious spider, like the naked lovers in some drained dam, entwined, the little death and the big death.[23] How awful to take the words of the Bard and put them to other uses, but I cannot articulate this inarticulate horror without. When they came with the news I felt you had betrayed me and I heard the words, 'Nothing in his life Became him like the leaving it: he died As one that had studied in his death To throw away the dearest thing he ow'd As 'twere a careless trifle.' But soon I will join you, planting my feet at your head, growing towards you.

When you came to my bed days after the funeral,[24] I realised that the guy in the crate could not have been you, only a stuffed dummy, a hollow man, but empty vessels make most noise. Air. 'Come, come, come, come, give me your hand. What's done cannot be undone.' And: 'The super-natural soliciting Cannot be ill; cannot be good.' Days, weeks, months, then years of watching your naked body in the studio, using you, stripping you further, reducing you to mere smudges and lines. Knowing your body better than you knew it yourself, showing your body in ways no mirror could. You were perfectly prepared to contort yourself into Tiepolo parodies, the *figura serpentina*, contrapposto, *sotto in sui*, poised on the edge of the upper loft. Very artistic.

At first a business proposal, then the payments became irrelevant, a standing order. You moved in briefly and out again. Your image hangs in Washington and New York, St Petersburg and Paris. There is an art-school adage that the model is often likely to resemble the painter in his drawings, his egomania and his familiarity with his own body imposing his features on the unfortunate irrelevant. Not you. Not me. Your beauty was something else and your quietude, your awareness of corporeal existence without the inter-ference in social mores, made you even more exciting to capture on paper.

Then you walked out. No goodbyes, only a postcard saying you were in Malaysia somewhere, readying to fly out to a reforestation programme in some unpronounceable place, combating soil erosion and setting up a more eco-nomic management system for the logging industry, before it gobbled up all the trees, the jungle entire. Maybe there'll be a desert there one day. A desert like the one whose sand I slept upon, grainy and barren, after your departure. You had taken to sharing my bed when we returned from get-togethers where getting drunk was somehow *de rigueur*. I always drank less and lay staring at the stars, a tent above my middle, as you slumbered and crashed careless hands into me and teased my body with hypnotic half-caress. I would fall into fitful sleep with the totemic exclamation mark and wake with another or maybe the same one and struggle up to cram it into cramped slips to crush out the blood and quell the desire. Then I'd make breakfast and draw you eating it, the duvet tantalisingly rearranged to support the tray and expose more flesh. Once you pushed the cover back to reveal Bacchic arousal. Again I drew, as you lay like an odalisque, eyes closed and a vague smile of self-satisfaction playing above the prong of your conceit. I had never imagined you'd be so unabashed and I couldn't decide if it was reward or further torture.[25]

When I told you about the first lover I had, the boy I had in school and afterwards, the boy who died in a car crash with no other vehicles involved, on a clear road on a clear night . . . when I told you those things, I never imagined you would be taken as casually and unpredicted. To be there, then to not be there. No more. He too is made of air.[26] I told you of the night we all went to a party in the hall in the next village and when the cars had ferried most away, only he and I remained. He had gone back to the boarding house and returned in the balmy evening wearing only midnight-blue pyjama trousers: a bizarre display; a strange idea – getting a lift back to a party that had finished, in next to nothing. I sat cross-legged on a yard-square table in the centre of the pine floor and he danced round me like Puck or Pan or Oberon.[27] And in the white-light glare of suspended bulbs, his torso was chipped from Carrara and the turn of his ankles like that our ancestors spoke of glimpsing under a farthingale or gown. I should have known he had come to court me, but I did not. Perhaps you did the same, but still I did not. We were in the theatre of the absurd but never reached the final act, or was it deliberately withheld as part and parcel of the plot?

Sodomised by a ghost and turned not to stone but to wood, a mendacious Pinocchio reverting to his primal state. I think about Baucis and Philemon and their spiritual reward. A pair of peasants who showed beneficient largesse to the gods travelling incognito who called at their door. They welcomed Jupiter and Mercury, who made their wine jug ever-replenishing and promised to ease the sadness of whichever of the couple survived the decease of the other by metamorphosing the pair, in extreme old age, into an oak and an elm or a linden, to grow side by side. But telling the story like that misses a couple of things, things which deprive it of its tragic element. The gods had gone about the village

194

seeking shelter, only to be refused. The inhospitable were later punished for their impiety when, after dining with the generous Baucis and Philemon, all four climbed a hill to watch the valley converted to a lake, the inhabitants drowned by their lack of grace. The old couple's humble dwelling had meantime become converted into a temple. There they served as precinct attendants until their own transformation. And of course there had to be a comic element. Once the hosts realised the passing strangers' divinity, which had caused the wine jug to be constantly refilled, they had endeavoured to make their repast more worthy by killing the goose that guarded their property. But the wise snow-white bird had evaded their doddering attempts at capture by hiding between the immortals. They decreed its life be saved because of its crafty escape.

I told you, too, of the next time that I saw him, at a party crammed full of revellers in a student house in the district around the tech. The drug squad or at least officers of the law, in night-coloured cloth, raided the place, called to cull the noise and seal the doors from spilling rabble and rebellion into the road. He and I and a friend and another climbed out of an upstairs window and over an extension roof and into the garden and off. We wandered in a cannabis haze[28] past river meadows and botanical gardens to a massive Victorian pile subdivided to accommodate the studious, those at the university who could pay more and more easily appreciate Mackmurdo and Morris, Tiffany and Webb (they sound like pop stars, but are architects and decorators). The boy whose lodgings we invaded said to me that he'd like to sleep with the first boy in town to admit he was gay so openly, but I refused and clustered on the rugs, under a blanket shared by us three waifs and strays. With what contortion did the boy who danced round my table and I contrive the slurp of sex,[29] and with what miraculous godsent narcolepsy did the boy on the other side of us not realise the agitation of the floor, the crumpling of the blanket and the desperate yell held in check as I climaxed into his elfin mouth? In the morning, he had a bath among the outmoded plumbing and I sat on the thunderbox and watched his hands dance over the body I was properly seeing for the very first time. I was sad, for I knew I would lose him: he would be sleeping with women as often as with me,[30] but I didn't know how soon he would crumple the roof of his father's car and crush himself out of this world for ever. I told you I didn't go to the funeral because I was too upset, but I had been to similar events where the whole performance seemed exactly that, a meaningless deposition of a box in the ground.[31]

This is being taken down verbatim.[32] There was once a woman who loved me, still does for all I know, but I could not follow the example of the boy in filmy blue, the boy under the blanket, the first boy in the box, the car-crush, car-crash kid, and sleep indiscriminately about. I should have slept with her. It would have rid me of her. I would have been shown to be just one more male chauvinist pig out for a poke, incensed that something so little could matter so much.[33] I wonder if my ghost will visit her, my faithful Beth, or whether she will imagine it? At least she will not see me boxed and buried in the brown.[34] My leafy presence as a visitation would be too extreme to be believed – a tree materialising at the end of the bed, waving branches against the Artex, a face in the half-light that a switch would dispel as the bedside lamp restores the nightmarish masks of child-hood imaginings to mere knots in the furniture veneer, sports of nature, tricks of the eye, pure self-deception.[35] Ridiculous.

The ghost that visited me was no gory-headed threat but a golden temple attendant[36] bringing the sun to my feast, banishing all fear from my mind. And now all I can do is have my passing noted down and ready myself for the final transplantation.

Notes

1. Swelt'red venom sleeping got. (4, I, 8)
2. Had I but died an hour before this chance
   I had liv'd a blessed time; for, from this instant,
   There's nothing serious in mortality –

196

All is but toys; renown and grace is dead,
The wine of life is drawn, and the mere lees
Is left this vault to brag of. (2, III, 89–94)

3. And good men's lives Expire before the flowers in their caps.
(4, III, 171).
4. That seems to speak things strange. (1, II, 48)
5. Guardian of their bones (2, IV, 35)
6. Let us seek out some desolate shade. (4, III, 1)
7. As from your graves rise up, and walk like sprites,
To countenance this horror. (2, III, 77)
8. To feeling as to sight? (2, I, 37)
9. Shake off this downy sleep, death's counterfeit
And look on death itself. Up, up, and see
The great doom's image! (2, III, 74–76)
10. Let the earth hide thee.
Thy bones are marrowless, thy blood is cold,
Thou hast no speculation in those eyes
Which thou dost glare with! (3, IV, 93–96)
11. And put a barren sceptre in my gripe. (3, I, 61)
12. Where violent sorrow seems A modern ecstasy. (4, III, 169)
13. And nothing is but what is not. (I, III, 141)
14. That memory, the warder of the brain, Shall be a fume.
(1, VII, 65)
15. Angels are bright still, though the brightest fell. (4, III, 22)
16. Now, God help thee, poor monkey! (4, II, 57)
17. To cure this deadly grief. (4, III, 215)
18. Who can impress the forest, bid the tree Unfix his earth-bound
root? (4, I, 95–96)
19. Whose heavy hand hath bow'd you to the grave. (3, I, 89)
20. The sleeping and the dead
Are but as pictures; 'tis the eye of childhood
That fears a painted devil. (2, II, 53–55)
21. A deed without a name. (4, I, 49)
22. Poor prattler, how thou talk'st! (4, II, 62)
23. As two spent swimmers that do cling together And choke their
art. (1, II, 8)
24. Why, what care I? If thou canst nod, speak too.
If charnel-houses and our graves must send
Those that we bury back, our monuments
Shall be the maws of kites. (3, IV, 70–73)
25. Better be with the dead,
Whom we, to gain our peace, have sent to peace,
Than on the torture of the mind to lie
In restless ecstasy. (3, II, 19–22)
26. I am for th' air; this night I'll spend
Unto a dismal and a fatal end. (3, V, 20–21)

27. Let not light see my black and deep desires. (1, IV, 51)
28. Stones have been known to move and trees to speak. (3, IV, 123)
29. Whom the vile blows and buffets of the world
    Hath so incens'd that I am reckless what
    I do to spite the world. (3, I, 108–09)
30. Could not fill up The cistern of my lust. (4, III, 62)
31. Into the air; and what seem'd corporal, melted. (1, III, 81)
32. But I have words That would be howl'd out in the desert air.
    (4, III, 193–94)
33. Under a hand accurs'd! (3, V, 49)
34. Are ye fantastical, or that indeed Which outwardly ye show?
    (1, III, 53–54)
35. A dagger of the mind, a false creation,
    Proceeding from the heat-oppressed brain (2, I, 38–39)
36. Most sacrilegious murder hath broke ope
    The Lord's anointed temple, and stole thence
    The life o' the building. (2, III, 65–67)

Pause

CONCRETE, CONCRETE, THIS story is encased in concrete.
And concrete is as concrete does.

The Keepers have all had one thing in common. For them
there could be no question of monkish celibacy, but neither
any possibility of procreation. The strictest sexuality guaranteed them their inability to offend against the sisters of the
Goddess, proscribing the planting of the demon seed in
the dark furrow that so abhors and fascinates. They didn't,
couldn't, wouldn't, share their fellows' obsession with culti-
vating that certain soil, watering it, seeing life burst forth
after a smooth-curved graph of growth and months of development. The grain these heretics would rather gather
remained without harvest barren. For every succeeding neo-
phyte, the sacrament celebrated on burning beds served, like
all such rituals, to commemorate the impossible as though
it were true or imminent. Each father was also a mother,
engendering her own son by obnoxious self-pollination, the
gulp of Khepera. Normal mechanisms of parenthood had
been somehow stoppered. Nothing sprang from their love-
making, their vain fertility. Before women they were as
eunuchs, yet passion and promiscuous scattering governed
them. Progeny born of clay carried within them the female
image, great in strength and of great wealth. They loved
themselves as the earth loves herself. She was fatigued by
the awful destruction and disordering of her children. Their
enclosure or exclusion may have been rooted in jealousy. For
all through their filthy coupling they retained more of their
self-knowledge than their counterparts, keeping their purity
and their freedom by becoming enslaved to depravity, the

act denied its meaning, becoming mere act, they, forever actors.

Grey was the concrete. Grey, grey, grey. It was the deadening admixture of black into white. It was dull. Its surfaces, whether roughened or smoothed, absorbed the light and gave back poor reflection. The plug of homogenous material had intruded itself into the variety of the strata, a man-made vulcanicity, the colour of solidified lava, basaltic. The bunker was deep, deep down. A place to die, away from the frenzy of atomic bombardment on a particle-purged surface, a lifeless void following the advent of another war. The pigments of warfare are grey too, muddied, sullied, soiled, made bleak. The souterrain tunnels curved, not in a satisfying innovative architectural style, but out of functional necessity, carved by some senseless mechanical mole.

Along with the inverted climes of worst-case scenarios, we must conjure up a secret cult with secret aims and watch for their demise.

Across the surface of the Mother there once crawled a sacristan, echoing her changes, predicting them in ways scientists would scorn with their precision. By becoming her servant he had become something other than other men. When he was caught and imprisoned, the know-it-alls prodded him for answers he would not divulge. His body was riddled with disease and, as it took its course, he found that being locked into the secure isolation unit prevented him from pursuing his quest for a successor, some young man to whom he could impart his supposed secrets. His ramblings were ascribed to senescence and inadequate circulation. The blame for the parched meadows and swamped coffee crops was attributed with meticulous inaccuracy to this or that form of global pollution, this or that abuse of the earth's generosity, but the sole heir to the age-old inheritance of invented hierophants thought that the time 'when she, with my passing, passes' would soon arrive.

When the plague came, the man chosen to carry the learning of the ancient order accidentally fell victim to it, ironically infected by the poisonous spill from an amaryllis-coloured flower head nestled between the legs of one of the

200

holy sinners. All things come from the earth and the sexton could not rationalise the process whereby she had spawned a brood of millennia-destroying microbes in the bulbs and roots of her most-honoured gardeners' stock. He assumed them sacrosanct.

As he became more infirm, the items on the news became ever more hopeless. His skin developed a sarcoma and part of China became a raging sandstorm. The radiation treatment made it glow like the tracks of electrons in a bubble chamber. The animals choked and had their heavy hides depilated, their eyes grew dull or inflamed. They stood, eyes rheumy and tight-lidded, like Egyptian tomb sentinels now guarding the tent-shaped sarcophagi of the moribund nomads at the edge of the Gobi. The man watched the screen in his hermetically sealed, glass-fronted chamber and the blurred film of stock-still beasts reminded him of the heretical pantheon of ancient times. The Nile civilisation held that the earth was a man-god and the sky a woman, a sacred but profane cow. That particular society had perished, but the logic that now governed the rubbing-out of this other blistered terrain eluded him. He knew that worldwide the cult of the giving *tellus mater* had become confused or had lapsed completely. Even so, the reports from the more remote corners of the globe suggested an incipient apocalypse that would scourge initiate and preterite alike. He could not draw a parallel between the decay of the world and that of his own body because the maps were not available and the correlation of data would require a powerful computer, duly attended by competent programmer-operators, as altar boys at a Mass, going through their paces without fully understanding the meaning of bells and burners, chalice and pyx.

The man, in pain and on drugs, wandered the library of his mind, pulling out volumes and glancing at arcane illustrations and obscure hieroglyphs, unable to decipher their message. His lover had died and the body had been restructured using lasers and pressure chambers, the molecules reordered before the debris was sealed in a metal tube and conveyed to the disused mine to join the infill of canisters and concrete at the shaft-bottom.

Almost every night, however short, however long, the man's dreams contained the metaphysical landscapes of depopulated towns, emerald forests, arctic, antiseptic whiteness, or glittering desert dunes over which his dead lover walked, sacerdotal, naked and smiling, often erect, frequently dribbling pollen on to the ground, phallus engorged, putting back his head to let a roar issue from his mouth which in turn charged the blue air with the ghosts of birds with orange eyes, each holding a faint golden fruit in beak or claw. He woke drenched, sometimes with an oil slick of semen mingling with the sweat on his stomach or his thigh. Deluges fell in arid areas and creamy white tidal waves swept over coasts in Europe and North America. And as he dried his skin, rapid gusts of hurricane force tore down the Alpine valleys or rolled flat tracts of Canadian forest. As he began to waste away, the rocks of mountain ranges seemed to become more craggy and fissures appeared in the crust, seeping noxious salt water which contaminated the drinking supplies and killed the fish and cattle.

The governments of some countries enacted Draconian measures to combat the spread of the disease and drew up contingency plans about the increasing inclemency of the climate. Ministers of natural disaster were appointed. Prophets of doom, usually men, usually oldish, always heterosexual, proclaimed from pulpit or soapbox the coming dissolution of absolutely everything, while more fundamentalist strains looked for a section of society or a poorer power to blame, at whom to shake their fists. The consensus was that divine retribution was being brought down on the many because of the indiscretions of the few, those undermining family life, those whose aloofness smelled of conspiracy, in an obloquy of desperation. This was declared to be a nonsense by the scientists. The church, allied to the state as it was almost everywhere, denied that the responsible were responsible. Elected and ordained potentates changed their tune when the seething masses raised one voice, proclaiming that the plague-carriers were the bringers of evil and, with a watertight proof in mind, deciding that anyone disagreeing was part of the pattern of disintegration and decadence.

Theoreticians were often unmarried or unconsummated, the hallowed community replete with those disinclined to marry or conjugate, prone to harbour victims in their midst, to the point of hiding the infected from the authorities.

Extrapolating the plots only leads to dire results.

The laws were tightened to include the internment of those only suspected of contamination. All opponents of repressive regimes could be labelled as 'diseased' and be quartered for the good of themselves and the rest of society. A register of Those Known to Consort with Those Known to Be was drawn up. Compulsory neutering of all in either category was proposed and the impregnating of one sex by members of the same sex was made totally illegal, consent irrelevant. It was claimed that enactment of such measures was to calm the contagious fears of the right-thinking, right-fucking majorities.

Intelligence agencies cooperated and the power lines linking one database to another shuttled improbable impulses every second of every dot-dash combination of blacks and whites strobing the earth from space. Every theory was to be tested on electrical models, with predictions and extrapolations punched in by machine-women called audiotypists who secretly maintained the crisis was male-engendered, engineered, but also felt empathetic to the plight of Mother Earth and the warlike winnowing of her sons. Those of the population who had stricken children denied it to their neighbours. Others tried to quash rumours that their unmarried boys were spunk-swallowers or were brought up badly enough not to be sure which hole to plug with their round pegs.

Since the man wasn't allowed out of his box, he did not know how many others inhabited the warren. It had been built against the possibility of nuclear attack, he mused. Visitors weren't allowed. No one was supposed to know where the place was or even that it existed. Nearly all the attendants were female, staying there in the belly of their mother to minister to those who could have been sons of theirs, had they had sons. Most were young, idealistic, inexperienced. They found it odd to be communicating through an intercom and passing trays of food into hermetic hatch-ways. An incinerator within each cell disposed of the remains. There was a shower *en suite* and a TV and VDU, which allowed access to books and newspapers, digitally retrieved from libraries.

Many countries had similar installations but certain places, which did not, liquidated the plagued in more direct ways. Ovens were supplied by the wealthier nations as inter-national aid, while they themselves kept specimens alive, not for humanitarian reasons, but so as to observe the progress of the germ and experiment on pathogen-infested flesh. The highly qualified geneticists were all male. The tampering with the bodies of other males did not deter them, nor did the supposed distraction of the nubile attendants, whose caring was mediated by electrics and curtained by glass.

In the computerised Reading Room in the British Museum, meanwhile, an archaeologist was pouring over copies of tomb inscriptions concerning the predictions of the demise of the last dynasty. They dated from just before the final collapse, painted in obvious haste on the south wall of a chamber once housing the body of a priestess, near the city of This, under the tutelary jurisdiction of Anhur or Onouris. The burial had been desecrated several times and her name had been scrubbed out. The rest of the pictograms remained untouched, so this was no random vandalism. No sarcopha-gus had been found, but a recent re-excavation of the site revealed a skeleton below the floor with an amulet beside it encrypted with the message: *This is the real body – with it everything finishes; the days will change places – the desert will bloom but grow cold and dark.*

The report he had just read, a transcription from a journal, pointed out that the remains had been those of a man, and recorded that the bone tissue seemed to have been ravished by some unidentified disease, though the size and shape of limbs indicated a person in the prime of life. The pectoral jewel showed, besides the inscription, a picture of Isis re-assembling the body of Osiris, at the point in the story when she realises that the genitals brother Sutekh had removed while dismembering the corpse could not be found and would not be found.

From the careful watercolour copy of the wall, the archaeologist translated the ancient words:

I . . . [name missing], last priest/priestess of the cult of the earth, see the future draw near and see the sex of my sky, my ground, my devoted followers, change. I . . . , son/daughter of all and none, feel the wind rise in the Sahara, feel the sea rise where before it stood off, sink where before it made harbours havens for vessels and fishers; the pyramids turn upside down, the mountains walk to the new shores and grind like millstones about to break. The women watching their work, work no longer, not needed, finished, ended. The corn will not be harvested by men, nor ground to flour. I . . . see my last son uncut, intact, imprisoned in the ground alive, near-dead. I see his impotent penis starved, limp in its field of reeds, his skin a field of poppies. His lover's remains are stored in Canopic jars but there is no body. You who read this will look for mine in vain. I am a woman who is not a woman, I . . . have thirsted after the men along the banks of the Nile and in years from now, when the sky is the earth, the earth the sky, I will continue to look to their help. There will be a new priesthood and as my last descendant prepares to go back to his/her mother I will linger a while. They will see that I . . . was right and that my loss will be repaid by their loss. The world will begin again, looking for that which is missing. If my name is obliterated, then the solution will not come. I will be sealed as he/she will be sealed for ever, without reason. There is no reason. I died slowly. The priesthood, years from now, will die slowly. I . . . commend my memory/memories to those that follow.

As more and more people died or were injured in the disasters around the world, concern about the plague and the finding of scapegoats began to diminish. The operation of the subterranean complex continued as before. The man whose ills reflected those of the world grew steadily worse. He began to burn up and the blotches on his once beautiful skin spread at an alarming rate as if to join together, to flay him. He lost weight terribly and moving to the hatch became almost too much. The bones of his spine protruded and blood soaked the sheet so that it stuck to his back. The regulations had been relaxed so that these indignities could be managed by the attendant staff, at last able to act as nurses rather than gaolers, shrouded in protective clothing which could be disinfected at stations along the corridor.

Subsequently, his penis had been catheterised to void emissions as much pus as piss. He would be periodically wracked with convulsions and the earth would judder with him. Many of the healthy inhabitants of cities or coasts had moved into rural enclaves to avoid falling masonry or crashing waves.

The deciphering savant sent a copy of his findings to the ministry, prefacing his remarks with excuses and expressing a desire not to be considered another doom-monger. He drew careful parallels between the two moments in history and underlined the strangely hermaphroditic doubling of subject pronouns. He elucidated the reasons for expecting a female occupant of the specific tomb type, the surprise at the uncovering of a male. He conjectured that the veiled references about sex referred to a cult involving homosexuality or castration. Then, scrupulously avoiding hysteria, he enquired if the information agencies knew of any obscure surviving sect having a heretical deviant as its head. He suggested further investigation so that a name be found before its being lost for ever. The undersecretaries were used to the crankiness, but more staff had already been drafted into the department to follow up every conceivable lead, scientific or not. Pleas from moribund plague victims and letters from disgraced thinkers were being collated and researched. Time seemed increasingly short and the voices of the shrill prophets grew more and more credible as the earth rocked and reeled.

The archaeologist found himself asked to attend a meeting in the depths of a basement in decrepit Whitehall. The sky was leaden. It threatened sleet. It was June. A collection of medal-toting top brass in the grey-walled room, and on to a screen a projector shining images of archaic writing and heraldic insignia culled from obscure manuscripts. Another specialist, expert in medieval alchemy, began to lecture about the symbols' significance. Every so often he sought confirmation or comment from the digger. It appeared that predictions were not exclusive to the apparently immolated Egyptian heresiarch, but were laconically penned by various magicians of the Middle Ages and by the Rosicrucians. Interpretation of these texts yielded a traditional belief that in time of plague and impending global annihilation one, not male, not female, would be needed to answer the questions of mankind's continued existence. Some said more specifically that the saviour would be an infertile husband or a castrated youth, others that he or she should come from a given religious background rather than an oppressed clique or coterie; that he should shout his worth before a crowd of unbelievers and be unbelieved; or that she should be put to death; that he should die before he could save the human race; that her knowledge would never be extracted by torture or that she would deliberately withhold the secret, determined to bring about Armageddon. Many of the scripts seemed to imply that the One would not relish his position and would seek concealment or substitution. They claimed that the price of saving the rest of the people of the earth would be too great for him. The similarity of detail of so large a part of these unrelated prophecies declared some underlying principle, something more than mere coincidence: plagues, earthquakes, oppression, freak weather, untold scores of deaths, and ultimately governments rendered helpless – all were predicted in these diverse Jeremiad prescriptions. There were other clues besides: many said that a queen or female ruler would reign in the country where he'd be found; many that he'd come from the north; and many that he'd be found living in a cave at the hour of greatest need.

The general explained that at the time of speaking there were thousands of incarcerated plague-carriers throughout the world, but a search among those countries that 'chose' to kill their unfortunates could be ruled out unless the reluctant redeemer were to be in a place of safety, hidden by family or friends, although the oppressive regimes had passed such tyrannical counteroffensives to lay waste to all those even suspected of harbouring the unsafe, the unsound. It was, therefore, totally unlikely. Orders had been given, here, to collect records of all those in accessible isolation. Note would be made of religious affiliation and any criminal activity such as civil disobedience. The information was being compiled as painstakingly as possible, but the vast quantity of material needing to be processed gave room for little hope. A directive had been issued to all the doctors and administrators in the warrens of the dying, insisting that the state of each patient should be monitored so that systemic checks could be made on those closest to death before they could expire, going to their eternal rest with the secret untold.

The bunkers were very secure. The events of the outside world were relayed into the old mines and fallout shelters, but they seemed distorted by the layers of concrete or strata, nearly impossible to correlate with the mass of individual illness inside. To say patient Q, or patient V, was 'connected' to external reality seemed a hideously tasteless game.

The man was close to death. He was being kept alive by metabolism-slowing chemicals, as were hundreds of others. The atmosphere in his cubicle was still carefully controlled. It was free from microbes and all dust had been electrostatically precipitated. Temperature, light levels and vibration were being arranged to minimise discomfort and stress. Vitamins were being pumped in and food drips were connected to his flayed arms. Air cushions supported his body as his backbone became a dorsal fin and his cock shrivelled to a putrid fruit. Liniment-soaked swabs were dabbed into place. Sensors noted every change. But this treatment was the same for everyone at death's door. The guardians were determined to prevent him crossing the threshold. The outcasts were now being scrutinised, afforded individual, imploring attention. There were many more interviewees than interviewers and the precise question to ask to avert the demise of the world was unclear. The answer could be equally unobvious. The man could be anywhere. He could hold his tongue. The whole idea could be based on a false promise, but by now clutching at straws seemed the only thing left to do. Time and temper were short, desperation the order of the day.

The dealers in temporary oblivion had a field day. Suicide became commonplace, more common than ordinary casualties. Fear stalked the earth. The hospitals couldn't cope. The cabinet had directed that the care of the clandestine army of perverts be stepped up, even at the expense of the broader health budget. Hordes of people wished to be out of it before the final curtain fell. Many fled in a blaze of green, purple and cyan as they threw themselves from new cliffs or tumbling buildings, as high as kites. Fathers died with no news of their sons, sons who had disappeared during the purges. Announcements on the radio, shrouded in tactful double-speak, asked anyone aware that their son held strange ideas to inform the authorities, even if the boy were numbered among the officially unknown. But nothing and no revelations came.

The supercomputer began to list possibles, probables, maybes. Everyone was investigated. The investigators feared they would miss something, either in their interviewing or in their attempts to tie medical records to the string of happenings throughout the world during the past year or so. Meanwhile, the man, our man, had passed into a coma. The catalogue of weird events seemed to come to a halt. There was a clammy, grey calm everywhere, as if the world were slowing. There was no air of rejoicing, but a feeling that there'd be a brief pause before the Four Horsemen finally tramped the righteous and the sinful regardless. The voices on the radio expressed hope devoid of encouragement, the announcer obviously reading what he considered patent rubbish. No one listened any more, anyway. They just watched and waited.

'Log all those in coma, catatonic or trancelike, all those on life-support systems,' ordered the commander. 'I want my man!'

Food was getting scarce, but only the few seemed bothered. The probes on his hairless skull registered that the last hope of mankind was closing down for ever, the brainwaves reducing to the smooth textbook squiggle, with an equation for the gradual planing of the rough places easily calculated and solved. Hourly the peaks and troughs grew more slight. Externally applied stimulus brought no response. The troops of researchers, only likely survivors of the final act, were frantic.

Then they found the perfect fit. The fluctuations in fever, the spread of illness, its peculiarities, matched the map of world disruption and decay. They had their man. The doctors added backup machines to the welter of electrical devices, but with the immune system failing completely, the circulation of the blood only conducted each bacterium from one point of the ruined country, down red roads, to anott for it to make a new home and multiply. Transfusions of uncontaminated blood helped, but supplies were scarce.

'Find this boy's mother, will you?' barked the captain.

'He's an orphan, sir.'

'Find his lover, then, damn it!'

'Died eighteen months ago, sir!'

'Can no one be found to get through to him? This is deliberate, isn't it?'

He would have shaken the corpselike body, but it was now enmeshed in electrodes, ducts, airbags, in a framework that would turn it automatically. The barrage of equipment at the edge of the bed made it look like GCHQ.

'We have to get him to wake up, to tell us what he knows.'

'I don't think he knows, sir. His records show no illegal activity, no bizarre religious beliefs, nothing out of the ordinary except, perhaps, that he spent a great deal of time travelling a few years ago, as if searching for something. Twenty-nine countries, hundreds of cities, towns, villages. Not excessively promiscuous. Stuck to his kind. Not especially camp. Self-educated and quite an expert in Egyptian mythology.'

The head of the useless army raised his eyebrows.

'And there's a year, when he was fifteen, when he ran away, which has no records at all. Nothing until he turned up outside Paris. Seems that that was when he got his taste for travel. Good patient. Slipped into coma – '

'I know when he "slipped into coma", thank you,' he interrupted. 'Is there any other way to get him out of it?'

'We could try the experimental drug Sebennytus, but it's very risky. About 50 per cent of those to whom it is administered die. It's only used *in extremis*. It induces a massive surge of multipolar neurone activity, like a brainstorm, from which he might pull out or fold completely. The heart could pack in, everything at once.'

'Try it!' He knew the proper procedure involved asking the government its opinion, but he also knew this shell of a body wouldn't hold up much longer.

The doctor fetched a syringeful of the miracle-worker and then refused to inject it himself. He explained that he didn't have the necessary authorisation and that if the general wished, he should puncture one of the drips and pump it into the liquid. It would then take up to an hour to enter the bloodstream.

After a moment's hesitation the general plunged the needle into the plastic bag and squirted the contents into it.

Forty minutes of pacing around the buried premises, smoking in an environment supposedly free from such pollution. The generators whirred in the stony silence. In the event of atomic winter the complex would sustain life for at least two years, but was there that long left? The doctor, the commander, the orderlies and nurses had a glass of medicinal brandy each as the half-hour passed. Sitting back at her screen, the woman in charge of monitoring the data announced that the drug was beginning to take effect. The orogeny of seismic scribble settled into less alarming patterns though no rhythm could be detected: long pauses, then dancing snakes; snakes, then gentle waves. They were clustered round the set rather than round the mechanistically sustained body.

'This is the crisis,' the doctor said. They didn't know it, but on the surface above their heads the sky was falling, the ground splitting, surging up to meet the drooping clouds. Tremor, tsunami, rumble, grumble, groan, screams from the scattered few clinging desperately to life.

Then the waves quietened. The man opened his eyes. They

211

looked over at him, not daring to move, expecting a paroxysmal end at any moment. His throat tried to work. A nurse went over and moistened his lips. He tried a 'Hello', which came out as a primordial croak.

He didn't stay fully conscious for long, but in reply to the numerous questions, he said that the secret was that he didn't understand the secret. He surmised that the only cogent explanation was that he was to be the last, but maybe each of his predecessors had thought the same. He said he had found no one to pass the arcana on to, but had imagined the boy whose ashes now lay in a steel tube in a coal mine up north could have been the one. But the plague had carried him off before he could abdicate from his throne.

Everything up above returned to normal and remained so, even as he slid back into blackness. The body would not support the mind, would not maintain itself wracked by such pain and palaver, too much stimulus on one front, too little on another. Skin grafts were performed and silicone flesh implanted; the pristine cell that surrounded him became still more technocratic. Three independent power sources were installed. Units that automatically manufactured oxygen and nitrogen were incorporated into the rig. Tanks of plasma enriched with additional nutrients were connected to a spaghetti network of tubing to obviate the necessity of frequent manual changeover. The cradle that turned him was still in place. A stereo or TV was left on throughout the artificially regulated day. There was a backup of over a hundred thousand hours of programmes that could be randomly selected in the event of a break in broadcasting. The care staff were encouraged to talk to the man on his machine-catafalque. This reassured the attendants of the probable quality of life of the Messiah. The man himself remained silent.

The plague ceased to spread as the remaining incarcerated died and the condition of the planet quietened. The immortality sought by the Egyptians had eluded the mummified. The immortality of idea had been achieved through a trick, requiring an ever-renewed line of successive 'immortals'. Now a third form of immortality would be tried: the fate of the world would lie in the bowels of the earth and a conspiracy of silence hide the existence of the Saviour of Mankind from mankind.

Acknowledgements

IN NO PARTICULAR order whatsoever, I would like to thank the following people for their help with this book:

My editor, Jonathan Burnham, and my agent, Peter Robinson, because it is great good fortune to work with people professionally when they are closer to friends than colleagues. The staff at Catz, both academic and domestic, above all, Dr Paul Hartle, without whose kindness and assistance these stories would never have been sent for publication in the first place. My 'Reading Committee' who when they weren't actually reviewing what I had written were helping me over my next crisis: Luke Edwards-Stewart, Daryl Stewart, Steve Briscoe, John Austin and especially Erica Hodgkinson. Those who typed the original manuscript, before I learned to use the word-processor: Nigel Reader, Steve Lack, Brenda Scruby, Simon Plaut and the ladies at Copycats.
    And everybody else who knows me.